The Tiger's Share

The Tiger's Share

Keshava Guha

JOHN MURRAY

First published in Great Britain in 2025 by John Murray (Publishers)

1

Copyright © Keshava Guha 2025

A CIP catalogue record for this title is available from the British Library

Hardback ISBN 9781399813389
Trade Paperback ISBN 9781399813396
ebook ISBN 9781399813419

Typeset in Sabon MT by Hewer Text UK Ltd, Edinburgh
Printed and bound in Great Britain by Clays Ltd, Elcograf S.p.A.

John Murray policy is to use papers that are natural, renewable and recyclable products and
made from wood grown in sustainable forests. The logging and manufacturing processes
are expected to conform to the environmental regulations of the country of origin.

Carmelite House
50 Victoria Embankment
London EC4Y 0DZ

www.johnmurraypress.co.uk

John Murray Press, part of Hodder & Stoughton Limited
An Hachette UK company

The authorised representative in the EEA is Hachette Ireland, 8 Castlecourt Centre,
Castleknock, Dublin 15, D15 XTP3, Ireland (email: info@hbgi.ie)

To Ayesha

What's the use of getting a son,
if he's neither virtuous nor wise?
. . . Better that he die as soon as he's born,
Better even that a daughter be born.

The Panchatantra

I

The Ambassadors

My father had been retired five years when he convened a family summit. That sounds too grand for a meeting of four people, three of whom lived in the same south Delhi neighbourhood, two in the same flat, and one of whom, my mother, was never likely to be an important participant. But anybody who knew us could see that my father's request was unusual. I measured the potential weight of it by the fact that it had taken Rohit, my brother, less than an hour to respond, not with mere agreement but with his flight details.

When Rohit was still a student, it had been so painful to coax him back for short visits that we'd long since stopped trying. Now that he was in the final months of his Optional Practical Training, with no prospect of an H-1B visa, you'd think he'd want to hold firm to every day he had left in New York, and maybe steal an extra week or two there. From April to October, Delhi was too hot for him. From November through February, it was too polluted. That left March, where the weather might be doable, but even so, this was Delhi, so far from the action. The city was *dead*.

My mother visited him twice a year. Between visits, every few weeks she'd demand that I issue one of those embarrassing Facebook appeals, asking if anybody was flying from Delhi to New York. Sometimes I gave in, and some poor bakra was saddled with frozen parathas, bottles of home-made mango pickle and Maggi noodles. Then one of these kind couriers sent me a bill for his excess baggage fee, and I told Ma I was done indulging her.

As for my father: he had never visited my brother, neither in New York nor in London. Nor was Rohit ever known to seek out Baba's company when in Delhi. I don't wish to give the impression that they disliked each other. They just didn't quite know what to do with each other. They were the sort of people who, encountering each other as strangers at a party, would have diagnosed within five minutes a fatally mutual lack of sympathy. Thrown together irrevocably as father and son, they did what each must have regarded as his best. As a teenager, Rohit would rage against Baba's dullness, not out of resentment at the fates for having granted him such a father, but out of what he called love. And when Rohit, in the certain knowledge of failure, hadn't turned up for his Chartered Accountancy exam, my father didn't even scold him. The only consequences were his agreeing to fund successive foreign degrees in design and filmmaking. By then each had given up on trying to change the other. Even Baba's failure to visit Rohit wasn't personal. He never went abroad in his life.

Under normal circumstances, if my father had asked that we all talk, my brother would have suggested Skype. But – at least in Rohit's eyes – things hadn't been quite normal for some time. Baba retired on his sixty-fifth birthday. He'd announced the decision two years earlier, after Rohit's non-exam. With no one to leave his practice to, he gradually wound it up.

You can never predict how someone will respond to retirement, and with my father it was easy to be worried. How would he pass the time? All our lives he had worked twelve hours every weekday, and filled as much of the weekend as he could with more of his practice. My mother was not the sort to push back against this, but if she had, we all knew what he would have said: 'I owe it to my clients.'

His duty to his clients didn't allow for outside interests. There were, there must have been, things other than work that he did. Forty-five minutes in the park, starting 6.30 a.m. in winter, 5.30 in summer. Beyond a close reading of the pink papers, which was work, that is duty, he spent three minutes each on Dennis the Menace and Hagar the Horrible, and when he was done, if that day's strip was up to scratch, the mark of his satisfaction was a single yogic exhalation. In later years he added another five minutes for the Sudoku puzzle; if it took longer than that to finish he passed it on to my mother and got on with his day. Then there were those Sundays when India was playing Pakistan in Sharjah or Toronto, and his brother, my chacha Vikram, would come over for the free beer and larger TV. Baba, his beer pristine, would supply us with statistical permutations at the end of each over. But we knew that he couldn't spend his retirement analysing cricket scores.

More than worry I felt curiosity. I thought I knew him as well as anyone did. Others said better. And there was nothing stray or accidental in my father's days. Everything was planned and accounted for. It must be the same with his retirement.

He closed the practice on a Friday, and gradually I had my answer. My old bedroom, left untouched all the years since I'd moved to the next block, became his study. Now that he had saved the hour he used to spend commuting to and from Nehru Place, he took out subscriptions to the *Hindu* and the *Indian Express* and the weekly magazines, and he read these at the dining table before moving to his study for the equivalent of the working day.

None of us can say much about what he did in that room. No one was ever invited in, but he kept the door three inches ajar, and if my mother or I went in with a question he never seemed to mind. We found him at his desk, taking notes by hand as he read on his desktop or iPad. Sometimes it was a printed magazine or pamphlet, these often in Hindi, and he would place this on the desk with the pages facing up, so I never saw a cover or spine.

Like all lawyers in this city I speak formal Hindi well enough, but I read it only haltingly, certainly not well enough to make a useful spy.

Once a day, for a little under an hour, my father would close, but not lock, the door. This was usually around 4 p.m., the hour at which he used to pause his accounting practice for a session of hatha yoga. It had been decades since he'd needed a teacher.

Later, Rohit would argue that my apparent absence of curiosity proved beyond doubt that I had always known exactly what Baba

3

was up to. Of course I was curious, but I assumed that if we needed to know what he was reading and writing and thinking about, he would tell us in due course.

In the first year of my father's retirement, Rohit once speculated that Baba was unable to leave work behind and was in fact handing out accounting advice online. That was all I knew him to say or think of the matter, until we were four years into Baba's retirement and I began to hear from Rohit's Delhi friends.

These were boys already in the position Rohit would soon find himself: they had studied abroad and, unable to secure work or a visa, had returned to Delhi, one and a half eyes fixed forlornly on that lost world of mixology bars, Peruvian restaurants and blondes who did CrossFit and longed for an Indian man to teach them *authentic* yoga. Back in Delhi they spent sulky days at the family business, browsing bikini pics on *MailOnline*, pausing periodically to abuse an underling. Others simply drifted. They usually had some entrepreneurial scheme forthcoming, never actually going – something to make Delhi less unlike London and New York, to bring it into the twenty-first century. One of them once asked me to draft a pre-nup for his (arranged) marriage. I was willing, although I warned him of what in fact ended up happening: the girl and her parents didn't just refuse to sign, they decided to find a new groom.

All these years, that was the only case of my being contacted by a friend of Rohit's. Many of them probably never even knew that he had a sister. Until I began to hear from them at the pace of one a month.

Each time it went like this. The friend would message on WhatsApp (they were all born in the late 1980s, seemingly too late for email). **Hi Tara, he would begin. I don't know if Rohit told you that I moved back to Delhi. Anyway, it would be great if we could catch up some time over coffee. There's some stuff I'd love to talk to you about, someone like you who's a hotshot lawyer and really knows how to make things work in this city. I'm still trying to get a handle on it**

4

[university aside, every last one of them had spent their entire lives here]. **Rohit's always talked about how smart you are and how you're killing it as a lawyer. Really awesome stuff. Anyway, hope to catch you soon. Serious shit aside, will just be nice to hang! xx Pavit**

Pavit was the first, and he was representative. I grew quite fond of it all: the xxs, the agreeably fraudulent flattery, the growing confusion of tone caused by having to forgo the use of the word 'bro'.

We would meet at my office. They always wore a jacket but no tie, usually cufflinks, loafers or smart sneakers, chinos. Substitute the last for salmon-pink trousers, and it would be what they wore on cocktail bar dates. They would accept my offer of chai once I assured them it could be made without sugar, and then I would do them the kindness of getting straight to it.

'What can I do for you?'

They never needed any loosening up. A female audience for their passionate blabbering was theirs by birthright. Each time I learned anew about the places they had left, the buzz, the energy – the *frisson*, one said hopefully – and their student entrepreneurial ventures. Then they would drone on about their plans to shake up Delhi, and their families' boneheaded refusal to invest in their visions. 'My dad doesn't get it,' they would say. 'He thinks that because he's made money one way for the past thirty years, we just keep doing the same shit over again. His loss, he could have had a real stake in the future.' The more sentimental among them might add, 'Now he gets to watch someone else's son do it instead.'

I would be encouraging in terms general enough to avoid outright lying. 'Always nice to see someone who wants to take a real entrepreneurial risk rather than just join Papa's business. And you're right, some of our parents' businesses don't make sense going forward,' I would say, adding that I knew very little about this sector, but I could put them in touch with a former client of mine, etc.

5

At this point they would move on to their real business. 'I'm worried about Rohit.'

'Oh no, what's wrong? Ma speaks to him every day and she hasn't mentioned anything.'

With Pavit, that first time, I was genuinely curious.

'He's really worried about your dad. It's getting him down. I hate to see him like this.'

'That doesn't sound like Rohit. Besides, there's nothing at all the matter with Baba. He's in excellent health.'

'Physical health, yes. Touch wood.' This being my office there was plenty of wood to hand, and they always took the opportunity to touch. 'But hasn't he become, like, a hermit? Spending all his time hidden away, reading, and not talking to anyone. A lot of Sanskrit stuff, your mom told Rohit. And they didn't even know he read Sanskrit. And your dad's never been like, religious, before, no?'

'He's as religious as the next person. Plus I'm not religious at all, so I don't really know too much about that side of him.'

'But whatever it is, this isn't healthy. It can't be right for anyone to live like this. Rohit just wants to make sure that your dad's OK, that he doesn't do something silly. And everyone knows the bond you and your dad have. Only you can get through to him.'

On the first few occasions, this was the point where I decided to end things, so as to save them the strain of searching for ways to shake my evident lack of concern. 'There's nothing to worry about. No man in the world has ever needed less taking care of than Baba. But, since Rohit is so worried, I'll look into it a little more.'

And then it was the turn of Kunal, the friend of Rohit's that I knew best, if mostly by reputation. His sister, Lila, was my age, and twenty years previously we had been in the same maths tuition class. Since then she had been a person I met only once or twice a year, but was immeasurably fond of; a part of me had always thought we ought to be best friends, but was restrained by that other part that said that such fondness depends upon a

6

certain distance. Since she was married, and now a mother, I didn't think we would get any closer. New mothers of Lila's age and type seek out others like themselves: the childless no longer interest them. She had recently set up the Indian office of an American private equity firm. There were thirty partners, globally; she was the only woman.

Kunal followed the usual script, but something adversarial lurked beneath his words and tone. He had refused the chai, and each time I answered him he made it too evident that he wasn't really listening. I couldn't tell if this was because he simply didn't like me, or if Rohit was now frustrated at how little I was able to tell his friends.

As I began to say that I would look into it, he cut me off.

'No,' he said. 'Can you really not get it?'

'Get what?'

'This isn't just about your father's health. This is Rohit's future we're talking about. His rights as a son.'

'The right to know what my father is up to? What he's reading? As a daughter, I've never felt entitled to such a right.'

'So you don't get it. Or you *do* get it, but you get it too well.' Now he stood up, and took two steps towards the door, planting his feet so he stood at forty-five degrees to me for his valediction.

Lila was right about him: he really did take his ideal of dramatic conversation from the Angry Young Man era of Bollywood.

'Whatever shit your father is reading,' he said, 'it's easy for you to say it's not your business. You've always been his favourite. He's never given Rohit his fair shot. What kind of father doesn't appreciate a son, doesn't love and cherish him? God only knows. Rohit says he's gone religious, but I don't buy it. Our religion doesn't teach a man to betray his son. He's been brainwashed, and we all know what happens next. He will say he wants to devote his life to the poor and needy, go full Gandhi, and start giving away what is Rohit's. And Rohit will lose his chance. But Rohit's too nice to fight for his rights. Too soft. And you won't help him, you never have and never will. But I won't stand for it. It makes me sick to see this happen to a man like Rohit.'

It was only the next day that I realised that I had forgotten to close the door, and that the whole office – my three juniors, the clerk, the receptionist and the office boy – must have heard everything. At the time I found myself fixated on something else. Rohit was thirty, and this was the first time I could ever remember someone referring to him as a man.

Before the onset of Rohit's ambassadors, it had been many years since I had any cause to think about my father's money. I was financially self-sufficient, and so were my parents, and nothing was likely to change on either side. With no husband or children of my own, I didn't think of money as a bridge across generations, or of inheritance as a matter of right. Of course I was aware of the privilege that underpinned this lack of concern. At twenty-two, I could afford to pass up corporate law in favour of litigation because I had the option of living rent-free at home – most advocates pay their juniors less than their chauffeurs. Many of my classmates were expected to pay a family cess on their salary from day one, to go towards the medical bills of grandparents or a sister's wedding. My salary was really pocket money – tiny, but spent all on myself. After three years I started working for a senior counsel, and could afford to move out.

And then I was busy establishing my own law practice. You can succeed – which means survive – in litigation, or you can contemplate matters like your inheritance. That Rohit thought to have his friends scope me out suggests aspiring filmmakers have more free time.

But back when I was still dependent, I had felt the limits more keenly than the privilege. Unlike so many of his friends, and a few of my own, Rohit and I never had any prospect of going abroad for college. As accountants went, honest ones at any rate, Baba was successful, but not to the extent of contemplating dollar fees. When I finished law school, I thought briefly about asking Baba if I should look at an LLM in the US – a one year master's versus the four that college would have been. At that time India was opening up and felt new to the American touch, and even a slacker from my law school could get into Harvard or Chicago. But what would be the point? I didn't need an LLM to practise successfully in Delhi. In truth I thought Baba would say yes, and I feared this more than a refusal.

Then came Rohit's graduation, and his exam no-show. He started work at an ad agency, and said he liked it. I had moved out, but had dinner at my parents' whenever I got off work in time. Rohit, who ostensibly lived at home, was usually out with friends.

In those months I established a pattern that still holds. I never had to say in advance that I was going to be 'home' for a meal. I moved between my parents' flat and my own barsaati as if they were rooms of the same house.

This was why, when my father convened the summit, I thought immediately of the only previous occasion, six years earlier, on which he had actually requested my presence at home at a particular date and time: Sunday lunch. An hour later he had called again, brimming with apology. Rohit couldn't do lunch. Could I come at 11 a.m. instead? The thing was, he said, Rohit needs to be there, because we're going to discuss his future.

I had arrived that day to find my father at the dining table. Rohit was sitting next to him, but he had moved his chair to allow enough space for my mother to stand between them. She never sat if she could help it; it impeded the natural flow between kitchen, living room and bedrooms that kept the house going and her weight down.

Baba had arranged five documents before him, side by side rather than stacked. I recognised them as title deeds.

We had known, dimly, that Baba had always invested what he could in property, beginning in the late 1970s when he bought our Hauz Khas home. It was the first place anyone in the family had ever owned, other than lost village land that had passed from history into myth. But none of us – even my mother – had anything like a full sense of his portfolio. Until now.

9

'I've called you both here,' he said, 'because Rohit has decided to go abroad for higher studies. He applied some time ago; neither he nor his mother saw fit to inform me. He has been admitted to a college in London. I haven't heard of it, but he assures me it is famous in its field. Designing.' When my father had to speak at any length he did so in neat chapters, pausing to indicate a narrative break rather than to invite interruption.

Rohit may not have observed this habit of my father's, or perhaps he thought the point too important, and so he took the opportunity to say, 'Interaction design!'

Baba made no acknowledgement. 'Rohit tells me – I know nothing – that no designing college offers scholarships. In England the tuition fees aren't so high as America. But living is expensive. He says he can work part-time, but your mother says if he works it will distract from the studies that are the point of sending him. I agree. So the question is, how does he pay for it?'

He went through the options, making a show of the tokenism of the exercise, the fact that each had been pre-rejected. It was too late for external scholarships. Loans made little sense for a course in which immediate job prospects were dubious. The trust funds established for our respective educations had not been with a view to foreign degrees. Only then did he come to the point.

Our father, we learnt, owned five flats in addition to the one in which we lived. Each had been, at the time of purchase, in an unfashionable colony; some still were. But over time their value had grown by several multiples of ten. The cheapest would have funded an LLM twice over.

'Rohit can pay for this degree,' he said, 'if we sell one of these. Paschim Vihar is the one I have in mind. The price won't rise much further. I'm told that this is the right thing to do. It's our duty; it is an investment in Rohit's future. What is a flat none of you will ever live in compared to an education? All the same, I don't know. It's an asset. The rent alone is more than Rohit's current salary. Will he earn more as a designer? Maybe I'm wrong, and with the new metro line the value goes up. Plus, right now we own six properties. That's an even number. But if I talk like this, people will say, Brahm Saxena, he can only think like an accountant.'

It was never spoken but always clear: he was addressing me. And so it was I that resolved the dilemma.

Of course he should sell, I said; Rohit wanted this, and deserved it. He would justify it in time, I said.

The flat sold for so much that when Rohit had to leave London there was enough left over to fund another master's degree, this time in America. Every six months or so my father would remind me that he had never bought another property.

2
The Summit

Six years later, in the days leading up to the summit, I was forced to confront the prospect that my father was going to say what he planned to do with his properties. It was in his nature to want to explain his intentions so as to forestall the interpretive contest that a will might provoke.

I had known, of course, that the properties were on Rohit's mind. Maybe his impending return to India and the fact that he was now out of degrees had, for the first time, concentrated his mind on his financial future. Like so many other Delhi sons, the value of his potential inheritance was out of proportion with his own earning power. Whether he got half, or everything, the inheritance might determine the course of the rest of his life.

Why was he so worried? He couldn't seriously think that my father would give me his share. Baba and I might be closer, but my father was a man whose notion of dharma was the performance of duty, not the expression of preference. If he planned to disinherit Rohit, he wouldn't have spent all that money on his foreign degrees. Maybe it was that remark of Baba's, six years ago, that bothered Rohit. 'Right now we own six properties – that's an even number.' Then we had six; now we owned five. Maybe he had more subtlety than I'd ever credited him with, and understood what Baba meant by six being an even number. Six properties and two children: an easy division. Five properties and two children: a recipe for litigation.

On the day before the summit, I felt a wholly unfamiliar urge to pray. To whom or what, I didn't know. All I wanted was this: that my father's summit be about something other than dividing up our inheritance.

*

I saw Rohit first. This didn't look to have been an accident. Opening the door to me was his way of saying, This is still my home.

'Coffee?' he asked. Only later did he think to hug me. 'Not the usual crap. I've brought home an aeropress.'

'No thanks,' I said, adding, quite truthfully, that I was conscious of drinking too much coffee to get through the week and the weekend was a chance to cut down.

'You look well,' he said. Was that what you were taught to say in New York? Or London?

'I am well.'

It was a year since I'd seen him last. There had been longer gaps; but on those previous occasions I'd never consciously observed him, never focused my attention on whether and how he might have changed. Isn't that how it is with all siblings? I was six when Rohit was born, and for years I'd strained to hold on to every memory I had of life before him, fruitlessly. Siblings are the nearest thing our lives have to permanent fixtures, and they don't change even as we do – they might change to themselves, and to others, but not to us.

But this time I was vigilant for any sign that this might be a new Rohit. Not new to the eye – he still wore the old morning uniform of basketball shorts and Killers T-shirt – but I watched him as I hadn't done since he was *new*, newly born. I wanted to find evidence in his manner of the anxiety and ambition that had propelled him to send his friends to me and for him to rush back for this summit. They were qualities no one had ever known him to possess. He had 'ambitions', or said he did, but he had always expressed them in the manner of the child who is asked what he wants to be when he grows up.

I had refused the coffee, but he went to the kitchen anyway to get my mother, who went to get my father. I lingered by the front door, as if in a stranger's house, awaiting guidance as to where to place myself.

'There you are,' said Baba. 'Let's do this in the living room.'

13

This was the room in which we had always done the least living. We 'entertained' guests there – but we received guests rarely, by Delhi standards. Growing up I had associated it with the TV that Baba didn't believe in us watching. Unlike other fathers, he could express this opinion without hypocrisy, because he didn't believe in watching it himself. The room itself could go weeks without anyone entering it except to dust or mop. Its soft red sofa and armchairs must have looked staid on the day they were bought, but twenty years later they looked new, in the sense of being unused.

This meant that none of us knew where to place ourselves. Unlike those families who do TV dinners, or enjoy a nightly routine of four-way conversation, we didn't each of us have our spot.

Rohit sat first, manshrinking, occupying as little as he could of the sofa to make clear to my father how much space was available. But my father didn't sit down at all. Unless I sat, this would leave Rohit as the only one sitting, which was untenable. It took him a minute to stand back up, more confused than irritated by the rest of us. I thought this set-up perfectly appropriate: we were standing to attention.

Ma placed herself behind me, in the space between the chairs and the wall, technically inside the room but outside its social space, as if to mark herself as only an observer to the summit.

We stood, and no one said anything. At least on my part this was deliberate. If the summit was what I feared, I wanted to hold it off as long as I could. And I had the harmlessly cruel thrill of watching Rohit's curiosity – would it swell up and show on his face, like that of a man who is stuck in a long meeting and needs the bathroom?

Baba, I was certain, had planned every word of what he was going to say. That didn't mean he knew how to start.

But Rohit, this new Rohit, surprised me. He gave Baba his cue. 'Let's go, Daddy?' If this was a new Rohit, what else didn't I know? Maybe Rohit knew what was coming – maybe Ma had given him a preview. But that meant *she* knew, which meant too much revision of a life's worth of assumptions about my parents and their marriage. No, all this meant was that Rohit had prepared.

Going by his sending the ambassadors, he'd been preparing for a whole year.

'We should sit,' I said, so finally we did, except for Ma, who drew closer and placed her hands on the back of my chair.

I felt a shimmer of regret at getting Baba to sit. Standing up, you could properly admire his unblemished slimness, the little miracles of his waist and stomach, his shirt tucked in with the fitted ease of a second skin.

'OK,' said Baba. 'I know you want to know what this is about, and I don't want to keep you waiting unnecessarily. But I also have to tell this the right way, in the right order. I have to tell you why as well as what.' He fingered the ball-point pen that stood in his shirt pocket, as of old. 'I have been five years in this stage of life. What people call retirement. I went into it without plans. Where was the time? Ever since I arrived in Delhi I had known what to do. It was simple – first right foot, then left. Every day I had to look after my clients, provide for the family. But now that had stopped. That work was done. I'm sure you didn't ask yourselves why I was retiring. You probably thought, everyone retires by sixty or sixty-five. I didn't ask myself, either. I just knew – this work is done. But I was healthy. I didn't feel old. I could die any minute, but I could also live thirty more years. Not being Bhishma, it wasn't in my hands.'

He made his first pause. Had Baba scheduled these pauses, when composing his monologue?

Rohit, the new Rohit, the one who had prepared, had been waiting. 'You don't have to explain all this, Daddy. *We get it.* You were looking for a new source of meaning. Something to give purpose to the rest of your days.'

Baba looked at new-Rohit with the unfamiliar satisfaction of having been understood. 'Yes. Although you make me sound important. I simply wanted to occupy myself. I *needed* to know what to do with myself.'

'It's OK, Daddy! It's the universal human experience of retirement.'

'Why don't we just let Baba say what he wants to say?' I said. 'I know he's thought through all this very thoroughly.'

It was only later, replaying this scene, that I stopped on my use of the words *I know*. I knew what Rohit was thinking: Fucking hell, she already knows.

Baba looked gratefully at me, as he had at Rohit a moment before. Whether or not this really was a new Rohit, this was a new Baba – one who was unsure of himself; one who, for the first time in his life, needed someone else's support and approval. 'Yes, thanks, Tara.'

I felt Ma withdraw a few feet behind me, to my left. As we waited for Baba to find his place, I saw that the pink dust-cloth that always hung over the TV had been folded back. Ma clearly watched it these days.

'At first I thought, let me just wait, and something will come to me. I had a vague idea – I have looked after the family, now let me do something for the society – but what? I had no special know-ledge or talent. So I started to read the newspapers in the morn-ing, and our scriptures for the rest of the day. Between them, I hoped for my answer.'

Rohit was nodding along, either as a cover for escalating panic or because he liked what he was hearing. Wasn't this what Ma had told him – Baba had gone religious?

'On Saturday I would take my walk with Vikram in his colony park, and we would discuss the world. He too was thinking of retirement.' Baba was still speaking of five years ago: Vikram chacha had been a full-time grandparent for getting on three years. 'You know Vikram – whatever you say, he will disagree. Normally a disease only lawyers suffer from,' he said, smiling at me. 'If I said I wanted to serve the society, he said there was no need, our duties begin and end at home. If I said I was reading all day, he said, do something useful with yourself.'

All this was most unlike Baba, who liked to approach the point with care, but directly, never telling you what you already knew.

'So what was it, Baba, that you decided to do?' I asked, with pointed gentleness.

I had scrambled the script. 'OK,' he said, 'maybe there's no need to tell the whole story. I have called you here to talk about the future. My little future' – he indicated how little with his hands – 'and your longer futures. But more than that – all our futures. The question is, what kind of future can you have? Can we have?'

I knew what Rohit was thinking. Something had gone badly wrong. If Baba was speaking this way about the future, with this much uncertainty, did that mean that Rohit's future, the other still unsold flats, the theoretical but surely real stocks and bonds, were built on sand rather than rock? Unlike Rohit, I knew that couldn't be what Baba meant. But what did he mean?

'Baba – who is we?' I asked.

Rohit looked confused; Baba, suddenly exultant.

'That,' he said, 'is exactly what I wanted to talk about. Look outside.' It wasn't clear if this was meant as a literal instruction. The living-room windows faced the street. The potted plants of the balcony obscured, quite successfully, the flats and houses on the other side. That left only the sky, which in March was a weak, watery blue; the winter smog had gone, leaving behind a thin film through which we now saw the sky.

'Is this,' continued Baba, 'a place fit for life? By future, I mean all our futures – all living things.'

'Whoah,' said Rohit, 'Daddy, you've gone full Greta. This is not what I was expecting.'

'No,' said Baba. And he made a face – of contempt, of hurt by association. I registered the face, but it would be months before I understood it. 'You think, son, that I'm talking about climate change. Climate change is only a symptom.'

'The *Anthropocene*,' said Rohit, using a word I had heard but couldn't precisely define, pronouncing it with a mocking drama that was surely involuntary.

Baba said, 'Do you even know what that word means?' Rohit composed an expression of sufficient abashment. 'No? Just a trendy word you know. Well, let me tell you. *We* – we humans – have decided that we are apart from life. Above life. Nature, after all, has rules that we don't set. It has limits. It has its own law of Karma. Everything you do has its consequence, has its response. We used to know all this. We have forgotten.

'Delhi,' my father continued, 'well, there is no better place to see this than Delhi. What was Delhi? A perfect oasis. In the middle of near-desert, a slice of green heaven, fed by a strong river. What have we made of Delhi? A place unfit for life. The river is a dry garbage dump. The water in our pipes is liquid refuse. The air – I won't tell you about the air. Every park is a monument to what we have done. What is a park? A temple of life. Our parks are temples of sickness. Every tree, every bird suffering, as if it has been told it must live but is stuck in a place no longer fit for living. Come to the mandi and you won't be able to show me one tomato that isn't sick and decaying.'

I could hear what my father was leaving out; how much he was straining against himself for our benefit. My father dealt in facts, which as far as he was concerned meant figures, the only facts you could be sure of. There was no doubt that he had in his mind every number that measured Delhi's unfitness for living. When I said at sixteen that I wanted to be a lawyer, he had said only, 'Of course.' But later, once I was a lawyer, he would occasionally express a sentence or two of regret. The law, he said, was not really about truth, not about facts: it was about who had the better story, and who told their story better. Now Brahm Saxena, whom they said could only talk like an accountant, was trying to talk like a lawyer.

'You think you know all this,' Baba said, skilfully looking at all and none of us at once, 'but it doesn't bother you. You complain

about the pollution' – this time to Rohit – 'but you're only thinking about how it affects you. You're thinking, "I don't want to live
in Delhi because of the pollution", or, "If I have to live in Delhi,
which is the best air purifier, which is the best mask for running?"
And at least you know there is pollution. The city is full of boys,
your age or younger, killing themselves slowly with every breath
and sip, and all they're thinking about is, "Which Chinese phone
should I get? Should I get a Voda SIM or Jio? Which will stream
porn faster?"'

Baba was speaking at a pitch and speed that I struggled to associate with his voice, his body. The familiar pauses were gone, too,
and with them any question of us interrupting. He had already
said more to Rohit this morning than he had in entire years.

'As I read more, I began to travel around Delhi to see for myself.
I saw the way things really are. I said to Vikram, What are we
doing? Why are we on this mission of collective suicide? Vikram
told me it was all the fault of the West. In the West, he said, they
think man is God, or can become God, can own and eat and have
everything. It is man's destiny to control Nature. But if that is
true, I told him, we Indians have the least excuse. Our religion
says that all life is equal, all life is sacred. I am no better than a tree
or an owl or a rat. Our culture says think about your children,
your grandchildren, all the generations to come. I said all this to
Vikram. He said, OK, maybe you're right. But why are you worrying about it? If you don't like Delhi, move to a hill station. You're
old. If you want to take our religion seriously, now is the time to
go to the forest. I told him, People like you are the problem. People
who think everyone should only think of themselves. And as for
the forest – the way we are going, soon there won't be one for
anyone to go to. Vikram said, You can talk all you want. But you
are a nobody. It's not like you can change any of this.

'So now,' said Baba, who looked like he wanted to stand up
again, 'maybe Vikram was right. Maybe you agree with him.
You're wondering why I'm wasting your time with this lecture,
I who can do nothing about any of this. Well, I don't care. And I

19

don't have a choice. With what time I have, I have to do what I can.'

Rohit was the first to stand. Baba and I followed. Rohit thought about hugging Baba, but instead he extended a hand. When Baba didn't take it, Rohit didn't look put off. He just beamed at Baba.

'Daddy, I just want you to know how proud I am. And I'm with you, one hundred per cent. We have to raise awareness. Whatever you want to do, I'm here to help you with. I might even have some relevant skills.'

Given everything that has happened since, I want to stipulate here that I don't believe Rohit was lying.

'Rohit,' I said, 'I don't think Baba is finished yet. Are you?'

'I don't know,' said Baba. 'The truth is that I haven't yet decided what I can do. I know what has to be done – people have to realise what's going on, before it's too late – but I'm still working out my own role. Vikram is right, I'm a nobody, but that just means I have to work harder to find my role, find my purpose. Later, I may ask for your help,' he said to Rohit, before turning again to face all and none of us, 'but that's not why I called you here today. I wanted to talk about how my purpose, whatever it ends up being, might affect your futures. I thought I owed you that. But maybe,' he said, looking almost sly, 'maybe you don't want to talk about that?'

'No, Baba,' I said firmly. 'We do.'

How perversely versatile that word, 'we'. Here was Rohit, who had waited at least a year for exactly this, now unable to ask for it; and here was me, commanding Baba to tell us what I didn't want to hear. But I trusted Baba to know all this, because I had always trusted him to know everything.

'Only if you want to, Daddy.'

Baba looked at me as if he needed further direction. When I didn't offer any, he said, 'Tara is right. Of course I must tell you.'

I felt my chest and pelvis contract. What mattered, what needed to be said – what Baba wanted to do with his life – had been said. What was to be said now, no good could come of.

I presume there really are perfect families, orbs of warmth and care and humour, like a four-person lunch that is simultaneously relaxing and invigorating, except lasting a lifetime; and that we don't see them because you have to be in one to know it, and don't read about them because perfection is thought insufferable when it isn't you that's suffering it. Unhappy families we all know. But most families are neither happy nor unhappy; they find their equi-librium, and as long as they hold it life is essentially endurable.

Our family's equilibrium contained only two close relation-ships out of a possible six, and one of those, me and my father, was close in an unexpressive, unphysical way. But the family still *worked*, as a whole and for each of its members. And it had long passed the point of improvability. We could hold our equilibrium, or we could lose it.

Ma drew close once again. I might have reached back and clasped her right wrist with my left hand, but we were not that sort of family.

'What I will do, I will do alone,' Baba said. 'I may ask for your help, but I won't expect it, and I will shield you from any conse-quences. But, all the same, my decisions may affect you. They may affect what you had planned, or what you were expecting. Not that I should presume those things.'

At what point, I wondered, had Rohit stopped beaming? I only noticed it now.

'When you were born, I wanted to make sure that you could take for granted what I'd had to fight for. I had to educate myself, and then I had to educate Vikram. I know that at various points you wanted more than I chose to offer. You thought I was too strict, and too kanjoos. You were jealous of other children, their toys, their fancy holidays. But I gave you an education. Not only an education, but the kind I never had. On that score, I denied you nothing. What I did not spend on the household and your studies, I saved and invested. Like anyone who starts early, and avoids bad decisions, I did well. Now, what does that mean? It means that, as long as your mother is alive, her needs will be taken care of. That has all been arranged. She has the best health insurance money can buy, and more than enough set aside for her day to day. Whatever happens, she won't need one paisa from either of you. You don't have to worry about that.

'When I understood what I wanted to do with my own life, I thought about my other duties. Vikram and his family are well settled. My children have been set up for life in the most secure way possible, through education. You can lose a house in an earthquake, you can lose any investment in a recession, but education you can't lose. I believe,' he said, looking straight at my mother for a few seconds, and then to Rohit and me in turn, 'I believe that to each of you I have done my duties, and that my duties are done. Fifty years of duties have passed, and now I am free.

'So all I have left to say is this. I will ask nothing from you. Not money, forget that, but nothing else either. I will not be a burden on you. But now that my duties are done, you can expect nothing from me. I have already given you what you needed. Anything else I have must now go where it is needed.'

When it came, could it really be said to be surprising? When Rohit, in New York, started to dispatch his ambassadors, when those ambassadors hinted that Baba had gone religious, wasn't it only this that he feared? Not Baba leaving it all to me – even Rohit couldn't fear that – only this, maybe not in its specific, well-past-Greta form, but in a general sense. Any worst-case preparations Rohit had made were for this. He couldn't be surprised.

Yet – *needed*. What could he say to compete with needed? You might fear it was coming, might have feared it for a year, but who's to say you were ready when it came?

Ma spoke first. 'Brahm, what is this bakwas? How can you say such things?'

We have to accept that we never fully know our parents. Maybe she'd used this tone with him before, but I doubted it. And – another observed first – he ignored her, and spoke instead to his children.

22

'Do you think what I've just said is nonsense?'

I looked back at my mother, in search of some appropriate follow-up to this brazen violation of wifely decorum as she'd always understood it – contrition, shock, embarrassment, even confusion – but found only defiance.

Rohit was recovering, or maybe he was finally able to access the responses he'd prepared. 'Daddy, don't you think it's a bit unfair to just spring this on us? Shouldn't it be a conversation?'

'This is a conversation. I'm happy to answer any questions you have. I offer total honesty.'

'But how can this be a conversation?' I asked. 'Surely what is Baba's is Baba's to decide what to do with. I don't think Baba is springing anything on us, either. It's not like we were promised something and he is now reneging on that promise.'

'Don't try to lawyer this, Tara. This is a family. Baba isn't your client. I'm not the other side. We're trying to work this out together.'

'What is there to work out? Baba has told us, and he's given us his reasons.'

'Brahm,' said my mother in Hindi, 'what are you doing?'

Before Baba could respond – if he was going to respond – Rohit returned to his script. 'Daddy, we are a family. We don't sign contracts with each other. You never said, I promise you this, I guarantee you that. But in a family, isn't everything shared? Nothing belongs to an individual, it belongs to us all. What's mine is my parents', and my children's, and my children's children, even if they haven't been born yet. I can't turn around tomorrow and say, "What's mine is mine, I won't look after my parents." How can we suddenly stop being a family?'

Ma looked at Rohit as if he were up on stage at school prize day receiving first place in elocution (she had come to prize day every year; he had never won anything).

Rohit's claim was baseless, legally: Baba hadn't inherited any of his property, so we had no intrinsic claim to it. And dubious factually: Baba had made clear that we would never have to provide for him or Ma. Then there was the hypocrisy of a guy who had spent a decade hankering after everything Western, individual freedom above all, appealing to Indian family values. But none of these arguments quite fit the rhetorical needs of the situation. I needed a different approach.

Baba beat me to it. 'We are a family. Who said we aren't? All my life my first duties have been to this family. But before we are a family we are vehicles of God's will, and of the ultimate. And that is why, having done my duties to you, I am proposing to serve other duties.'

I thought Baba would stop there. It was less a matter of what he had said than of how he looked as he said it. He had the calm certainty that is only exhibited by two kinds of people: lunatics and possessors of the truth. You can't argue with either, no matter how well you're trained, or how long you've spent preparing.

But he went on, and this time he addressed Rohit alone. 'You are saying this because you have had expectations. And for that I should take responsibility. Clearly, if you developed certain expectations, I have done something to give rise to them, or at least I have not done enough to prevent it. And for that I am sorry. But I don't see why you need waste your time with expectations of this kind. You have had the education you wanted. You have more, so much more, than I did when I was your age. To make of yourself what you wish to make, you already have everything you need.'

The summit was closed. Whatever else Rohit had planned to say, tactically he withdrew. No one confused this with acceptance. What I had feared was now real. My father had taken the equilibrium built up over the nearly forty years since he married my mother and wrecked it in a few minutes. Rohit might withdraw now, but only to regroup, to plan for a long campaign, perhaps years, as long as was needed for the old equilibrium to be restored, or a more favourable one achieved. Ma would be with him. She couldn't help it.

We weren't dealing, here, with a conflict of loyalties. My mother and I were not choosing sides. We each had our place, permanent and unchosen. No, loyalty had nothing to do with it. And no part of me wanted to further alienate Rohit, whose pre-existing alienation I had long regretted (without doing anything about); or to lose what I had with Ma. She and I were two people with nothing in common, no deep connection, exchanging nothing more than teasing jokes, but never less than glad of each other's existence. The best thing I can say about my mother is that I took her for granted. While she lived, the world was stable. The world was known.

I hadn't seen the summit coming. And as I listened to my father I wasn't instantly converted to his cause. I'm not even sure I understood him, really. But I'd felt the force of his certainty. And from my unchosen place I could see what Ma and Rohit couldn't: that if Baba had wrecked our equilibrium, it was because he had to. I could not doubt my father, not unless he began to doubt himself.

Rohit left three days later. His Optional Practical Training visa was due to expire in July, and he was sure to take a holiday after. I counted on not having to see him until August, and thus to defer the next phase of his campaign. I knew Rohit: his last months in New York, maybe the last months he would ever have as a resident of the West (his Twitter and Instagram bios read: 'Filmmaker. Dreamer. New Yorker via Delhi and London'), would be spent in a carpe diem frenzy, his inheritance at best an inconvenient itch.

I was wrong. Four weeks later Mr Chawla – father of his friend Kunal and my almost-friend Lila – died suddenly, and Rohit flew back to Delhi.

3
Our Fathers

Ma didn't tell me Rohit was flying back. While never referring to the events of the summit, and never showing me anything that could be called hostility, she made clear every time I visited that things had changed. There were no jokes from her, and when I made one she met it with a smile of practised enigma. Had I known Rohit was coming, I'd have assumed Mr Chawla's death was only a poorly chosen pretext. You flew back from America for the death of a relation or of a friend, not a relation of a friend.

It was at the chautha that I saw him: in a corner of the room, behind the bhajan singers, who were in the process of packing away their things. The prayer meeting was over, the tea-and-snacks-and-condolences beginning. He wore an off-white poplin kurta that I was certain he'd bought the previous day, and he was talking to Kunal. In the three or four minutes I watched them, only Rohit spoke. He leaned in close, not whispering, but definitely confidential, while Kunal looked forward, not at the room but into blank space, nodding every now and again.

I hadn't watched them together before, not as grown men. In Kunal's nodding silence, and Rohit's keen chatter, I saw the nature of their friendship; I saw who was boss. I'd seen this scene in many other places: football matches on TV, the assistant manager chattering while his boss looks exasperated or contemplative; big-time CEOs and their jumpy little-time subordinates; dynastic politicians and their cronies.

I could watch them so long because Rohit never looked away from Kunal, and because I was all but a stranger at this chautha. I had met some of Lila's friends, but I was well beyond the periphery of her circle. I had never met Mr or Mrs Chawla, which is why I thought of them as Mr and Mrs, rather than Uncle and Aunty.

It would be senseless to inflict myself upon Mrs Chawla amidst the general clamour for her time, although I was idly curious, as I always am about the surviving spouse at a chautha: was she numbed or overwhelmed by grief, or was she, if it isn't too sacrilegious to use the term, enjoying herself? Not the attention, but the occasion as a whole, its stately drama. If most of our lives are patterned with uneventful repetition, then it is the *events* – births, marriages, deaths – that structure the plot, make us feel like we are living *lives*, not just an aggregation of meals and tasks and visits to the bathroom. I thought about these things more now that it looked less and less likely that I'd experience them myself. You needed to have a spouse to lose one, and single parenting had never appealed to me.

I watched Kunal and Rohit because my only business was to find Lila, say what I had to, and leave.

She saw me first. 'Tara,' she said from behind me, in her voice that was never actually loud but always as loud as it needed to be. If you were transcribing Lila's speech, you'd never have occasion to use an exclamation mark, and if you couldn't see her, it was difficult to tell how far away she was. By birth or breeding she had many little talents of this kind, talents that one could envy but were far more pleasant to admire.

By the time I'd finished turning she was beside me. She wore a blouse, in the Western rather than sari sense, and cream trousers; she could have come straight from work, or be on her way to another appointment. It wasn't exactly chautha chic, whatever that was these days, but Lila had her own ways. She never bothered with dressing to expectations, or dressing to what others might think of as appropriate for her figure. She didn't need to. You rarely looked past her face. I didn't, anyway. It was what they used to call handsome: robustly symmetrical, the chin and cheekbones and forehead a set of planets that paid imitative tribute to the central star – a nose so strong and straight that you always, after looking at the face as a whole, zoomed back in to it. It wasn't the Delhi pretty-girl face, and some fools doubtless thought it masculine. On a man, some fools would have thought it feminine.

And now it smiled at me with a broadness that was a little too much for a chautha. 'How long has it been? Gotta be at least a year.'

'More than that,' I said.

'Unacceptable. Let's catch up properly? Next week? You'll text me?'

'Don't worry, we can do it when all this is over. Whenever things start to settle for you.'

'No. I know how these things work. Now we see each other, and we both very sincerely want this proper catch-up, but if we let it slide it'll be another year. I know how crazy your lawyer lives are—'

'Hardly! As if private equity lives are less crazy! Private-equity-dedicated, supermom lives.'

'Ah, but there are shades of crazy. There's organised crazy and disorganised. And you know which side is you and which side is me. Being a mother actually makes one *more* organised. So you text me a day and time, and I'll make it work.'

'OK, I will. Can't wait.'

You can see why I couldn't now say what one was supposed to: produce some not at all dishonest but still needless formulation beginning, 'I'm so sorry . . .'

Lila, however, grabbed my wrist and made one brief concession to the occasion. 'I know you don't know too many people here, but have something to eat, at least? The chaat is really excellent. Papa's favourite.' And then she released my wrist. 'The weirdest thing is that I keep thinking about how much Papa would have enjoyed this. Not listening to everyone saying how sorry they are that he's gone. But he just loved chauthas. He said it's the best place to catch up with everyone you know, and it's so much more relaxed than a wedding. At a wedding the hosts are stressed the whole time, and the bride and groom are shit-scared about what's to come.'

'Clearly your father didn't drink.' My unseemly remark catalysed the unseemly smile, broader still this time.

'No. An essential prerequisite for preferring chauthas to weddings. Although I should make clear that drinkers loved Papa, because he stocked the best single malts and nobody poured more generously.'

'Well, if we each get our own version of Paradise, maybe he isn't here but he's at an even better chautha.'

We hugged, and she went back to her duties. I found myself hoping that this encounter, lacking as it was in anything resembling the exchange of condolence, might have given her more pleasure than anything else that day. And then I decided that the chaat couldn't possibly be good enough to justify enduring the queue, so I left.

Mr Chawla's was the sort of life you'd point to if you wanted to tell the story of modern Delhi in a hopeful old Hollywood way, earned triumph following world-historical tragedy.

In West Punjab the family had a life not of wealth but of plenty, with wheat fields, and orchards that poured out Chausa mangoes in summer. Mr Chawla's father had gone to college in Lahore where, in 1947, he had a job as the young manager of a sporting goods store, with hopes of soon starting his own.

It is said of families like the Chawlas that they 'lost everything' with Partition. In their case, this meant not only their land, possessions, and way of life, but Mr Chawla's chacha and chachi. She was nineteen, and pregnant with what would have been his cousin.

In Delhi, a strange place without the old foundations, they built new lives. In the stories of that refugee-built Delhi, it sounds like a kinder, more neighbourly place than the one I've known, with each neighbourhood sharing a communal tandoor, just as they had in the villages they'd left behind. The crueller,

Darwinian elements of that life have been edited out. But whether Mr Chawla saw more kindness or cruelty as a child, he was propelled by that particularly high-octane form of ambition that is refined from injustice, from the feeling of having been robbed by history. He wanted to do much more than match his father's pre-Partition dreams (in Delhi, his father had eventually opened a shop, but one that sold stationery rather than bats and racquets). He wanted wealth; the kind of wealth that made one matter, the kind that would withstand history and last generations.

Mr Chawla did not die a famous man, nor had he ever been one. But he was wealthy. He was one of those businessmen that rose up in the Delhi of the 1970s. In that licence-permit-raj era, the barriers to entry were high, and establishing a business required a combination of connections and the ruthlessness that calls itself resourcefulness. But once you were established, you were secure, and in the right sector a licence was a licence to print money.

Mr Chawla's licence was for the manufacture of air conditioners, and he was particularly skilled at winning contracts to supply his ACs to government buildings.

Unlike Rohit, I'm old enough to remember the import-substitute window ACs manufactured by men like Mr Chawla. They grunted and groaned like diesel generators, and drank electricity with the desperate urgency of a man on payday before he has to hand his salary over to his wife. Compared with today's Japanese and Korean imports, they seem childishly primitive, but they were real luxuries. Later, of course, ACs became a routine part of Delhi's visual furniture. If you ever walk round the back of a south Delhi market, you'll see the LG condenser units installed behind every shop like basketball hoops on suburban American driveways.

Air-conditioning was just one of the sectors in which imports, usually superior *and* cheaper, had killed off the old licence-holders. Unlike many such businessmen, Mr Chawla had seen ahead. He quietly sold his factory in the early 1990s and became a dealer for a Japanese brand. And he invested in prime real estate well before the boom that started in the late nineties that, by the time it gave out around 2010, had allowed plenty of lucky people to think themselves smart. Mr Chawla had been both.

Compared with the old manufacturing business, the dealership was small beer. Perhaps Mr Chawla kept it going just because he liked the idea of having a live business. But for many years he had spent most of his time at the Delhi Golf Club, and, more recently, being nana to Lila's son. At the time of his death his aspiration had been to spend the rest of his life combining the two activities: his grandson was to be made into the first Indian to win the Open Championship.

It sounds like an idyllic retirement, and for the most part it was. But in those last years Mr Chawla, for reasons nobody ever understood, grew anxious. Anxious about his health; anxious about money. Eventually he settled on a creatively obsessive fear of dying. Not death itself, but the act of dying. Not yet seventy and healthy in every measurable way, he kept constructing new ways it might happen. After reading *The White Tiger*, in which a wealthy man is murdered by his driver, he began to lock his bedroom door at night, and avoid going out in the evenings unless Lila or Kunal accompanied him. It wasn't a specific driver he feared: they were all threats, or had it in them to be. He bought an expensively pointless anti-radiation shield for his cell phone, and began to import a German product that claimed to wipe pesticide traces from fruits and vegetables. And one night, waking up to go to the loo, he looked up in his bed and realised that right above his head was a potential murderer in the form of his two-ton Japanese AC. What if it had been improperly installed? What if there was an earthquake? From that day on, his greatest fear was death by falling air conditioner. All the ACs in the house were moved to positions no human might find themselves beneath. When walking outdoors, he kept a few feet away from the sides of buildings, ceaselessly vigilant for condenser units. If one fell, it would not find him on its way down.

In the event, he did die in bed: of a heart attack.

Like the Chawlas, my father had arrived in Delhi with nothing; not because he had lost everything, but because there had been nothing to begin with.

Unlike Lila, who knew all the major facts of her family history, my knowledge was thin and patchy, and acquired piecemeal. Mr Chawla, and how could you hold it against him, liked to talk about his journey, of how he had turned tragedy into wealth through sheer will. He had no first-hand memories of life in West Punjab before Partition – he had come to Delhi at thirteen months – but he *felt* history, he knew those places and that life in the marrow of his bones. He knew what had been taken away, and he could measure what he had gained against it.

Baba didn't talk about the past. You had to prise it out of him. Open-ended prompts were no good. You had to ask specific questions, and be persistent, and develop bat-ears for any stray statement or allusion he might make in the course of ordinary conversation. And because Rohit had never cared enough to do any of this, he knew almost nothing of what I am about to relate. Ma must have known all of it and more – or did she?

Of Baba's parents, I knew least of all. Not only had they died before Baba came to Delhi, but they had left nothing of themselves behind, or at least nothing that he chose to carry. An investigator could comb through every inch of our house, and my father's old office, and find no other evidence of his having been born to a family, with a history, other than a name, Ramesh Chand, which was on all Baba's official documents in the box marked 'Father's Name'. Most official documents didn't require a mother's name, except for birth certificates, and Baba didn't have one of those. His mother's name was Pushpalata, but the only evidence for that was Baba's memory.

Where were the photographs? He didn't know if they ever had been photographed. All my life, in the houses of friends, I had seen grandparents, great-grandparents, grand-aunts, grand-uncles; seen them watching TV, or talking on the phone, or at the dining table, and above all in photographs. To this day, if I am in someone else's home, and they step out of the room to use the loo or make a call, I make straight for the family photos, especially those of ancestors. I don't use these moments to attempt a dubious construction of what my paternal ancestors must have looked like but, rather, to see what can be learned from photographs; to get a sense of the kinds of things I'll never be able to know. If it's someone I know well, I don't mind them finding me at it on their return. 'Your grandmother was so beautiful. They look like they had a very happy marriage.' 'Photos can lie, in fact they're often meant to. They couldn't stand each other.'

Ma's parents had lived in Meerut. Her brother lived there still. When her parents were alive we had visited every few months: more rarely than seems reasonable, given the distance. But they had both gone by the time I was eight, and while we had photos of them, Ma didn't display any in the house, presumably out of a sense that the asymmetry would be inappropriate. Four weekends a year – once a quarter, like some accounting standard – she still went to Meerut to see her brother. But he'd never wanted to know us, which meant that with each passing year our link to Ma's family frayed further. Our nuclear family was now an island with no motorable bridges backwards in time. If Rohit never had children, there wouldn't be any forward links, either.

We were this way because my father, in circumstances less world-historical than the Chawlas, had built himself in Delhi, built without foundations, and without even memory.

Baba had been born in the village of his ancestors, but his childhood was spent in a then-new town called Balaramgarh. It is in Allahabad district and is today obscure even to Allahabadis. But it had life once, in the brief flicker of Nehruvian optimism: optimism about India, and about the capacity of the Indian state.

Balaramgarh was given a watch and clock factory. In fact it was made by the watch factory: three grim villages turned into a town. Baba's parents didn't work at the factory itself, but were part of the movement of people that came in to supply the goods and services the factory needed. A cousin of Baba's father had set up a shop that sold ready-made clothes, and Baba's father was hired as the manager. Manager in name, said Baba, peon in practice. There are few greater indignities, he'd said, than working for a wealthier relation. You get all the usual burdens of employment without any of the protections of impersonality. And you are there because you have no other choice, or at least no good choice. Any boss may oppress you, but your relation will oppress you while reminding you every day that he is doing you a favour.

And then, when Baba was ten and Vikram six, their parents went back to their native village in the next district to attend a wedding, leaving the boys behind in Balaramgarh. On the way back, their parents' bus hit a goods train at an unmanned level crossing a few miles outside the town. Twenty-seven passengers were killed. Most of the dead, including my grandparents, were migrants to Balaramgarh, their families far away. There were no funerals. My grandfather's cousin was sent to identify his kin. Baba and Vikram were never even shown the ashes.

Then came the years of which Baba didn't speak, and which I preferred not to ask about. In my imagination they resemble a Hindi adaptation of a Dickens novel. All I know is that Baba and Vikram were set to work in the shop, without pay, and that Baba was rescued by the discovery of his gift for figures. Rescued first from other kinds of work – by thirteen he was the shop's de facto accountant – and then by the arrival of a benefactory stranger. A garment manufacturer from Delhi who brought his wares to that part of Uttar Pradesh every few months took note of Baba and his ability. For a one-time fee, his father's cousin agreed to let him go to Delhi.

The stranger was not an altruist. He had bought Baba because he thought he offered good value. Instead of the familial feudalism of the Balaramgarh shop, Baba was now dictated to with a coldness that he cherished, because it contained no hypocrisy. But the food and quarters were worse in Delhi, and for four years he couldn't see Vikram. Even so, Baba said, he could only be grateful to the garment manufacturer, whose name he never told me. The man had brought him to Delhi, where he saw that there was a world: a world in which you could make yourself.

In those first Delhi years, Baba had two free hours each day. Think about how much that is, he said: 730 hours a year. Long enough, in four years, for Baba to begin to learn, on the streets and in markets and parks and cinemas, about the kind of self he could make.

He learned that, in the scheme of things, the firm to which he had been sold was a contemptible nonentity, no bigger than an insect. There were garment factories coming up all over Delhi, places that sold clothes to London and Paris and Chicago, not Balaramgarh. He offered himself to several of these places, like one of the boys hanging around hopefully outside Bombay film studios, until one took him in. He traded servitude for a job, with a salary that he would have to live on in the city; by now, he had worked out how this might be done. Within a year, he would send for Vikram.

From this point until a couple of years after my birth, there were two ways of thinking about Baba's story. There was what you might call the CV version: what Baba had achieved, and when. While at the garment export factory he had begun to study for a BCom by correspondence, as well as for the Chartered Accountancy exam. He had been articled to an older CA, Mr Asthana ('my mentor', he would say, followed only by frustrating silence). He had passed the exam at the first attempt, and worked for a few years at a cement company before starting his practice. Along the way he had put Vikram chacha through college, and found him a bride. Finally, he had found himself a bride ('through the Kayastha section of the matrimonial classifieds'). I was born, and soon after he bought our flat.

But there was also the other version, a matter of texture rather than event, and of speculation rather than fact: the answer to the question of how exactly Baba had become Baba. Not Brahm

Saxena, the successful accountant with six, later five, properties, and a wife and two children; but Baba, my father with his effortless discipline, his perfect regularity, his neatly defined face and figure, all of them the fruits of his absolute certainty about how to conduct himself.

Standing metonymically for all of this, for the achieved Babaness that was the only kind I'd known, was his English. English was the language of our household. But Baba couldn't have grown up speaking English. I didn't even need to ask about that to know. In the part of the world that he came from, unlike in, say, Bangalore or Calcutta, English really was a foreign language. Even in Delhi, it was a language of elite power, absent from most everyday commerce, emotionally alien to the vast majority.

But my father insisted on English, a language that he can't have learnt to speak fluently until his mid-twenties. This was not difficult to justify. With English, as with our educations, he gave us what he had had to fight to acquire.

The English he had acquired was unaccented. You could place him as Indian, but beyond that it had no regional markers – no clues for any Henry Higgins to run with. He spoke slowly, but this was in keeping with the deliberate quality of everything he did, so that it never seemed as if he was translating from Hindi. It was Indian English, the register always formal. He made fewer mistakes than friends of mine who had degrees from Yale or Oxford. What gave him away, even more than the absence of an accent, was the absence of idiosyncrasy. That was how one knew that his English had been acquired with pointillist care.

As a child, I had taken his English for granted. By the time I knew it was acquired, I felt I could not ask how. To ask, 'Who taught you English?' could be taken to imply that there was something unnatural rather than simply heroic about the acquisition. In fact, my father's path of self-making had made authenticity per se seem worthless to me. What mattered was the quality of what one was true to, not its origins.

*

For all the differences of wealth and history, there was something rather symmetrical about the Chawlas and the Saxenas. The father essentially self-made, the mother a housewife. An older daughter pursuing a meritocratic profession by conventional means: academic success, planning and hard work. A younger son, keen in theory to make himself as his father had, except grander, but burdened by privilege and yet to really assemble drive or purpose. Lila and I were born a few months apart; Rohit and Kunal in the same week.

Where the symmetry broke was that Kunal had been adopted. You could see it in his build. The genetic Chawlas were all well short of tall, and they had slight upper bodies. Mr Chawla was slight full stop, with the usual Indian male belly, timidly round, while mother and daughter carried most of their weight lower down.

Kunal was six foot three and built like a wrestler of old – what Punjabi mothers might call 'healthy' or 'well-fed' – lasagna layers of muscle upon fat upon muscle, with a face of unembarrassed chubbiness; the face that comes from a life of ease and vigour. As a boy, said Lila, they drowned him in milk and buried him in chicken; as a man, he followed a similar diet, with the addition of a weights-but-no-cardio workout routine. But part of it was his genes. In the Chandigarh orphanage he had been chosen for his size and his colouring: he was the heaviest and fairest baby.

When Kunal came to see me in my office, I hadn't quite forgotten that he was adopted, but nor was I reminded of it. But when I had watched him and Rohit together at the chautha, and read their dynamic – the kind of dynamic that could account for Rohit flying all the way from New York – I wondered whether I might have underestimated Kunal. I had had him down as another Rohit, except richer and more brutish. Now I wondered whether, in the fact of his being adopted, with an older sister who wasn't, he had been given a chip of motivating insecurity that Rohit lacked: the kind of thing that could propel true self-making.

37

I didn't text Lila after the chautha. I hadn't forgotten; I thought about it every day. I wanted to see her. But each time I pulled out my phone to do it I couldn't. Yes, she had asked me, yes, it seemed genuine, no, I knew it was genuine, yes, she said if we don't do this now it'll be another year, and she's right, and I don't want that. But her father had just died, and who knew how busy she was with the bureaucratic nightmare that follows an Indian death, on top of the ordinary demands of work and motherhood. Who knew how many closer friends, real friends, had been messaging her to meet. She had asked me to text, and she had meant it, but that didn't make it the right and proper thing to do.

I didn't see Rohit again, either. I would postpone that until his permanent return. Ma, who even in this new disequilibrium was not going to lie to me, said that he had stayed only four days.

A few days after he had left, a Monday, Lila emailed.

If I were to wait for you to text, we might meet in ten years, not one. But seriously, I actually *need* to see you. Could we meet this week? Need you, it looks like, as both friend and lawyer.

4
Disequilibria

When I was eighteen, half a life ago, I left home to go to Bangalore for law school. When I was twenty-five and had done two years as a junior lawyer, I was selected for a fellowship that let you shadow a senior London barrister, a Queen's Counsel, for two months. It paid for flights, accommodation and a modest daily allowance. My father gave me a little spending money on top. I didn't use this for clothes or better food, but to pay for the cheapest possible weekend trips to Paris and Berlin. By my twenty-seventh birthday I had saved up enough for flights to the US. I started and ended the trip in Boston, staying meanwhile on the couches of law school friends in New York, Chicago, Houston and San Francisco. That was my last trip to the US, as well as the last time I stayed with friends anywhere. By the time of the summit, I could afford a holiday every summer, and had decided that from now until the end of my days I wasn't going to let a year pass without two weeks of it being spent in Italy.

I had never *lived* anywhere other than Delhi, except a law school hostel, and college accommodation hardly counts as real residence in a city. But I had seen enough places, enough cities, to look again at Delhi not with 'new eyes' but with improved eyes; eyes that had incorporated new filters, new contexts.

In Bangalore people would tell me that Delhi was planned, Bangalore unplanned. Bangalore, like the British Empire, had expanded in a fit of absence of mind. When I began to travel to other Indian cities, to argue cases – Bombay, Jabalpur, Ahmedabad, Allahabad – I saw that all of them were Bangalores. They had grown without logic or restraint. If you wanted to be kind, you could say they grew not in the absence of mind but in a surplus of mindfulness, the attitude that all we have is Now. Sometimes the results were dystopian, sometimes merely the non-fatal dysfunctionality that an American ambassador once called India's 'functioning anarchy', a phrase we took as a compliment.

Delhi was different, but it took many foreign trips before I could put my finger on how. Delhi had a logic, an underlying principle. If other cities in India were, in a sense, non-cities, just patternless agglomerations of millions of people, then Delhi was the anti-city. Delhi took the logic of the modern city and inverted it.

In the modern city, density decreases as you move away from the centre. Let us take the very centre of Delhi to be Rashtrapati Bhavan, a presidential palace four times the size of the White House, on grounds eighteen times the size. Central Delhi – Lutyens' Delhi – was on the scale of a gilded suburb. Ministers, MPs, senior bureaucrats and generals, and a few businessmen – old money and new in equal proportion – lived in bungalows on plots of an acre or several. They were more likely to have a tennis court at home than to hear the neighbours having a domestic quarrel.

Then you had the gated colonies of south Delhi. Hardly any bungalows here, or large individual gardens. But the effect was still less than fully urban. The early houses had been replaced by builders' flats, often with stilt parking, but one flat per floor, and three or four floors at most. Much of the land of each colony was reserved for parks and gardens. Unlike the private squares of central London, you didn't need a keycard to enter one of these, but that was just a concession to disorder, not a democratisation of principle. In those colonies with a sufficiently large population of resident domestic staff, the children of the staff had their own park – smaller, shabbier, but its very existence a form of privilege when the children of non-resident staff, like most children in this city, grew up with no access to green space of any kind.

This was another way in which Delhi inverted city logic. If you looked at Delhi from above, the centre resembled a landscaped forest with broad green avenues and a light smattering of houses (assuming, of course, that it was summer or monsoon and you could see anything at all). As you moved away from the centre, you came eventually to a treeless world of streets the width of Lutyens' Delhi pavements, choked up with dust and flies, the buildings unfinished except for the facade, which might advertise a beauty parlour or a UPSC coaching centre. This world, where most people now lived, had no place in the public or private-facing image of Delhi, and was likely to have no role in its recorded history. It gave Delhi away as just another north Indian town.

The final sign of inversion was transport. The further away you got from the centre, the rarer cars became. If you were over thirty and travelled by metro or bus, the odds were that you lived in the treeless world. As for Lutyens' Delhi, south Delhi, my Delhi: if a sociologist were to examine our lives in search of a shared culture, shared ways of being, all she could be sure to find was that we got around the city by car.

Lila had three cars, one for her, one each for husband and son, and two drivers. Raj, her husband, drove himself. Lila preferred not to lose an hour or more of productive work each day.

I saw the cars before I saw the house. Two of them were parked on the street, outside the gate. The drivers were leaning over the gate and bantering away with a third person, inside the compound, who turned out to be the nanny.

When she returned from the US after giving birth to her son, Lila had decided to rent a flat in Sunder Nagar, which is possibly the only colony in Delhi to be accurately named. It was where I would have lived if I could afford it. If you excluded Lutyens' Delhi proper, with its mansions and avenues, no colony better embodied the inverted nature of our city. The streets were wide enough to allow three cars per family without risk of the daily parking disputes that had eradicated all traces of neighbourliness from Greater Kailash and Defence Colony. The parks and gardens were maintained with the year-round diligence normally reserved

41

for the bodies of star athletes, glistening green even in May, and they were indecently large. There was more pleasurable green space for the thousand or so residents of Sunder Nagar than for entire cities in Uttar Pradesh. In Jor Bagh and Golf Links, Sunder Nagar's rivals in the colony-prestige Olympics, the architecture could be relied upon for some compensatory ugliness. But in Sunder Nagar, the new unaestheticism was still outweighed by Art Deco and other legacies from a time when people with money had also had taste. Lila, who had both, could have chosen nowhere else.

And then there was the quiet. Sunder Nagar was surrounded on different sides by Mughal, Lutyens' and modern Delhi, off the busy Mathura road, next to a large branch of the Delhi Public School. But it was insulated against the city by a high wall, really an enceinte, and a wide inner road like a moat. Once you were properly inside, you were more likely to hear the howler monkey from the Delhi Zoo than any human sound from Delhi itself.

Lila came out while I was still watching the drivers. She was in yoga pants and a loose grey T-shirt, and led her son by the hand. All she'd given me was a time and her address. I hadn't thought about the possibility that she might bring her son.

I prided myself on my ability to get along with people across the generations, on being equally at ease with twelve and eighty-eight. But I couldn't do toddlers; children under the age of, say, six, who are automatically rather than deservingly called 'cute' – I was clueless in their presence, and grew testy in my cluelessness. I couldn't baby talk, or pander, or hand out false compliments; I didn't know how to choose the right present, or read out loud. I avoided the birthday parties of my friends' children until they stopped inviting me. And this was Lila, on whom for some reason I was always especially keen to make a good impression, to be the most likable and compelling version of myself.

'I hope you don't mind,' she said, 'Kabir has a play date in the park. We can sit and chat at a safe distance. Apart from every now and again he'll barely notice us.'

As we walked towards the park she stopped. 'How presumptu-ous of me. You don't mind doing the park in this heat?'

'Of course not. It isn't *bad* yet. And if we're going to survive Delhi, we have to learn to enjoy the heat, since we're imprisoned indoors almost all the time it isn't hot.'

'Indeed.' And she gave me a version of the smile from the chau-tha: not quite as broad, but deeper, as if I had reminded her that we were kindred spirits. It was the sort of smile that, once provoked, you want to provoke again.

Kabir, whom I took to be two or three, hadn't looked at me once. Now Lila belatedly attempted an introduction. 'Oh, gosh, you haven't met, have you? Kabir, this is Tara aunty, a very old friend of mine. She's a lawyer, like Sejal aunty. Come on, say hi.' He continued to look straight ahead.

'Don't bother,' I said. 'I can't imagine how annoying it is for children his age, constantly being introduced to people who need mean nothing to them.' I thought, but didn't say, People who they're unlikely to see again for years. I was wrong. In the months that lay ahead, Lila and I would meet again and again at this hour, in these circumstances. Our conversations would usually take place either over text or in this park, with Kabir a few yards away. Nobody planned this, or ever recorded its ascension to routine. We fell into it, because it worked for Lila, and I made it work for me. I never learned how to get Kabir to warm to me, but he grew used to me, and would say 'Tara aunty', willingly if without enthusiasm.

As we entered the park I asked, 'He knows what a lawyer is? That's impressive.'

'He knows the word. And he likes it when I mention Sejal because she lives in New York and he was born in New York, and that fact is very important to him.'

Kabir's friend was already there, a little girl, unmistakably half-white, accompanied by a nanny rather than a parent. She was in a blue dress that looked far too fancy for an outing to the park, and she raced at Kabir, who dodged out of the way.

43

'He'll ignore her for the first few minutes.'

'Power move?'

'Yup,' said Lila, with pride. Of course she'd rather be the mother of the child who made the power move than of the pathetically eager recipient.

We found a bench. The sun was softly reddening as it set. It was still hot, but, if you sat still, in a massaging rather than grilling way. We sat beneath an amaltas tree, beloved redeemer of the Delhi summer, just coming into full flower in that Platonically ideal yellow, the colour of laughter and of the perfect reading light. No one could wish to be anywhere else. It was rare for me to think that way about Delhi.

Lila sat facing me, one foot on the ground and the other leg folded up on the bench. I paid the children more attention than she did, out of some subconscious fear that it would be rude to tune them out altogether.

'Who's the friend?'

'Mila, like Kunis. Lives nearby. Her grandfather is my landlord's brother.'

'And one of her parents is foreign.'

'The mother. American. I'll tell you the story sometime.' With this, Lila was signalling that we didn't have room for today to be a free-flowing catch-up.

'OK, so I've had four days to wonder what you meant by "lawyer as well as friend". Put me out of my misery——?'

'Thank God. It's so hard to find someone else in this city who likes to get to the point.' She looked to Kabir and Mila as a way of finding time to settle on her phrasing. Then she looked at me more directly than I was accustomed to, from anyone. 'I don't normally have feelings like this. And when I do, I don't make decisions on the basis of those feelings. You know, that's how most Indian businessmen justify their decisions: "I feel it in my gut." Well, I have a functioning brain, so I don't need my gut to multi-task. Usually.'

I had no idea where any of this was going.

'I've always liked you, but somehow, after that first summer, we've never gotten close, never gotten to know each other really well. But when I saw you at the chautha, I had the feeling. And then I had it again and again. It's a hard feeling to precisely verbalise, but let's put it this way. A feeling that you would get it. And that I could trust you.'

'Get what?'

'You'll see. Tell me, have you spent much time in Sunder Nagar?'

'A bit. Mostly just the market. But enough to know it's the best.'

'Let's say you were to spend an hour walking up and down the colony, long enough to walk past every single property. I'm not suggesting you do this, it wouldn't be very interesting. But one of the things that would strike you is that a quite absurd number of these houses are empty, and some of them have been empty for decades.'

'Property disputes. Inheritance. The story of Delhi.'

'You say that, but it was new to me. When I first moved here, I'd take Kabir for a walk around the colony most evenings, and I couldn't believe it. Parents die, and whether there's a will or no will, the children contest it. And they'd rather let the house rot empty, a house worth dozens of crores, than come to a reasonable settlement. Anyway, the more houses like this I saw, I told myself, Thank God we're not that kind of family, and I will never let us become that kind of family. And Papa's been dead two weeks, and it looks like we might have been that kind of family after all.'

'Surely your father left a will?'

'He did. Basically everything goes to Mamma, for now. But that doesn't help. In fact, it might make things worse.'

'But, Lila, if everything is hers, and you're all in mourning, then surely at the very least inheritance questions are postponed? Your mother is healthy, isn't she? And not yet seventy. Why worry about any of this right now?'

And then Lila told me why she needed a lawyer as well as a friend; and why I, not even her closest lawyer friend, was the person she knew she needed.

What she didn't know was that in almost fifteen years as a practising lawyer I had avoided property disputes, even though they made up the bedrock of so many Delhi practices. When I told her this she said it didn't matter.

Lila and Kunal had never exactly got along. She admitted to resenting him from day one, acknowledging that that was both entirely normal in the circumstances and entirely unfair to the baby Kunal. But as he grew, resentment became chronic irritation and eventually contempt. Unlike the original resentment, this contempt had been thoroughly earned. At home and in school, he had been a bully. While Lila had gone to the US for college and then business school, Kunal had never left Delhi, except as a tourist. His mother had wanted to keep him close, and he had heard that college in the US was harder work. It was at Delhi University that he had met Rohit. By then the school bully had grown into the college dada. Rohit was first among chamchas, but there were several.

Lila almost never spoke to Kunal when she was in the US. On visits home she was forced into his company, and she saw that he had all of the vices of Punjabi masculinity without any of their father's virtues. He was fawned over at home, by everyone, although she detected that for one or two of the staff this was a compliant facade. She wondered if his character could be excused on grounds of being spoiled, and decided that once you were a grown-up, you alone were accountable for yourself. But she was civil to him, for her parents' sake.

After the first few years she had never again felt that their love for him threatened their love for her. If anything, she took pleasure in the comparison. The adult depth of her own relationship with her parents stood in pleasing contrast to their mollycoddling of Kunal. As to the future, inheritance and all that – she had assumed her father had decades to go. But when the time came she'd have nothing to worry about: her father's closeness to her, and her son, spoke for itself.

'I have only one regret,' she said. 'Maybe regret is the wrong word. One thing I didn't do, which I ought to have done. I never gave any thought to how Kunal might feel about me. I didn't think it mattered.'

In the days after the death, Kunal ostentatiously took charge. Lila let him do it; this was not the time for conflict. She took upon herself all the tasks she knew he wouldn't think of, from the death certificate to emails and calls to friends and family around the world, and allowed him to own the public business of funeral and chautha and notice in the *Hindustan Times*.

Their mother, immobilised by shock, had said to Lila how proud she was of Kunal; if only Mr Chawla could be there to see him stepping up to his role. Lila hadn't contradicted her. Letting Kunal have this moment, she told herself, cost her nothing.

Most weekends since he had learned to walk, Lila had taken Kabir to spend a day at her parents' 'farmhouse'. The Chawlas were like other families of their kind in having a weekend home in what had once been farmland and was now south-west Delhi. They had garden parties there; Lila had been married there. Kabir and his friends could swim and run around and, most importantly, play games that did not involve toys or screens. On Saturday and Sunday mornings Lila would check the Air Quality Index. If it was below 200, they could go to the farmhouse. On farmhouse days Raj played golf.

The Sunday after the chautha was hot and clear. Summer had begun, but not yet turned dusty. Mother and son set off for the farmhouse. But when they arrived, they were confronted by an unfamiliar security guard who refused to let them in.

'He said he didn't know who we were. I said, "This is my house, and I don't know who the hell *you* are." I showed him my keys, he said, "How did you get those?" Can you believe it? I called the cook and gardener; their phones were switched off. Later I learned that they'd both been dismissed, and their phones confiscated.'

'Holy shit. How long had they been with you?'

'The gardener was new-ish, but the cook, maybe twenty years. He was part of the family.'

'So what did you do? You weren't going to involve your mother, not at a time like this.'

'That's the point. Kunal knew that. He knew, also, that Kabir is old enough to be affected by a scene like this.'

Kunal had left her with no choice. She had called him, and the security guard had let her in. But neither Kunal nor the guard had apologised in the usual way for the misunderstanding.

'Because there was no misunderstanding,' I said.

'You should have seen how pleased Kunal was, on the phone. He had the gall to say, "Glad to hear the new chowkidar is doing his job. The old one was useless." And the guard – I don't know what Kunal said to him on the phone, but when he let me in he acted like I was being done a favour.'

'Sounds like he was very well instructed.'

'I wanted to kill him.'

The guard or Kunal, I didn't ask. Either way, she clearly still wanted to.

'Tell me – you couldn't call your mother that day, but surely Kunal couldn't fire staff without telling her? Wouldn't they go to her for rescue?'

'That's the thing. The staff always answered to my father, and only my father. Kunal will have said to them, I'm the boss now, and I'm throwing you out.'

'And what are you going to do about Kunal? This is clearly the first move of a long campaign, on his part.'

'You can see why I need *you* for this—?'

I could see. It was the symmetry of our families. The older daughter, finding success through brains and application, dutiful to her parents while expecting nothing from them, self-reliant and free from entitlement; the younger brother, ill with entitlement, thirty and with nothing of worth to show for it. Lila saw herself in me, and in my position. 'Because I understand it, not just legally or intellectually?'

She laid a hand firmly above my wrist, not squeezing, but pressing down.

'Exactly.'

'There are many layers to this. And I don't want to predict the future. But as far as the legal side goes – what are your concerns? Let's be totally practical. You think he's going to intimidate your mother into leaving him everything?'

Kabir came bawling towards us. The palm of his left hand had been punctured by a rose thorn. Lila soothed him with efficient grace, like an expert dog-trainer, and sent him off again.

'Do other mothers often say to you, "You make it look so easy"?'

'No, but I hope they're thinking it. Don't you find their whining exhausting? All these trendy novels about how awful motherhood is. You know, if you're an inept narcissist, sure it's awful, but have you thought about how much more awful it is for your child to have you as a mother?'

'Ah, but they'd just say, "You would say that, with all your privileges."'

'Oh, give me a break. It's privileged ones that whine and can find an audience for their whining. Whining *is* a privilege. Mothers who don't have privileges are too busy keeping the wheels turning. Sorry, you were asking me about Kunal. I know I don't have to spell this out, but let me do it anyway. You know I don't need the money. Not one rupee. Nor do I feel entitled to it. If my father wanted to give it all to charity, that was his right. Not that he'd do that in a million years.'

'But—?'

'But, my concern is with justice. Sure, I've wished every day for thirty years that my parents hadn't brought that creature into our family, but I've accepted him. I don't begrudge him his share. But he's not going to bully me out of mine.'

'And there's more than money to this, anyway.'

'That's it. The worst part isn't him going after the inheritance. It's this head-of-the-family crap. That's what he was trying to show me with the way he handled the chautha and everything else. Well, he can tell himself whatever he likes, but he'll never be my father, and he'll never be my father's son. He had thirty years to learn from Papa, and he learned nothing.'

Legally, there was nothing to be done, not yet. That time would come – you could be sure of it. As a friend and as a lawyer, Lila had called me in now because she wanted me to be prepared, and because she wanted a teammate, a second. I wanted to *do* something immediately; I wanted to show that she had the right lawyer, the right friend.

'What are you going to do, short-term? Try to have a conversation with Kunal about where the two of you stand? Is he capable of it?'

'He isn't and, let's face it, we aren't. We don't have a real relationship.'

'Why don't I go and see him? The way I see it, the escalation that bringing a lawyer in implies actually makes sense in this case. You don't think of him as your brother, but as an irritant who is now an adversary. If we go by the all-bullies-are-really-cowards principle, we have to pre-emptively show him you're going to fight. And he already dislikes me – maybe because I remind him of you.' I had told her about Kunal's ambassadorial visit to my office.

She nodded appreciatively. 'Thanks. If you're sure you don't mind.'

As we walked Kabir back to the house, I declined her offer of coming up for a drink. As ever, I had a long evening of work ahead. I'd take my drink at home, with a file.

We hug-kissed goodbye and Lila said, 'Please go and see him. But what we need is a weapon. Something to scare him with. I think you're right, he'll scare easily, but just a visit from you won't do. Try to think of what might?'

Since the summit I had only spoken to my father twice, both times with my mother around. I was lucky to have chosen a profession that I could always bury myself in.

At this point I was handling two complex telecom cases, in both of which I was briefing a senior counsel; and a range of other matters in which I acted on my own. In recent years I had acquired a minor reputation as a good lawyer for students suing universities. Female students naturally preferred me to a male Delhi lawyer whose honeyed tongue was often an appetiser to wandering hands, but a couple of prominent successes had meant that men came to me too.

One of those cases had concerned a provincial university which, after holding its annual entrance exam, had decided to alter its admission criteria, increasing the weight allotted to the interview. It was credibly rumoured that the reason for the change was to ensure the admission of three sons of local politicians who had scored poorly on the exam. As with every such case of everyday Indian corruption, there was no way to directly make this accusation in court, let alone prove it. But thirty students who had been denied admission as a result of the change decided to sue. Technically they filed thirty individual suits, and there were at least a dozen lawyers involved. I only represented two of the students. But I was the youngest and hungriest of the lawyers; for the others, this case was a side piece at best. I offered many services to the other lawyers and their clients, asking for neither payment nor credit. Word spread in the town that I was really the main lawyer, and the local press got to know me. When, eventually, the court ruled in our favour, and reinstated the original scheme, it was covered in a small way in the Delhi press, and I was the only lawyer mentioned.

This success was not a happy one. It came with a large serving of unpleasantness, and cost me more than one friend.

The court wasn't the only place the case was being argued. On the streets and online – social media was beginning to take off in Hindi-speaking India – it was fought by other means. The involvement of the politicians' sons, inadmissible in court, was widely disseminated. But it didn't stop there. A local right-wing outfit, loosely but not officially tied to the Hindu nationalist party, began to allege that the politicians' sons were just a front. The real story, they claimed, was that the rules had been altered to favour Muslims.

Anyone who had studied the case knew this was nonsense. Exactly one additional Muslim had been admitted under the new rules. Muslims were fifteen per cent of the population of the state, and under five per cent of the student body at this university. In what we can now see as a portent of things to come on a national scale, those essential facts remained in the station waiting room while the campaign of lies boarded trains for every corner of the state.

When the bench ruled in our favour, I began to get calls from other Delhi lawyers. How could I let myself be a willing accomplice to Hindu majoritarianism? Didn't I know that the case had been decided not on the merits of law, but because the judges had been swayed by the campaign?

Most days I told myself that the social media campaign was deplorable but had nothing to do with me. I had argued a case I believed in, and won it on the merits. But I didn't have either the facts or the arguments to dissolve the other side completely. Every honest lawyer knows that there may be times when a favourable judgment has been bought by a client, not by paying for your legal skill but by buying the judge. I couldn't prove that the judges in this case hadn't been influenced by the campaign.

Eventually I had gone to Baba to ask him to settle my conscience. I laid out the facts, and diligently put the case for the prosecution. But he refused to rule.

'If your conscience wasn't clear,' he said, 'you wouldn't have come to me. You think you did right by your clients, which is your first duty. What you want from me is something else. You want me to tell you that the cause itself was just. How can I judge that? There are only two judges. Every individual, and the ultimate judge.'

That was the last time I had explicitly asked him for advice or reassurance. I had sensed in his answer an implicit rebuke, or maybe just an exhortation: be responsible only to yourself. Be like me – not that he would have been capable of forming that thought.

That was the nature of our famous closeness, in the old equilibrium. I wanted to be like him and, after a point, that meant letting go of the question, What would Baba do?

In the new disequilibrium I could no longer know where Baba and I stood. After the summit I waited ten days to go home. If I stay away any longer, I told myself, I won't just be accepting disequilibrium. I will, as mediocre therapists say, be co-creating it.

I went when I thought dinner might be ending. In retirement, my father ate slowly. This wasn't a matter of more chewing, but of breaks between chews, breaks between mouthfuls. It may have been the only way in which he was less efficiently purposeful at seventy than he'd been at forty. Ma ate as quickly as ever, and while he finished she commuted between kitchen and table, brewing her ginger tea, drinking it, and with inhuman swiftness completing the cleaning of vessels and surfaces that, in an orderly household, certifies that a day is done and the next fit to start. Only the most obvious of the many ways in which I could not be my mother.

I aimed to arrive during this phase, Baba finishing, Ma shuttling. No summit, I told myself, could change *these* rhythms.

Ma came to the door, and she let me in as wordlessly as ever. Her teapot was still on the table. My father wasn't there.

If I said to Ma, Where's Baba? or, Has Baba gone to his room?, would I be saying, in effect, that I was there to see him? Had I merely miscalculated the time, or was he now leaving the dining table sooner, to get away from Ma?

Before the summit I'd have sat with Baba, and mainly I'd have talked to him. But every three minutes I'd have called out in some way to my mother; mocked, for the millionth time as if for the first, her refusal to sit down, the liturgical rigour of her kitchen scrubbing.

Without Baba, could I sit at the table on my own? Or trail her unhelpfully? Domestic help from me was much worse than no help.

At first I sat, opposite my father's place, in the chair that had been mine since this table arrived twenty-three years prior. Moving out hadn't meant giving up my title to that chair, and to the best view the world could offer of Brahm Saxena's face. I sat, and with no father opposite, no evidence in plate or crumb that he had ever sat there, I felt as little at home as someone visiting her ex-husband and his new wife.

From Kashmir to Kanyakumari, on every street that evening a mother and daughter were settling down to chat, in warmth or rancour. Those mothers with distant daughters were waiting, depending on time zones, for the grandchildren to be put to bed or for the daughter herself to wake up. For the call. From San Francisco to Sydney, my law school friends called their mothers. Every day, for hours. 'With her, the hours just disappear.'

Not with us. Or they did, but never in talk.

Still, on this day I tried. There was no question I could ask my mother to which I didn't know the answer. I couldn't press her for the details of her day without seeming unhinged. So I asked about Rohit, at the risk of seeming something worse – tactical.

'Why do you ask?'

I couldn't say: Do I need a reason, Ma? What did it say about me, that she thought I must? 'No reason. He must be sad about leaving New York.'

'He's not sad.'

Unable to take it at the table, I was now standing in the kitchen doorway. I didn't go further with Rohit. I started talking – about work; about Deepti, the friend of mine Ma knew best; about how Ma, the only woman of her kind without a smartphone, was kept safe from Manju chachi's daily projectile vomit of grandchild photos. I had no idea how to talk to my mother – I'd never had to – and I was hoping the effort might speak for itself.

Outside, in the stairwell, I looked at my phone and saw that I'd been with her eighteen minutes.

The next time I came earlier, early enough that if Baba wasn't at the table, it meant he was eating in his room. I brought work, and Mathura pedas.

My parents were eating together. Since Baba's retirement he'd taken all four meals – breakfast, lunch, tea, dinner – at the table with his wife. They could pass entire meals without so much as one sentence being spoken, but they were never less than gratefully companionable. My parents shared their silences more happily than most couples in Delhi shared their chatter. Shared, or had shared?

I couldn't look at them and tell that this silence was different, because I couldn't know that I wasn't just seeing what I dreadfully expected. I sat in my place, they in theirs, next to each other. In the usual way I started to tell Baba about my ongoing cases. I didn't look for ways to include or engage Ma.

My father never appeared to be anywhere other than listening to me. But he didn't ask a question. He showed no signs of boredom and no signs of interest. I don't think anything he said that evening would in grammatical terms constitute a complete sentence.

I couldn't wish the summit hadn't happened. I could wish my mother wasn't there tonight, and I could despise myself for it.

When Baba was done he got up and went to his room. I thought of staying at the table, opening my file, and thought again.

On my way out, my mother placed the unopened box of pedas in my hand. 'Give these to your juniors, beta. You know we're too old for sweets.'

Rohit, when he could tear his attention away from the seductions of his last New York summer, must think that Baba and I had been brought closer; that, whether or not we'd been colluding prior to the summit itself (which remained the likeliest scenario), we were definitely conspirators now. He saw what had been our family as two rival partnerships. Maybe he told himself it had always been that way, and the summit had merely brought the unacknowledged into the open.

If I hadn't yet got Baba on his own, it was at least partly because I didn't want to prove Rohit right.

*

55

I had Kunal's number from the time he came by my office. I asked him if we could meet. I didn't offer a reason.

He asked me to come to his office, which was in Defence Colony market. Only on the way did it occur to me that I ought to have been surprised that Kunal had an 'office' at all. I had no idea what he did, beyond firing gardeners and hosting chauthas. Did he notionally run the AC dealership?

The office was on the first floor, above a shop that sold stationery and greeting cards. The building itself was run-down, like most of its kind, but in a way that we no longer noticed, like thick scratches on a phone screen that the eyes filter out after a day or two. External shabbiness was a given in Delhi markets. Only interior appearances mattered.

There was no sign visible from the street. So it was only when upstairs that I saw what I had come to. There was a gold-plated signboard to the left of the glass door, and the same text printed on the door itself, above an outline map of India with a sun across the centre.

ADHIMUKTA BHARAT
ENERGIZING INDIA'S YOUTH

The door opened into a reception area. A girl in her early twenties sat behind a laminate desk, another Adhimukta logo behind her. To the left stood the office itself: an open-plan central area with four rows of young men at desktops, three private offices and a conference room beyond. One of the offices was twice the size of the others. The overall effect was irritatingly close to a law chambers, but the young men added a small-time tech-start-up vibe which I chose to focus on.

I knew which office was Kunal's, and I also knew that he was the oldest person there.

The receptionist took my name and said the Chairman sir was in a meeting. Would I care to sit? No, I would care to stand. Please sit, she said, switching to Hindi, it will take some time. I'd really rather stand, I said in English.

The idea that one would rather stand than sit is gravely troubling to the urban Indian mind, as perverse as choosing to take the stairs when there's a lift. There was something about this girl that made me want to be troubling. I stood in front of the desk, three feet away from her, and I didn't even have the decency to pull out my phone. I just looked at her.

No offers were made: no tea, coffee, not even water. Was this how Chairman sir's guests were typically treated?

I grew bored of the girl and walked over to the central area. I placed myself by the wall closest to Kunal's office. The young men ignored me. The other two offices looked empty. Kunal's had tinted windows, but I thought I could trace the outlines of two empty chairs in front of the desk. He wasn't in a meeting, unless of the video kind.

The receptionist got up and came towards me, heavy with tension, perhaps from the effort to be polite and hostile at the same time. Please, would I sit? I'd be much more comfortable that way. No, I'd really rather stand. You can't stand here, she said, please come back to the waiting area. Then Kunal came out, in a white Chinese-collar shirt, khaki trousers, and what used to be called a Nehru jacket and had now been rebranded a Modi jacket, navy.

'Tara. Come in.'

I followed him in and deliberately did not close the door behind me. The well-trained receptionist girl closed it from the outside.

'Wow,' I said. 'I had no idea this was what you did.'

'This?'

'Ridding Bharat of Adhi. By the way, what is Adhi?'

'It's *Uh-dhi*, not *Aadhi*, firstly. And – why don't you go look it up for yourself.'

The name, and my general sense of Kunal, had led me to conclude that the place was a vehicle for political aspirations, and I was pretty sure of what tendency.

'I thought all that mattered was that Bharat be Congress-mukt?'

'There's a lot you don't know. Now listen, I don't know why you're here, and I don't know about you but I don't have all day and certainly don't have the time to educate you.'

'I'm sorry, I didn't realise you were in such a rush.' We were both standing: him behind his desk, me between the door and the two guest chairs I'd traced through the window. Unlike the receptionist, he seemed at no pains to get me to sit. On the desk stood a jumbo-sized iMac, three photos – one of each parent and one of the two of them with a teenage Kunal, on some European ski jaunt – and a pile of three books. The spines pointed away from him, towards the visitor. The *Bhagavad Gita* was on the bottom, The Constitution of India in the middle, and *Inner Engineering* by Jaggi Vasudev on top. Behind him were three more shelves, largely empty but with around a dozen books (politics, business, spirituality), and two gilded brass mementoes that on closer inspection turned out to be awards given to Mr Chawla by the air-conditioning industry. A window that presumably looked onto the market was covered by a grey roman blind. Most of one wall was occupied by an OLED television, and most of the opposite side by a very comfortable-looking plush analyst's couch.

My own office's absence of nappable couch came sharply into focus.

'May I sit?' I took a chair before he could answer. He kept standing. 'I'm here on Lila's behalf.'

'She needs to send emissaries to her own brother?'

'Not as her emissary, which is a role you know all about, isn't it? As her lawyer.'

'Ah.' And now he sat in his Herman Miller chair, a year's salary for a young barrister with an unusually generous employer. 'And why do I need to deal with her lawyer?'

'Let's not be coy, Kunal. Apart from anything else, it always wastes time, and you've already said yours is precious.'

'My father has been dead less than a month, and my sister is sending lawyers at me. Does this shit have to start *already*?'

'This shit never *has* to start. It's better if it doesn't start. And even when it has started, there's a small window where you can backtrack. Call it a false start, it'll be as if it never happened. We're still in that window.'

As I spoke I was straining to read his facial expression. When he had come to my office this had been easy. But this was a different Kunal. Perhaps it was as simple as a matter of habitat. This was Kunal in *his* kingdom. Here he was Chairman sir.

He said nothing, only kept looking at me with just the ghost of a glower.

'Let's take what happened last weekend. It could be the start of the shit. But it doesn't have to be. All I'm really here to say is, it's up to you. Lila, like any reasonable person, has enough shit of her own. She doesn't want any of this. If you backtrack, if we call this a false start, you can be assured that she will never instigate anything. And we can all move on as if nothing happened.'

'*Like any reasonable person.* Of course. Don't think I don't know what that means.'

I didn't know what he thought that meant. 'If I didn't think, if Lila didn't think, that you were a reasonable person, I wouldn't be here. That's the point. Everyone involved is reasonable. Which is why—'

'You shouldn't have come,' he said, and you could see how much effort he put into saying it softly.

'What does that mean?'

'She should have come herself. But, actually, it doesn't matter. She wouldn't understand, just as you don't.'

'Try me. Or, actually, don't count on me understanding. Just count on me being able to remember. Whatever you want me to tell your sister, I will.'

There was a long silence. It's always instructive to see how someone will react to a silence. I looked at his cheeks, chubby-strong like the love handles on a young buffalo, and at the thick black mass that looked like it had been poured onto his head with an ice-cream scoop, and I saw how unlike Rohit he was. Rohit and every other one of his friends had some asinine trendy variant of the short back and sides, and they dressed and spoke as if they inhabited some adult extension of an international school in which there is one universal culture and its two sources are California and London. Lila, too, could fairly be accused of importing a New York life to Delhi and adding the Indian trimmings of cook and chauffeurs. Even I had my Italian longings. But Kunal seemed content with Delhi, content with India. His desires were Indian, so too his insecurities. If he was dissatisfied with anything, he wouldn't look beyond Delhi for his answer.

Unlike me, and unlike Lila, unlike even Rohit, Kunal spoke Hinglish rather than English. My record of his speech should be taken at least partially as a translation rather than a transcript. Every time he opened his mouth I thought, Have there ever been two siblings whose accents and diction were so different?

To my amazement, I found that he was interesting me. I had to remind myself that there was nothing wrong with this.

I broke the silence. I hadn't anticipated having to do this. 'You could tell me, for instance, why you pulled that stunt about the farmhouse. OK, you don't like me calling it a stunt. And your staff management practices are none of my business. But you knew Lila used the farmhouse every weekend. You knew about her relations with the staff. You knew, in fact, that they had much more to do with her than with you. So why not consult her? Or even just keep her in the loop?'

As I spoke I watched his anger puffing out, as if it were an inflatable ball and each of my words pumped in more gas. The ball originated in his chest and by the time I was done you could see it on those buffalo cheeks and you could see it in the clenched fist of his right hand. And then I watched him let it deflate, not all the way, but enough so that he could congratulate himself on his self-control. And when he spoke it was again with that strenuous softness, like a man who has been accused of wife-beating trying to come across all patience and discipline in court.

'Do I really have to explain these things to you?'

60

'I told you, just think of me as a messenger. You're not talking to me, you're talking through me, to Lila.'

'I mean, why do I have to explain at all? How can you not know the answers to these questions? Which country are we living in?'

'Kunal,' I said, using his name for the first time, 'if there's one thing practising law teaches you, it is that nothing is obvious. When you know or understand something, you think everyone does. But it isn't so. So spell it out. Maybe I'm just ignorant. But I'm sure I'm not too thick to understand, once it's explained to me.'

When he spoke he was soft again, but in a different way. 'This is India. Our country. You're Indian, right? Did you know that Lila's son is American? They waited till he was born to move back so he could get US citizenship. Not an option for Lila and Raj, because for Indians the green card pathway is *blocked*.' He grinned, drawing out the pleasure of this word, as if describing to me his enemy being stuck for hours on the Gurgaon–Delhi road. 'So they're still Indian. My grandparents risked their lives so they could be Indian. But apparently, I have to now tell her, *through you*, about India. How Indian families work. Amazing what people can forget, in their own country.'

I wasn't going to say anything until he was quite finished.

'Lila didn't get the green card, but she has still tried to make herself American. I guess you've done that too, without even leaving India. But as long as you have Indian parents, Indian brothers, you live in Indian society, you can't just do that. My father has died. When a king dies, his son is the new king. When a father dies, there's a new head of the family. It happens instantly. There is no break.' He pointed to something I hadn't noticed, a calendar on his desk, and began to turn its leaves. The months alternated with patriotically Photoshopped images of Indian Air Force jets. 'Just like how the earth keeps going round the sun. One year ends, the next begins, but there's always a year – it's 2016 and then it's 2017, there isn't even a millisecond where it's neither.' Maybe he had actually read some of the spiritual books on his shelf, and acquired a profundity of the kind that escaped me. 'I'm the head of the family now. I have to take decisions. I have to keep the family safe. I have to do what's right for the family.'

'And who appointed you head of the family? On what grounds? Your mother is alive. Lila is older.'

He looked at me with pity, outrage and amazement. 'You *know* how it works. Don't try to piss me off, please. I get that lawyers try to argue everything, but there's a limit.'

'I'm not trying anything. I'm asking a perfectly valid question. Who appointed you?'

'Whatever you say, you know how it works. Lila has her own family now. That's what happens when you get married.'

'When a girl gets married?'

'When a daughter of the family gets married.'

'Kunal, that may be how it works in some families, maybe most. But is that how it works in your family?'

'Lila is part of a different family now.'

'She has kept her name. Your name.'

'That doesn't mean anything. She has her own family. Raj is the head of that family. Not that he does his job.' He grinned at me as if inviting complicity; he wanted someone to share in his contempt for Raj's unmanliness. He got nothing. 'But those things can happen. The king can be so weak that the queen rules. Doesn't matter. The king is still the king. The queen rules because he lets her rule. He rules by right.'

'Do you think Raj thinks of himself as head of his family?'

'OK, you have a point. There are some families where a woman can be the head. But not our family.'

'I ask again, who decided that? Who appointed you?'

Up until now he had been sitting away from the desk, his left leg crossed over his right. Now he rolled his chair forward, placed both feet on the ground and leaned towards me. 'I didn't want to have to say this.' He was being soft again, but this time with pained condescension. 'It's not a nice thing for Lila to hear. It's better not to have to say some things. But you're not giving me a choice.'

'We're all grown-ups here.'

'I'm different. From you and from Lila, and from Rohit. From most people, although there are a few others like me. Most people have no purpose. Their birth itself is random, accidental. They are born to a family, but only because one out of millions of sperm happened to win a race. The whole thing has no meaning. But I am not an accident. I have a purpose. I was marked out. I was chosen.'

'You were adopted and Lila wasn't,' I said, violating my vow not to interrupt him, 'but no one has ever treated you differently because of that. You and Lila might not be close, but you are her brother. You're both your parents' children. You are equal.'

'But that's the thing,' he said, his eyeballs now glossy with pleasure, 'we aren't. Lila was an accident. Her birth in my family was random. I was chosen.'

'This is wild. You're making the claim that when there is a biological sibling and an adopted one, the adopted one should take precedence, because they were "chosen"?' I made the air quotes. But he didn't see me. He was somewhere else, filling up on the serotonin rush that accompanies the contemplation of a man's chosenness. And then he was with me again.

'Do you know why I was adopted? Has Lila ever told you? No? I wonder if she can even admit it to herself. Why are most people adopted? The mother is infertile. She can't have any more children, or can't have them at all. My mother was never infertile.'

'They must have tried again, after Lila. You're quite a bit younger.'

'They could have had another one like her, another random child. They could have had ten. But every time is a coin flip. And they didn't want to keep gambling. They wanted to be sure. You get it now? They had to have a son. A son to keep the family going, to be head of the family one day. They chose me. You know how many boys there were in the orphanage? One hundred and seventy-seven. They spent two days looking. They saw every single boy. They chose me.'

63

I was getting distracted from my purpose. I was meant to be there to talk sense into him, negotiate with him, scare him if I had to, but I was getting caught up in what he was saying: whether there was any merit to any of it, what were the philosophical implications. So far I had achieved nothing. I had failed Lila.

'Of course your parents chose you. But that was thirty years ago. I don't get what it has to do with right now, and how you choose to behave with your sister.'

His eyes had dulled; he was no longer ecstatic. He addressed me in a Chairman sir voice. 'Lila just has to accept that I am head of this family now.'

Embracing defeat, I rose to withdraw. 'OK. I'll deliver the message. But I wish you'd see how unnecessary this all is. A family doesn't even need a head, you know.'

'If you don't want a family with a head, or don't want to be part of a family at all, that's your life. I was chosen to be head of this family.'

As I was opening the door – he had stayed seated – he said, 'Wait. With all this talk about my family I forgot. Rohit tells me you're not an expert in family or property law. Whatever you and your daddy are planning, forget about it. Your daddy is clinically insane. So, no decision he takes will be allowed to stand. It'll only be embarrassing for your family if all this has to come out in public. So let's—'

It was childish of me, and I lacerated myself later for it, but I left the room as he was speaking. As I closed the door behind me I nearly walked straight into the girl from reception, who was carrying in a tray with an ice-filled glass and a can of Red Bull.

5
Darwinism

I am technically a millennial, but only in the way a tomato is technically a fruit. The arbitrariness of these classifications shows up around the edges. In my cohort, supposedly the first of the millennials, I knew people who lived on Instagram and people who had only vaguely heard of it. I had never had an Instagram account, or a Twitter. I did have Facebook, used occasionally to check messages from law school batchmates, but then Facebook was for old people: if it was your primary social medium, you weren't much of a millennial. I used to have LinkedIn for the purpose of researching clients or adversaries, but I hadn't used it in years. That was it for me and social media, but for Wojciech.

Wojciech was my most recent ex-boyfriend. I had started to think of him as the Last Boyfriend. Even if there were other serious relationships in my future, which one ought to accept was far from certain – I had been training myself, with conspicuous success, to like the idea of spinsterhood – I would soon be at the age, if I wasn't there already, where the essential silliness of the term 'boyfriend' emerges from its wrapper of social acceptability. I know that in the kinds of families where the parents get divorced in their fifties or sixties, once the nest is empty, the children can shortly be heard to say, 'My mother's got a new boyfriend.' But there's always either disapproval or a giggle in the term. It's never simply declarative, in the manner of, 'My mother's got a new car.' Some Indian aunties and uncles used the word 'friend' to cover anything short of affianced. That wouldn't do. The next time I had a chap, I'd decided, that was what I was going to call him: my chap.

But he was the Last Boyfriend for other reasons, too. I was repurposing the old folly of finality. The last boyfriend is supposed to be the last because he graduates from boyfriend to life-partner. When I broke up with Woj – a break-up without a cause in the Mangal Pandey/Franz Ferdinand sense – I knew that I wasn't doing so because there was better out there (there's always better out there, but that doesn't mean *you* are going to land better), but because 'good enough' wasn't a good enough reason. 'Good enough' is just a euphemism for the fear of spinsterhood, a fear I refused to be ruled by. When I left Wojciech, I was leaving boyfriends behind altogether.

(Woj, which is what I usually called him, rhymes with boy. The W is really a V. 'ciech' is basically 'check'. My parents insisted on calling him Wojciech, which they pronounced with great care. He told me he wanted them, my mother at least, to address him as beta. That never happened.)

But no embrace of spinsterhood can ever be allowed to be pure, not in this world. He wasn't just the Last Boyfriend, he was the only boyfriend with whom permanence had approached plausibility. He was *the* road not taken, the opportunity cost, the unlived life to measure spinsterhood against. He was daily evidence that it makes no difference if you have one life or several, because you only have one life at a time. Nobody needs a road not taken; what one needs is a control group, the ability to be with Woj *and* to be on my own, and then decide which is better. Most of the time, almost all the time, I was happy enough with spinsterhood that while I thought of Woj at least once a day, it was without nostalgia. My years with him were a period I was happy to have lived, and happy to have passed through, and weren't even defined by him anyway.

But that was now. What if, in five years or ten, I woke up one morning and had the same horrifying epiphany about my spinsterhood that Isabel Archer had had about her marriage, and knew that I was every bit as condemned as she was?

What was worse, if that happened I'd be proving Woj right. He said it to my face, the day I told him; he said it in a letter, later in emails and phone calls; and that's not to count the times he must have inflicted it on friends, or said it to himself while brushing his teeth or having a contemplative shit.

I can't believe this. You're better than this. This is the biggest mistake you're ever going to make. You don't understand what you're doing. You know what you're doing, but you don't understand it. I've never been so disappointed in a person. I've never been so wrong about a person. You are never going to fulfil your potential now. You are never going to be the person you tell yourself you are. In five years you'll wake up and you'll understand. In ten years you'll wake up and you'll really understand. You had one chance to be the person you could be and you're blowing it. Instead you're going to be picking the scraps off the plate of Delhi men. *Delhi men*. Instead of being with me. Once you understand, you're going to spend the rest of your life regretting this. Leave me in haste, repent at leisure.

I made that last one up. The rest I've heavily compressed. When he got going, whether in person, in print or on the phone, he built up a Philip Glass opera of repetitions and indistinguishable variations. These were his notes and he was going to keep playing them.

And I let him play. I replied to his letter in terms that made clear that I'd read it. Every time he called I took it, and I listened quietly until he was done. OK, 'listened' isn't strictly accurate – I might have been cutting my toenails or filling out a crossword, but I let him think I was listening, and I didn't push back. I had ended the relationship, I had hurt him, badly; I thought I owed him this much. None of my friends, even the ones who had liked him, thought I owed him any such thing.

He had been back in Warsaw over a year, and no longer called. But I knew he was single, because he would have had a friend let me know if it was otherwise. And if he was single, a part of him, maybe most of him, was still confidently waiting for me to come to my senses. We still exchanged texts every few weeks: this movie/article/store sign made me think of you. He didn't play the old notes in the old ways, but they were still audible in the background, not as echoes but as if they had simply been turned down.

Wojciech was almost my twin: he was only three days younger. And we had bonded initially over the affinities between childhoods in 1980s Warsaw and 1980s Delhi. But he was a millennial like a mango is a fruit: the original species. He was ahead of the curve on most superfoods; by the time a new diet became a fad he had already moved on. He never went on a run without posting it on Strava, and I used to joke that every time he had a thought about The World he immediately activated one of three buttons in his brain: Twitter, Tara, Both. Somewhere between sixty and eighty per cent of the time he pressed Both.

But Instagram was where he really lived. It seems incongruous. Wojciech, the Polish intellectual with his Cambridge degree, 'the only cultural attaché in Delhi who is actually cultured', quoting Słowacki and Valéry in the original, Cavafy and Faiz in translation. That line about him being cultured was attributed to a well-known art historian in a Sunday newspaper feature that hailed Woj as the man who had placed Poland on Delhi's cultural map. For the rest of his time in our city he wore it on his person like a tattoo. In the shorter term, he put a screenshot of the article in his Instagram story, with this quote in big white letters, followed by a #sorrynotsorry.

If I'd never used Instagram, how did I know this? Sometimes he showed me. More often, Deepti showed me. My friends were more or less equally divided between Woj fans and Woj sceptics. But of the latter, only Deepti was open about it; the rest I identified by inference. Only Deepti disregarded the principle, one of pragmatism rather than morality, that you should never be too free with your reservations about a friend's partner, because you're more likely to alienate the friend than succeed in extricating her. Deepti understood that the principle was never likely to apply to me. So she sent me screenshots, unaccompanied by editorial commentary. Poetry, obscure Delhi monuments, gym selfies.

It was really only the last category that counted. The gym self-ies were the reason that the best predictor of being a Woj sceptic was following him on Instagram. There are circles of friends where the gym selfies might have generated Woj fans. Mine was not such a circle.

More often than not he was bare-chested. Just once, Deepti couldn't resist adding a caption to a screenshot: 'Wojciech's gym sessions are like Salman Khan's movies from the 90s. It's in his contract that he has to be shirtless at least once.' Later she told me what had bothered her so much about that particular photo – it wasn't even a selfie. He had asked someone else at the gym to take it.

Unwritten but vividly legible behind every screenshot was this: *Tara, this guy is a narcissist. How can you of all people be OK with this?*

I didn't owe her a reply, but the implication was that I owed myself one. The closest I came was the notion, not quite a theory, that I didn't understand Instagram, and this was presumably just what the medium was like, just what these times were like, and Woj was generation-conforming in a way that I wasn't. Mostly I preferred not to think about it at all.

Of course I'd never told Woj about Deepti's messages, or let him know in any other way that I was aware of the gym pics. But I knew what his defence would be.

Woj was proud of his body in the way that people in the past might have been proud of their knowledge of Sanskrit or needle-work. His body was an accomplishment. The first time he showed me a photo of his father, his purpose was to illustrate this point. Look at him, he said, without fondness; the man loves his beer and bread. Only vegetable he eats is potato. And then Woj indi-cated his own legs and torso. Now you've seen my genetic inherit-ance. *This* is all pure discipline and hard work.

The comparison was intended both to measure the span of his accomplishment as well as to put Delhi men in their place. He meant the Delhi men he knew: middle-class or higher, upper caste. He meant the set of Delhi men I could conceivably date or

marry. Delhi men, he said, had no accomplishments, only entitle-
ments. They were the crossbreed products of a global strain,
patriarchy, and an Indian one, caste. Everything in life was
handed to them: a job in Daddy's business, a house, servants,
eventually a wife. Most of them got no more exercise than reaching for the beer and kachoris while watching Manchester United.
By the time they were thirty-five every sexual encounter was a
near-death experience for the wife, because the husband was
now built like a hippo and insisted on being on top. The ones
that did work out went only for bulk, in the belief that size
conferred masculinity, and out of an inferiority complex towards
Western men. And even they invariably skipped leg day. Woj
himself was built, or had built himself, like a cyclist: tautly sleek,
a McLaren not a Hummer.

Woj might have gone on about this a little too often, but I didn't
exactly disagree with him. After all, I was the one who knew what
it was like to have sex with an Indian man. My exes were all nerds,
and skinny-fat rather than bulky. The first time I fucked Woj I
really saw what I had been missing by shopping in that particular
aisle all my life. I'm not saying a Woj-like body guarantees good
sex, but it doesn't hurt, and when first experienced it comes as a
set of explosions of concentrated exhilaration. The feeling of his
love-handleless hips and lower lats as I moved my hands over
them, a purely admiring thrill, like that of running your fingers up
and down an Ionic column; pressing myself down against him
and receiving the repeated tiny shocks of his firmness, the absence
of the familiar give, the familiar squish; then him springing up
like a cat and the shocks, not tiny, of the grace and power of his
movements. Those were the explosions; for many weeks to come
there were aftershocks, sometimes during sex itself, sometimes
when I was in the office or, most inconveniently, in court. I was
once arguing before a judge who was ugly by Delhi judge standards, with lumpy cheeks and hair that sat glued in shiny discrete
patches, as if his head had been desecrated by a rat rather than
balding by a natural process. One second I was trying to look in

his direction while not actually seeing him, the next I was looking at Woj's naked back.

It didn't last. I came to convince myself that I had imagined the third explosion, the grace and power. I came to find his movements robotic. Maybe they were just repetitive. And, like everything about Woj, I saw them through the filter of a break-up that I alone chose.

Regret and vindication aren't the only two possible emotional narratives that follow the decision to leave someone, but most of us tend inexorably towards one or the other at any given time. My time for regret might come, but it hadn't yet. Vindication didn't mean dislike. My prevailing feeling for Woj was fondness. I don't believe in judging someone for how they act when they've been dumped. I preferred to remember the things I still liked about Woj; but there were fewer of these left.

First came the text: **Have you seen this???** And the message on the top of the app screen that said he was typing.

Then a YouTube link arrived. I read Woj's comment before I read the YouTube caption itself. He said: **He's really lost it this time. My God. What's going on? It has 25k views. In one day.**

I was in the High Court, waiting for my case to come up, so I muted my chat with Woj and closed the app. On my way home, a little after 10 p.m., I opened it up again. He had been sending me hourly updates. **27k. 30. 33. 35!!!** And finally: **Why aren't you replying? Are you in on this too?!? It's Jordan Peterson meets Bjorn Lomborg.** One of those names meant something to me, not much; the other, nothing.

Only at home, on my laptop, did I click on the link: **WHY 'ANIMAL CONSERVATION' IS A DENIAL OF OUR PURPOSE AS HUMAN BEINGS.**

It had been uploaded by an account calling itself 'The Human Future'. I forwarded the link to Lila, and I poured myself my nightly gin and soda, four ice cubes. Then I started watching.

First there was a young American woman, pale and with hair

the colour of a rotting apple core – a colour that has always irritated me for its inexplicable ability to scramble the minds of otherwise sensible men. She asked me to subscribe to the channel. Then Rohit came on.

When Woj said 'he', I hadn't given any thought to who 'he' was. The exact second I saw him, Lila texted. **I'm watching.**

Rohit wore a white shirt, the sleeves dragged rather than rolled up, so that they always looked a second away from sliding down again. You couldn't say where the thing had been shot, because they'd placed him before a background of liquid grey, the same grey of Delhi mornings in early November while the farmers of Punjab and Haryana are burning their paddy stubble and the smoke floats over to kill us slowly.

'*Have you ever wondered,*' Rohit began, '*what our purpose is as a species? I know you ask yourself every day about your purpose, your goals, your aspirations. But you aren't just you. Now I want you to think about the last time you saw a lion. It could have been in a zoo, on Animal Planet; it doesn't matter. When you saw it, you thought of it as that lion; but you also thought of it as a lion. But when you think of yourself, you're just you. The lion doesn't forget that he's a lion. We forget every day that we're human, the same way a tree is a tree, a lion is a lion. I'm asking us to remember.*'

Lila texted. **I thought you had your very own Kunal. I was waiting for the day when your parents finally declared that R was adopted. Never knew he was a philosopher!**

The unexpected philosopher proceeded to unwrap our true species-purpose. All it took, he said, was to truly remember that we were human. This knowledge was already within us. When we came into the world it was *all* our knowledge; then society made us forget, education made us lock it away in a sealed compartment of the brain.

'*I am here to break the seal. Break the seal, and remember that you are human. And the awareness of this one fact will flood your brain, forcing back all the irrelevant, toxic garbage that has been*

72

holding you back from understanding the human purpose. And then you will remember, and you will see.'

Even at the time, knowing and thinking as little about these things as I did, I figured Rohit couldn't have done this alone. Someone had helped make the video. They had paid for the editing and for the redhead and the 35,000 views. This someone had more than money; they had institutional capacity. They had a small army – they might call it a team – of minions, that they might call employees.

We were both thinking it, but I texted first. **Whether or not he's Kunal 2.0, he's Kunal-aided. How is the question.**

And why, as in what's in it for Kunal.

Lila, I now realised, knew nothing about our summit or my father's plans. I said I would tell her about what might be in it for Kunal in person.

In that case, in person means tomorrow.

I pressed Play. Rohit began to accelerate.

'What is our species-purpose? You think the purpose of every species is survival. Wrong. If survival is winning, what makes one non-extinct species better than another? Sheer numbers? That would mean ants are more successful than humans, and bacteria more successful than ants. Come on. Survival is the minimum. Let's pause to take a look at how our fucked-up use of language reflects our fucked-up mental states. You know the words "survive" and "survival". You also know the word "thrive". You know that survive and thrive don't mean the same thing. In fact they're close to opposites. Do you want to survive, or do you want to thrive? And yet we have the word "survival", but we don't have the word "thrival". We don't have the word because we've locked up the truth. There, friends, is our purpose as a species: not survival, but thrival. Thrival means dominance. Thrival means greatness. Thrival means glory. Thrival means we don't just live in the world, we choose it. We make it.'

Will you tell him, or should I? Rohit, stop trying to make thrival happen! It's not going to happen!

Actually, though. Lila replied to herself. **Maybe it could catch**

73

on? Maybe Rohit did actually learn a trick or two in his year at the ad agency . . .

'*Animal conservation,*' continued Rohit, '*is the very opposite of thrival. Find me another animal that puts other animals before its own interests. Find me an animal that throws its own out of their homes to make space for another animal. Not just another animal but an animal that given half the chance will eat your cows and goats and dogs, and eat you next. That's what we do in India every time we build a "tiger sanctuary". How do you create the sanctuary? You kick the humans out. Humans who have lived there for thousands of years. Humans who have seen off the threat of tigers to make their own lives. And we want to destroy these people to protect an animal that sees us as lunch! Can you imagine a tiger building a human sanctuary? For a tiger, a human sanctuary is called a buffet. All-you-can-eat.*'

Now we were treated to a brief montage. Rajas on shikar, Brits on shikar, Teddy Roosevelt in Africa standing over a rhino (of a subspecies that I learned, not from Rohit's video, was now extinct) he'd just shot.

'*We used to get it. We used to know that thrival means dominance. To hunt for survival is great; without survival you can't have thrival. But to hunt for dominance, for glory . . . when a man hung a lion head up on his wall, his house became a temple to human thrival.*

'*And now? We put hunters in jail. Doesn't matter if they hunt for glory, or because they're supplying sick people in China with medicines that they badly need. We call them poachers, and we think that what they do is worse than killing one of our own. We are sick. As a species. But it's not too late for us to get better.*'

Cunning appeal to the Chinese audience right there. Too bad they don't have YouTube. He needs to have it dubbed and uploaded to Youku.

'*Now, here are the three thoughts I want to leave you with. One: man is the only animal that has forgotten his purpose, but it's not too late to remember. I have remembered, and so can you. You are not just you. You are human.*

'*Two: the human purpose is thrival. Say it to yourself as you brush your teeth every morning. Spell it out. T-H-R-I-V-A-L. It's the only mantra you'll ever need.*'

Now it became clear that someone had told Rohit that every video needs three takeaways, and he only had two. He wore the hangdog smile of a chap who has just asked a girl out and been politely rejected. He played it pretty cool, I thought. Without fading, his smile tightened into something secure.

'*Three: this is not just our purpose. This is our destiny. We will defeat those who thwart us. We will win. We will dominate. We will thrive. See you all soon.*'

And then he made a surfer sign with both hands.

He was Rohit, not Kunal: deeply unthreatening, ultimately harmless, somehow sweet. Rohit never could understand, much less admit it, but I have always been fond of him.

I slept well.

That summer we were all but spared the Loo, the caramelising wind that terrifies beast and plant alike. But even sans Loo the city was parched and brown. Inside our flats we lived as cheese and chocolate do in India, refrigerated; except in the bathroom, where there were two taps, both of which issued water warm enough to brew tea in. We had geysers, and fridges, and ACs, but no one seemed to have invented a device that *cooled* bath water; maybe no one but me felt the want of it.

The parks emptied. Their trees and bushes began to aestivate, shedding life and colour like layers of clothing. The lawns were intermittently patchy, not through human abuse but as a measure of how much resilience individual blades could summon against the force of a north Indian May. The devil take the hindmost.

That was how things stood in my securely privileged bit of south Delhi. In the parks of Sunder Nagar the lawns were fit to start Wimbledon on. The trees had merely changed to a different shade of green, like those men who have linen suits for the summer. But even here no one had worked out how to cool the open air. A park into which one could comfortably fit three railway platforms was ours alone. This time, Kabir was friendless: the little half-white girl and her family had removed to Connecticut for the summer, and no other child had parents willing to expose them to this heat.

Kabir was putting together an installation that involved pulling out clumps of grass, which he arranged along with twigs over the edges of a thick sheet of red cardboard he had brought from home. Then he went on an expedition that took a surprisingly long time, all the way to the other side of the park, back to us and back again and back to us, until he had found the right five pebbles of equal flatness to place in the centre of his piece.

'What are those pebbles meant to be – a religious symbol, or secular? The whole thing looks like a map to me – a country, a city, maybe a world.'

'God knows,' said Lila. 'You must think I'm not curious because I see it every day. Quite the opposite. I'm as easily and endlessly fascinated as any overloving parent.'

'I know what *really* pleased you, though. Not Kabir's imagination. His persistence. The fact that he kept going until he found exactly the right pebbles. While being cooked in a tandoor.'

And I got what I had wanted. The smile, strong and radiantly wide, the rays giving her cheeks a halo that lightly coated my own.

'You know me better than friends who have spent literally a hundred times as much time around me. Which says plenty about you, but also speaks to how much time I've wasted not seeing you. And I feel like I don't know you half as well. Speaking of which – want to tell me what's up with Rohit and Kunal?'

Lila approached conversation as an efficient conductor: of an orchestra, or of rush-hour traffic. I didn't digress with her; I suspected tolerance of digression was not one of her strengths. In half an hour I'd told her everything.

'I have to go. And I know you should, too. You're always too polite to tell me how much work you have, you just take it out of sleep, but don't think I don't know.'

'There's always work,' I said. 'I'm grateful for that. The alternative is what scares me.'

'Let's do this time next week? And each of us takes that time to come up with a plan.'

I had been going to say: No, Lila, we don't need to think of this as a campaign, not yet; these are just facts to be aware of, nothing more. But then I found myself saying, 'I've just thought of something.' I really just had. 'I have an intern. Thus far she's just been vegetating, poor thing. But now I've thought of a use for her.'

Lila rose to go. 'Great. Let me know how that goes. But as I said last time, what we really need, my dear, is a weapon. A Brahmastra.'

It was the first time I'd seen her make an Indian cultural reference of this kind, but it didn't bear much interrogation. She wasn't any more like Kunal than I'd thought: she'd just been reading her son Amar Chitra Kathas.

It was a mark of the distance that accompanied my long-standing fondness and short-standing intimacy with Lila that I couldn't say, Wait, you didn't let me finish. You don't know what I'm going to do with my intern. Maybe it wasn't a matter of distance, which is implicitly shared. This was all me: my desire to impress Lila, to be invulnerably poised and sure. Her active show of apathy was a defeat and, however small, I felt both the defeat and the strain of covering the feeling.

That was a Friday; this particular intern had the weekend off. So before I could move on that I went home and showed Rohit's video to my father.

We watched it at the dining table, on his iPad. I had checked in advance to confirm that Ma was out. When she wasn't visiting her brother, Saturday was errand day. You could have counted on that for at least a decade.

What I really wanted, which was to watch Baba watch it, I

77

denied myself. I stood behind him, so I couldn't see his face. His head was monkishly still. So were his hands, which sat on the table like nailed-down coasters right up until Rohit's final word. Then he paused the video, and I waited for him to speak.

'He's a fool,' said Baba, eventually. 'And yet . . . he's almost, almost, there. He is making progress. No, that's not right. It is as if he is passing by the right path, on a parallel path . . . all he has to do is jump across.'

'But he won't.'

'He can't see how close the paths are. He *thinks* he's going in the opposite direction. You see, my love, he thinks he is fighting me. You see how close he is? No? He is saying we shouldn't just think about ourselves, our lives, our families. He wants us to think as a species. With a broader purpose. What did he call it? *Species-purpose*. If only he could see that before we are a *species*, we are life. All species are life first, life together. Sometimes it might look like we are in competition, but that is an illusion. At most it's a little pond compared with the bottomless ocean of our interdependence. Maybe he will come to see that. By moving beyond himself, he has already made a huge start.'

This was the closest Baba ever came to being proud of Rohit. Certainly it is the only time I can remember Rohit rousing Baba to some visible emotion. I noticed that at some point I had taken Baba's hand, or he had taken mine.

'Baba, not today, but some other day, when you have the time, when I have the time, I want you to educate me. About all this.'

'All this?'

'All that you've been reading and thinking about. All that occupies you now.'

'I am no one to educate you. At best I can give you things to read, videos,' and now he looked to the iPad and smiled, '*other* videos to watch. But even there, I may not choose the right ones. Rohit is close to the right path, although he doesn't know it. I know very little, and I know it.'

'No, you misunderstand me. The education I'm talking about has to do with you. What's going on inside my father's head. Where you are and how you got there. In much more detail than you could give us that day.'

And my father withdrew his hand and folded up his iPad and said, 'Your mother will be back soon. I'll go to my room. You stay here and wait for her.' He walked slowly to his study and before going in he said: 'Perhaps next time we can go on an outing.'

I stood by the table and I can't say which I heard first, his closing the door which except for yoga had always stayed ajar, or my mother coming in.

We faced each other and I knew what I should say: 'Ma, Baba and I were watching Rohit's video.' Don't accept disequilibrium, fight it with the truth. If I said that, what might I say next? 'Baba didn't agree with some of what Rohit was saying, but the video is so well-made, so professional.' No, I couldn't platitude, and I couldn't lie. Ma would see through me so straight that I'd get moral sunstroke. In that way we were like any other mother and daughter.

As I left I must have said something brief and pathetic, not, Sorry to miss you, Ma, but something like, I have to go back to the office.

Most of my interns came from the newer five-year law schools that hoover up the cleverest Indian teenagers who can't or don't want to either become engineers or go to America for college. They weren't yet much use, law-wise, but then the transaction was not meant to be equitable. Everyone knew that internships existed for the sake of the intern: to give them a sense, however necessarily partial, of what the life of a lawyer looked like, and of whether litigation might be for them.

I ignored those interns who were quiet or earnest or clumsily ingratiating, and was grateful for the others, because they livened up our chambers. Not that I engaged much directly with any of them, beyond checking in at the end of each week; but by keeping my door open, and turning visits to the bathroom into slow circumnavigations of the office, I could eavesdrop on their conversations with each other and with my juniors. I could learn about how the College Student of Today fell in and out of love.

But this intern was an irregular matter. She was the first and last I ever took on who was not a law student. She was at college in the US; or had been, until she had come home with an illness, unspecified and therefore assumed by me to be depression. She was the daughter of a client; a lucrative client who was likely to have plenty of future business to offer. He asked that I keep her for three months, longer than any actual law internship. I agreed, telling myself that if she was going to be useless, she could be useless for as long as she liked.

Her name was Jahnavi, and she was unusually tall and unusually strong and unusually mousy for a rich Delhi girl of her age. The mousiness, I decided, was temporary, a product of the illness. In healthier times, I decided, she must be not only a basketball player but a team captain. For now, she was going to prove how little I knew by being not only not useless, but the first ever intern to invert the usual arrangement and be actively useful – to me. What I could offer her was something that might lead her out of the imposed mousiness.

When she sat down in my office she looked, poor girl, as if she'd been brought in to see Principal.

'Jahnavi,' I began, with a smile of cranked-up kindness, 'you haven't been happy here.' She missed or misread the smile. 'Please don't pretend. I'm not offended. The failure is ours. We haven't been able to find you things to do.'

'That's not true!' She named my juniors in turn and how helpful each of them had been. She wearied me with the energy of her lying. She thought I was trying to end her internship two months early.

I held up a palm. 'I've called you here because I *have* found a use for you. Until now we haven't known quite what to give you because we're only used to law students. But now I have a task that isn't for a lawyer. A task that needs different skills; skills that I very much hope you have. Skills that I need you to have.'

She tightened, with energy rather than anxiety. The strength we'd all seen in her calves and shoulders began to show, for the first time, on her face.

'Now, Jahnavi, I am going to do something that is totally unlike me. I'm not someone who places any great store on my instinct. If I'm going to do something, I need to be able to tell myself why I'm doing it. I need to build a rational case. For what I'm about to do, I don't have a rational case. I only have what I usually don't allow myself to trust – my gut. But I'm going to trust it. Which means this is what I'm going to do – I'm going to trust you.'

This was for show. Less euphemistically it was manipulative. The spiel about this being unlike me was intended to convey intimacy and respect, the prerequisites for complicity – and thus to generate loyalty and, I hoped, discretion. After all, I *was* trusting her.

'What I'm asking you to do isn't just non-law, you could argue it's non-legal. Not illegal, mind you – but potentially in a grey area, in the sense that it may involve some degree of deception or concealment. God, I can see I'm confusing the hell out of you. I need you to be a spy. My spy.'

Jahnavi was, I later reflected, not in all ways ideal. She was too large and too robust and too capable of defeating a man at arm-wrestling. Kunal and anyone likely to be his crony presumably wanted girls to be self-evidently *feminine*. Sufficient femininity could be achieved in more than one style: you could be slight and waiflike, or voluptuous and proprietorially sexual, or caring in a maternal way, or caring in a servile way. All of these, even the last, were beyond her. Besides, she wasn't pretty. She wasn't ugly or plain; just awkward, sadly in a way you don't grow out of.

But she was available, and willing, indeed delighted. When I said that I couldn't tell her until after she was done why I'd need her to be installed as an intern-cum-double agent at Adhimukta Bharat, not only did she not push back: she thrilled to it.

6
One Flesh

The following weekend, I knew, Ma was scheduled to spend in Meerut. I messaged my father and asked if we could have the proffered outing that Sunday. In the meantime, I set about placing Jahnavi at Adhimukta Bharat.

I wrote the cover letter that accompanied her unsolicited application for an unpaid internship. It began by declaring that its purported author was a young patriot who intended to dedicate her life to the glorification of her country and wanted to use this sabbatical (taken 'for family reasons') from her studies to get started on that life project. I named the business her family owned ('founded in 1911, the year Delhi became India's capital') and claimed for it a century-plus record of national service. I expected Kunal to know the name, and if he didn't, I knew he would look it up. And then I played my trump. Jahnavi's grandfather, I wrote, had been a friend of Mr Chawla's, and Mr Chawla had often spoken to him of his pride in his son and the organisation he was building. Jahnavi's grandfather, I wrote, had said to her: Kunal Chawla is someone you should look up to, and learn from.

I was lying, of course. But Mr Chawla wasn't around to contradict me. Jahnavi was accepted immediately, and told she could begin the following week. I said nothing to Lila of all of this. I was waiting for something concrete to give her. I told Jahnavi to come by my chambers each Friday evening to deliver her report.

Baba had asked me to meet him at Hauz Khas metro station, by the kiosk that sold bottled water and antique samosas. I was there a minute before the appointed time. Baba was looking at the samosas.

I placed a hand on his shoulder. 'Where are we going, Baba?'

'We'll take the Magenta Line to Kalkaji Mandir, then we change to the Violet, and from Govindpuri – well, we could walk, but we can take an auto.' I didn't point out that he hadn't actually answered my question.

The driverless Magenta Line was then new, and slow to catch on. It didn't stop at any of weekend Delhi's favoured markets or monuments. When we got on, a young woman, presumably a college student from the North-East, wordlessly gave Baba her seat. She stood up and walked to the other corner of the carriage so as to disarm him of the option of refusal.

I took the seat while Baba stood. 'Nice girl,' I said. 'Hopefully she doesn't stay in Delhi long enough to lose her manners.'

Baba looked anthropologically around the train, not reporting back on his findings.

'If the metro had existed before you retired, you'd have taken this line to work every day.'

'Would I? Do people like us take the metro? No one who can afford a car does. Why would I be different?'

'Baba, you are different.'

'You remember me in my working days. Was I so different?'

Different to others, or to his new self? The father who had sat at the dining table with his newspaper while I left for school each morning was the same father who now declined to tell me where he was taking me. Nested within my certainty that Baba must be right was the certainty that Baba could not change. Was Baba unchanging like the force of gravity on earth, or was he unchanging like the truth, that is, always changing and always true? Either way, he was right. The Baba who had commuted to Nehru Place every day would not have taken the metro. That Baba had served different ends, different duties.

At Kalkaji Mandir we changed to the Violet Line – overground, and more crowded. No one offered Baba their seat. It was only one stop from Kalkaji to Govindpuri. We ought to have got out and taken an auto from there but in those two minutes the logic of Baba's route-planning came into view. Where on the Magenta Line he had looked within the train, here he only looked outwards, across south-eastern Delhi, like a god surveying the fall of his creation.

At Govindpuri metro station Baba walked to the row of autos and got into the first one, which was empty. When the driver arrived Baba said, 'Take us to the mountain of trash.' That was what he literally said, in Hindi: Kachra ka pahar.

For a few years now there had been one or two news stories a year about a famous landfill in Ghazipur, in north-east Delhi. The headlines usually framed the situation in terms of architectural achievement: Delhi's garbage peak is now higher than the Leaning Tower of Pisa, now the London Eye. Nearby residents would be quoted complaining about the smell. The rest of Delhi shrugged, as people do. In a minor way, Ghazipur had become something of a local tourist site.

But that was Ghazipur – which, if you lived in south or central Delhi, was as far away, as easily ignored, as Azerbaijan. The mountain we were going to was in *our* Delhi, in Okhla, home of textile workshops and start ups and the India Art Fair.

The driver did not own his auto. He was employed by a cousin. He shared this fact without evident resentment, but still my father could not help himself.

'Son, don't work for your cousin. Find something else to do.' The driver shrugged with apathy or resignation. 'I'm serious. I will help you.'

It was through a scratched and blotchy windscreen that we first saw the mountain. It entered the scene, or we entered its scene, and as it began to take up more of the frame it didn't stop looking like a geological feature, an Okhla Uluru. Not even when we got out of the auto, and my father pointed out to me where we stood.

'The landfill is next to a *hospital*?'

'A government hospital. Central government.'

Mountain and hospital stood cheek to cheek, like Fred and Ginger. Is a hospital a temple to life, or death? You came to the hospital to die, and the mountain was the last part of the living or dying world that you saw. Or you were born in this hospital, and the world in which you would live and die began for you with the mountain of garbage.

We walked past the hospital to the open gate that led to the landfill. Here Baba stopped.

'You don't want to go in?'

'I have been, many times. I don't need to go again. There's no need for you to go at all.'

'Then why bring me here?'

'You can see enough from here.'

And with all my years of training and practice I tried to see what he wanted me to see. Not people – on this day the only other people there were two men, sharing a beedi by a stationary JCB grader. Not even the mountain or massif itself, its slopes and ledges, the changing patterns of its fabric of mud and refuse. He wanted me to look to the very top. He wanted me to look at the animals.

The mountain had a table roof. And on this roof dogs trotted back and forth. These were not the familiar stray dogs of south Delhi colonies, that livened up the days and nights of security guards with distant families and sparked civil wars between young dog-lovers and elderly park-walkers. The trot of these dogs was robotically regular, more perfect than any dog-show champion. Nor were they scrawny. They looked strong. They looked – *adapted* to their habitat.

Above, the crows and black kites carried out their surveillance, swooping down occasionally to claim a prize.

'One reads,' I said, 'about how many species humans are pushing into extinction every year. But looking at this, you start to wonder if we should be worrying more about the ones that will survive.'

'You understand. It is the height of human arrogance to think that death is the problem. The question is not, Are we causing death, the question is, What are we doing to life?'

And I finally saw what Baba had meant when he said that Rohit was 'almost there' – that he and Rohit were on parallel paths. They were so close to wanting the same thing – call it thrival, not survival. The difference was that one saw thrival as victory in a contest in which every species was a contestant, and the other saw life as the only contestant.

Well, there was another important difference: by this time next year, Rohit would have moved on. He thought with all the passionate brevity of a teenage crush.

Neither of us spoke and, after a few minutes, while my eyes didn't move from the mountain roof and its dogs and birds, I began to zone out. I was thinking about what might constitute the range of reasonable responses to the mountain of garbage. The vast majority of people – from Lila to Deepti, to every politician, judge or petty official, to the tens of millions who had walked or ridden past it at some point – would push away *any* response. The mountain couldn't be called an aberration; compared, for instance, with the air that we breathed, it was little more than a footnote in the story of what we had done to Delhi. And how many people actually thought about the air? They got on with life, as people do. Like the dogs and black kites they adapted. They coughed and wheezed and on average they died younger than they might have if the air were clean, but not younger than they used to when the air actually was clean. In the time of the emperor Akbar, the air was immaculate, and life expectancy was thirty.

But if you chose to dwell, even for a few minutes, you might summon sympathy for the garbage pickers or the animals; or outrage, which tends to come more easily. The pickers *or* the animals – almost never both. If you had been educated at JNU or on Twitter, if you made your living as some kind of intellectual, you might look at the mountain and think, Capitalism. Baba wouldn't do this, not only because I'd never heard him use the word, but because he was too familiar with other structures of oppression, and it was precisely what you could call capitalism that had freed him from those structures. Wojciech wouldn't, either. He was, after all, Polish, born the same year as Solidarity. He called himself a social democrat, not a socialist. When he saw a young Delhi lawyer or academic offering a free lecture on the capitalist origins of climate change, he'd say: Don't tell me about socialism. I come from socialism. Every socialist regime in history has been addicted to pollution. The only difference between capitalism and communism is that the communists would have either shot Greta Thunberg or put her in jail. The capitalists will soon give her a Nobel Prize.

As for me – I had no response. I was there for one reason alone: not to better understand myself, or the world, only to better understand my father.

'Time to go,' Baba said.

He had paid the auto driver to wait for us. This time he took us straight to Kalkaji Mandir. At the station Baba asked for his number, and then insisted on giving the young man a missed call, so that he could confirm it was the right one.

As he drove off I said to Baba, 'What will you do for him?'

'I can see it so clearly. He despises his life and he thinks he is stuck. I'll show him he isn't stuck.'

This was not a new Baba, nor the old. He had never been given to random acts of altruism. And the new Baba that I was trying to understand was thinking in the widest terms of all: the interests of all life. This was the rarest thing with my father. An exception.

'It's not like you to interfere, Baba.'

'You are right. I won't tell him what to do. Just tell him what he might do, and offer to help him.'

I held his hand as we crossed the road from the metro station to our colony. Father and daughter in the first throes of a new complicity. I took his hand again as we said goodbye outside in the street.

'Thank you, Baba.'

'Thank *you*, child.'

*

87

I was walking up the steps to my flat when Lila called. She was one of those people who always texted first, so that an unheralded call declares itself an event before a word has been said.

'I need to see you. What are you doing right now?'

It is an indefensible policy, and maybe a sign that I am fundamentally out of sympathy with Delhi, that spontaneous city, but I will not agree to meet someone immediately. Not even Lila.

'Is anyone dying?'

She laughed in an odd way, as if at a private joke she did not yet care to share. 'Unfortunately not in one case. Unfortunately already dead in another.'

'Kunal and your father. What's up?'

She would not tell me over the phone. I could see her the next day, I said. For a nightcap.

Lila had last come to mine maybe a decade prior, when I lived in the barsaati that I'd moved into when I left my parents'. The occasion was a birthday party, thrown against my will by Deepti. We were all then close enough to or nostalgic enough for undergraduate life that a certain atmospheric crumminess and Blenders Pride whisky with food of the kabab-and-rolls kind, plates and cutlery either plastic or theoretical, was to be expected, and accepted. No one complained about these things. We were young enough that reverse snobbery was the only acceptable kind.

I had loved that barsaati. I threw parties often. My landlady, who lived beneath, defied every malignant stereotype that Delhi Punjabi landlords have earned themselves in the decades since Partition. Her sons lived in Canada and visited rarely. She said she needed me to 'keep her young'. I went down every morning to see her before work, staying for tea on days when I had my shit together in time. She usually greeted me with, 'What's the gossip?' and, as I lamely tried to provide some, she'd say, 'I'm craving some really excellent gossip.' She said she looked forward to my parties because the mornings after were the only times I gave her any.

But she smoked her way to a heart attack at sixty-nine and the sons who had found so many reasons to avoid Delhi in her lifetime now took an assiduous interest in her property. The day the paperwork was sorted the builders arrived to demolish the house and, two years later, four flats stood above stilt parking, identical to neighbours east and west. As colony after colony was emancipated from height restrictions, barsaatis, like vultures and blue skies before them, were shifted from the life of Delhi to its history.

I moved two streets away, to a newish third-floor flat by a park. By any standards my new quarters were more attractive (the rent was four times what I'd paid for the barsaati). Most recent Delhi flats have one bedroom more than the square footage should sensibly allow, but this one had been designed by an enlightened family rather than a market-conscious developer, so there were two bedrooms rather than three, built around a living-dining area and balcony that looked over the park. In the late afternoons light flooded the flat, making it seem twice as large. After work I could usually be found in the balcony with my gin and a book, the only other company a gulmohar tree that an averagely athletic rhesus monkey could access from the balcony. By some strange miracle the balcony stayed dry in all but the strongest showers. The happiest hours I've ever spent in Delhi had me deep in a long novel while the rain briefly cooled and exfoliated the air and thudded away all manmade sound.

The flat was made for entertaining, and in my first year there I hosted as often as I had in the barsaati. Why I stopped is difficult to accurately account for. It wasn't just that work picked up. I had peers, as busy or busier than I, who entertained more avidly than ever. It wasn't Wojciech. He loved parties; he needed them the way Bollywood stars do their periodic beautifying trips to Swiss clinics.

Now, at the office, I mentally scanned the contents of my liquor cabinet and fridge. In these realms, my tastes had ascended with age and income. I need have no fear of inadequacy. (I didn't really even know if this version of Lila drank. I hoped she did.) But the flat – the flat was another matter. The flat and I, I knew, were like a married couple far gone into sad neglect. I lived in the flat but I had stopped looking at it, years ago. The walls had needed repainting for three years – or was it four? For at least a year the living room had been half-lit, like the head of a person who ran out of hair-dye midway through. Was I going to have to buy lightbulbs on my way home from work? Even if I made it home by eight, which was ambitious, I couldn't reverse neglect in two hours.

Lila was certain to be one of those people who enters a home and sees everything. Lila would see your flat and judge the state of your marriage, your career, your fitness to be a parent.

I bought the lightbulbs. Right outside the electrical shop stood a florist – I couldn't say if he had stood there weeks or years – and I chose a bunch of large white liliums that I hoped would suit Lila's taste, for I had none of my own, florally. I didn't believe these efforts would convince Lila that I cared about my home. If she saw through them, all the better, really; it's always gratifying to know that someone has gone to special effort for your benefit. It didn't occur to me that she might have quite enough on her mind already.

From a quarter to ten I was alive to the sound of the lift. Lila took the stairs, and she rang the bell at 9.55. She wore a loose white shirt and jeans and three flights in this weather had been enough to coat her neck with a thin lacquer of sweat. She panted.

'What was the need to race up like that?' I smiled. 'What are lifts for?'

'Lifts are for the proliferation of diabetes and heart disease. Best thing we could do for this city's public health would be to abolish them. First lifts, then escalators.' She looked at me as if to measure my response. 'What do you do for exercise, huh?'

I ignored the question. 'Shall we sit in the balcony, with the fan? And what will you have?'

She smiled when I told her what I would be having. 'Soda instead of tonic? Health-wise that just about makes up for your taking the lift.' She followed me to the kitchen and after examining my liquor cabinet she said she would have the same as me, with the addition of a measure of Campari. She looked approvingly at the liberality of my pouring, and after I was done she went back for more ice.

Only when we sat down did I notice that her bag was a laptop bag.

'OK,' she said, laying a vast grey MacBook on the coffee table. 'Mind if we get straight to it? What's your wi-fi password?'

'beckysharp. All lower case.'

'Huh. Always found her annoying, myself.'

'Woj said she's the sort of woman women don't like but men do. He chose the password, actually.'

She grimaced. 'Wow. What an "insight".'

'Remind me. Did you ever meet Woj?'

'Twice, but never with you. No time for that right now. Later, though, when this is done.'

Lila was opening up a cloud storage app. She clicked on the first folder: CCTV FOOTAGE 97 GL. 97 Golf Links was the address of the home in which she had grown up, where Mrs Chawla and Kunal still lived.

'Kunal,' I said. 'I figured that much. Want to tell me what I'm about to see?'

'First we watch, then we discuss, then we watch again. The advantage of having had to wait thirty hours to see you is this footage has now been efficiently edited. OK, here we are. In the kitchen. Two months ago.'

The timestamp read 1.23 a.m. The kitchen was empty. I marvelled at the sheer size of it; it must have been recently expanded. My eye was drawn to an island over which you could have placed a baby's cot. In our parents' generation no wealthy home bothered with a large kitchen, because no wealthy person spent any time in one.

'Why do you have CCTV in the kitchen? A thief on the staff?'

'Hush.'

The door opened, more slowly than a kitchen door ever does, and Kunal entered. He wore a white kurta-pyjama, unrumpled.

He went to the fridge and extracted a bottle of milk. Then he picked up a beer stein and placed it on the island. From the drawer below he pulled out a blender. From another cupboard emerged a green bottle, the size of a bayan. I recognised the brand as the same South African one Woj had used. He had complained constantly of the unavailability in India of decent protein.

'Funny time for a protein shake.'

Kunal went back to the fridge for ice. He plugged in the blender and filled the stainless steel container with his ingredients. He was bizarrely stingy with the protein powder, so stingy that you wondered why he bothered with it, or with the blender. It seemed a cumbersome route to a glass of cold milk.

Now Kunal got on tiptoes and unlocked a drawer above the fridge. Reaching in with both hands he picked up a covered pot perhaps half the size of the protein bottle. A thing of brass and copper, usually reserved for storing water from the Ganga.

'Kunal is adding Gangajal to his shake? Hope it's been purified.'

He placed the pot next to the blender and reverentially opened it with his right hand. He put the lid down and lowered the same hand down into the pot. He made some kind of stirring motion for a few seconds before retrieving . . . not water, but another powder. He held a pinch of this second powder between three fingers. Cupping his left hand below his right, he raised those fingers to his nose and sniffed. He then dropped that pinch into the blender container and dusted his hands to make sure not a grain was wasted. He turned to something we couldn't see, some-thing beneath the camera, and paid obeisance as if to a deity. Then he covered the blender and turned it on, and Lila paused the video.

'We aren't going to watch him drink it?'

'You can. I don't want to see that again.'

I had spent the past several minutes watching both Kunal and Lila watching Kunal, and I had never found her more difficult to read. Her face had shown horror, and triumph, and contempt, and confusion. Now she looked grave, which I hadn't seen on her before.

'Tell me, Tara. What did you think we were watching?' Before I could reply, she went on. 'Fine, I don't think it'll make any difference, but if you want we can watch him drink it.'

She closed her eyes and pinched her face tight as he ran the blender. By the time her face eased he was drinking: first sips, then mouthfuls, then the rest of it in one clean draught.

'I'm not sure exactly, but it's pretty clearly some sort of religious thing,' I said. 'Actually, religious isn't quite the right word, but you know what I mean. It fits in with what I suspect he's doing at Adhimukta. The second powder was presumably something that once emanated from a cow. Dried gaumutra? Is that a thing? And before blending he did his namaskaar to a picture or idol of some god – Hanuman? Ganesh?'

'There are no gods in our kitchen.'

'Then?'

'The namaskaar was to a picture of my parents.'

'And the powder?'

She closed the laptop and stood up. I led her back into the living room. 'A refill?' She gave me her glass.

'The first powder was presumably what it says on the label. The second is my father's ashes.'

Lila's expression had settled into a faintly ironic calm. But in it, and in her voice, I detected notes of each of the faces I'd seen as we watched the video.

'Jesus. You're not joking.'

'I said we needed a Brahmastra. Here it is.'

When I returned with our refills she was at the dining table, the laptop open again.

'What you saw was the first time, to my knowledge, that he drank that particular blend. The week after the funeral. Since then he's been back, not every night, but most nights. I have it all here. I could show you more instances, but I'm going to presume you get the point. He never takes more than a pinch, whether because he doesn't want to actually taste it or because he's drawing out the supply. I'm sure we'll find out, when we want to.'

'Lila, before we talk about *this*, I need the background. Why is there a CCTV camera in the kitchen?'

'They're everywhere in the house. Papa, as you know, was . . . losing it a little. He was afraid of the servants. Not of stealing but of murder. He thought the cook might poison him, for instance. I did it to shut him up for a few days. He was always happier when he thought something was being *done* to forestall his murderers. I have an app on my phone that receives all the footage. Not that I routinely look at it.'

'Then how did you come by this? What made you look?'

'The staff. Over time he's become less careful. Once he forgot to properly shut the door of the shelf where he keeps the ashes. Rakesh bhaiyya – he's been with us for decades – saw the open door in the morning. He saw the pot inside and he called me immediately. Then I checked with the drivers. Kunal was supposed to go to Beas in Punjab to immerse the ashes. He had gone out of town once for a couple of days, but he hadn't taken any of our cars, and there was no evidence he'd taken the ashes. Both Rakesh and Jagmohan – the cook – noticed that he'd been using the blender at night. He left the container in the sink. They were used to him drinking protein shakes, but only in the morning. This was new.'

'Tell me something. Are the staff simply loyal to you? Or do you pay for this information?'

My question pleased her. 'Let's say it's a little from column A and a little from column B.'

'And you've gone home and confirmed that the pot contains your father's ashes?'

'That they are ashes, yes. And whose else could they be? Unless they gave him the wrong set at the crematorium which, you have to admit, would be pretty funny.'

'You'd be cool with your family being given someone else's ashes?'

'What difference could it possibly make, Tara? When you've had a father, you know that there is nothing of substance of him in a pile of dust. I'm not delusional.'

'How did you open the cupboard? Kunal had left it unlocked?'

'He didn't exactly make it difficult for me to find the key.'

'One last question. What does Kunal know about the CCTV situation? Does he know that the cameras exist, and that the footage is sent to you?'

'I'm all but certain he doesn't know about the cameras. He was very impatient with Papa's paranoia, when he bothered to engage with it. Papa never went to him for help or reassurance. And you've met him – you couldn't call him bright. Or observant.'

Couldn't I? Not bright the way Lila was, sure. If Kunal was bright, he was bright in ways Lila couldn't detect, forget respect.

'Now,' she said, 'we figure out how to nail him. We have our weapon – just need to work out the details of deployment.'

There were too many things I wanted to say. I wanted to ask if she was sure she wanted to escalate. I wanted to ask if the priority now shouldn't be protecting her mother. What came out, as usual in these situations, was something unplanned.

'Lila, how do you *feel* about this? What do you feel when you're watching it?'

The irony of her expression grew brighter. 'Therapist as well as lawyer? I feel a lot of things. But they're all obvious enough that you could infer them. Horror, mainly. Contempt. Outrage. Not so much about him doing this to Dad's ashes – as I said, those ashes aren't my dad in any meaningful sense – but at the way he makes everything about him. We've lost our father and he's using it to medicate his own insecurity about being adopted.'

I had told Lila about Kunal's dichotomy of his chosenness versus her randomness, but we hadn't dwelt on the theory or its implications. As with everything Kunal said, she refused to take it seriously. Now I caught myself wondering whether the insecurity that propelled him to the kitchen at night was also behind his weaving of chosenness into an identity, or whether there was a genuine paradox here between true insecurity and its seeming antithesis, true confidence. Lila was the wrong audience for these speculations. I searched for something more appropriate to say.

'You didn't mention being weirded out by it. Aren't you? Are you at least surprised?'

'I mean, I'm literally surprised in that it never crossed my mind that someone could do this. And sure, it's weird, but I kind of take for granted that the world is full of weird things and just like it rains more in some places than others, there's more weirdness per capita in some places, and Delhi we know is pretty far off on one end of that distribution.'

'Do you think this is a thing that people do? And not his unique contribution to the annals of human eccentricity?'

Briefly she looked interested in the question. 'Don't call him eccentric, that's too nice. Statistically, the odds of a "unique contribution" from anyone are . . . Can we get back to talking about how we destroy him?'

'What exactly do you have in mind when you say destroy him?'

'Show him his aukat. Put him in a box that he will be confined to henceforth.'

'A metaphorical box, right?'

'Of course. Not a jail cell.'

'Not a jail cell, but you need my legal advice?'

'The idea isn't that he *end up* in jail. But surely there's more than enough here to make the threat so tangible that he can begin to smell the cell walls and taste the jail dal, with its garnishes of pubic hair and sweat.'

'Lila, is there something I'm missing beyond what you've already told me? Isn't he still your brother?' I didn't say: Lila, why are you enjoying this?

'Is he behaving like a brother of mine? A brother of yours? A brother of anyone's?'

I didn't say: Lila, what does it mean to *behave like* a brother? To be a brother is a fact of birth and/or law, and unlike being a husband, it is irrevocable and not subject to standards of conduct or mutuality. Surely the fact of Kunal's adoption didn't impose on him the requirement of having to earn the status of brother? Would she talk like this about a brother who hadn't been adopted?

There were plenty of reasons not to ask any of this, but I settled on a good one. All you had to do was look around you, in any Delhi colony. If you were a lawyer you didn't even have to look. The people of south Delhi were almost as a rule no respecters of the fraternal bond, uterine or otherwise. They might love their siblings in childhood, but later on, when it came to property, to inheritance . . . Was Gandhi quoting a Chinese proverb when he said all men are brothers? In our Delhi, for reasons unconnected to any one-child policy, there were no true brothers.

I turned my attention to what Lila wanted of me. Whether or not Kunal's smoothie recipe *was* unique in our strange city, we could count on finding no precedent or close analogue in case law. This meant no obvious place to start; no ready fit between action and statute. Lila, of course, was a few steps ahead.

'I haven't even Googled any of this, but I have had some time to think,' she said. 'We start by accusing him of cannibalism.'

'I thought you said ashes weren't your father.'

She looked more disappointed than annoyed by my obtuseness. 'The point isn't what *I* think. If you ask a hundred people in Delhi whether their father's ashes are important, what will they say?'

'Got it. Go on.'

'There's obviously no law that directly deals with eating ashes. But we can argue it is cannibalism, and wouldn't quite a few people see it that way? That's the big charge. Then we can tack on a bunch of other stuff. Maybe there's a law about defiling corpses? And who do the ashes belong to – my mother, surely?'

'There's also a potential religious angle. Were the usual Hindu rites performed at his cremation? If we want to be creative we could cite IPC 295a, say he's committed an act of sacrilege. And if I'm not mistaken' – I knew I wasn't mistaken – '297, not that I've ever actually seen that section invoked, deals more directly with the question of burials and cremations.'

97

She was pulling the Indian Penal Code up as I spoke. 'You're right. "Whoever . . . offers any indignity to any human corpse." Indignity – that's putting it mildly. Up to a year in jail. Too bad.'

'Too bad he'll never actually see the inside of a jail?'

She nodded.

What was the truer duty – to be Lila's willing charioteer in the pursuit of victory? Or to guide her towards a different pursuit – equilibrium?

'Lila, can we try to be clear about what our goals are here? And what we want to avoid?'

'You know the situation. You met Kunal. What's in doubt? I didn't choose this war. He did. This allows us, hopefully, to end it quickly.'

'What about your mother?'

'What about her?'

'She *is* your mother in a way Kunal isn't your brother. I don't mean biologically. You know what I mean. Protecting her – not hurting her – that's the primary consideration, right? One that precedes destroying Kunal.'

For the first time since she'd rung the bell she paused. Eventually she said, 'This way my mother never has to know there was a war. When we go to Kunal with what we have – can you imagine him letting her know he's doing this? He'll do anything to prevent it. Her thinking less of him might well be scarier than the thought of jail. With the threat of Mamma being shown this footage hanging over him? My brother is going to be my little lamb. He'll dress up as a girl and perform at Kabir's next birthday party, if I ask him. Fuck, I never even thought of the Mamma angle. I was so busy thinking of ways to intimidate him legally. We don't even need any legal threats. We just say, Behave or Mamma sees this. And maybe, just for something on top, Behave and Mamma and Papa's friends don't see this.'

'Is there any chance your mom knows about this? Encouraged it?'

'You don't really know my mom, right? She's as thick as Kunal. There's a reason they get along so well – as a teenager, I sometimes wondered if he really *was* adopted. Don't look so scandalised. But Mamma at heart isn't like him – she's genuinely sweet and utterly conventional. She'd be horrified by this. And he'll know that.'

That Lila didn't really need me as a lawyer had been obvious weeks ago. What she wanted was a co-conspirator – not an equal, not a sidekick, but something in between, a provider of fellowship and reassurance and above all of understanding. She was open to advice – she would never let herself be the person who wasn't open to advice – but you had to be realistic about the limits within which she might act on it.

Lila asked for the loo and by the time she was back I had my direction.

'Quite a pile of books you've got in there.'

'Bad habit, I know. Also a privilege of spinsterhood.'

'Spinster, huh? Not yet, I'd say.'

'Very yet.'

'It's only a bad habit if the books are bad.'

'Lila, on this Kunal business, here's what I suggest. I agree with you that this is the Brahmastra. But the whole point of the nuclear option is you use these things when you have to. *If* you have to. And we aren't there yet.'

'So you say we just let him keep drinking Papa at midnight?'

'You yourself said he's not drinking your dad.'

'OK. But we have to do *something* now. Or soon. There needs to be a response.'

I told her about Jahnavi, and this time, unlike in the park, she listened and then she laughed. 'Look at what I've done to you, dear. I've turned this straight-laced lawyer into James Bond.'

'Never James Bond. Maybe George Smiley.'

She agreed that we wait for Jahnavi to start delivering her reports. After that no one said anything further about Kunal. We actually succeeded in pushing it from our minds; neither of us

99

referred to it even accidentally. She stayed another hour and we spent most of it laughing. We had at least two more drinks each.

Before she left, Lila spent several minutes examining my bookshelves in infuriating silence. She called her driver and I walked her down to the street.

'Tara, dear, have you ever tried dating apps?'

'Are you nuts?'

'We have to have that Wojciech' – she mangled the name without a trace of apologetic self-awareness – 'conversation next time. In a word, Yuck.'

'That's harsh.'

'You would say that. I don't mean to be insulting. It can happen to any of us. I have' – she signalled to her driver that she'd be a minute – 'an idea. For you.'

'Beyond turning me into a spymaster?'

'Someone I think you'd get along with. I'm going to check on his situation and let you know.'

7
The First Fish

The next time I saw Lila was by chance, the following weekend, in The Book Shop.

Not long ago when rents were lower and readers more numerous, the main branch of The Book Shop was in Khan Market. Now, its founder dead before his time, the shop lived on in Jor Bagh, in a market of luxuriant quiet, a market where you could always find parking and where a bookshop was not under threat from cocktail bars or Apple dealerships. It occupied a room smaller than some one-SUV Delhi garages, but like all good bookshops it was a world, complete and satiating.

Lila had come here nearly all her life. But I hadn't come from the sort of family that took its children to The Book Shop. I had discovered it as an adult.

To steal the title of a book I'd once bought there, The Book Shop was a territory of light. The light streamed out in comforting waves from the furniture and from the staff, but mostly from the books themselves. No matter the state of the weather or the air conditioning, you always felt as if it was early February and someone had just gifted you a fine cashmere sweater. It was the softest place in our hard city.

I found Lila flipping through a paperback that I recognised as *The Story of My Teeth* by Valeria Luiselli. She placed it back on the shelf when she saw me.

'I've read that, I don't think it's for you.'

'Too gimmicky.'

'That's an unfair word. But, yup, basically that. I liked it, anyway.'

Kabir was in the children's corner, cross-legged with an elbow resting on either page of his book. It looked a particularly comfortable way to read. I had a moment of regret that grown-up books weren't designed for it.

Lila went up to the till with her haul: three by Rachel Cusk and two business books that she said were for Raj. Whether they were her idea of what he should read or his, I didn't ask.

She spoke to the owner and her assistant with an ease so fluent it could only be of long standing. I had been in this shop enough to know that there were dozens, maybe hundreds, of customers who were this familiar with the shop and its people; there was nothing special about Lila. In watching her I was really observing myself in negative. For all the years I had been coming to The Book Shop, for all the happy hours I had spent in it, I had wilfully failed to get to know the staff. I never requested a book, let alone attempted small talk. Shopkeepers are used to all kinds, and they grow infallible instincts in these matters. They had written me off as antisocial and respectfully matched my silence. (Until that day. After they'd watched me behave like a regular human being with Lila I decided I'd better cut out the nonsense. We began to get to know each other. By the time the shop moved nearby to larger, even lovelier premises in Lodhi Colony, we were friends.)

As we said goodbye, Lila asked if I could come to the park the next day. 'I checked and he's single and he'd love to meet you. I'll tell you all about him tomorrow.'

In the office that evening I started watching Rohit's second video – MEET THIS MAN WHO IS FIGHTING FOR HUMAN THRIVAL – but I only got as far as the redheaded girl. I still can't tell you who the man referred to in the title is. Rohit had made a mistake, I thought – not that I know anything about YouTube – in putting 'thrival' in a title so early. You had to let your made-up words catch on, you shouldn't push them too hard.

This time was different. Lila had brought Raj. I tried to think if I had ever had an actual conversation with him. Raj's family was from Delhi, but he had grown up in Dubai and studied in the US. He and Lila had met in business school. It was a measure of where

I'd stood with Lila that when they married I was only invited to the reception, not the wedding or the mehendi or the sangeet.

I remember going for fifteen minutes tops, partly out of politeness – not that my absence would have been noted – but mostly out of curiosity as to the chap who Lila had chosen, of all chaps, to hitch to herself for life. Lila would not divorce. There was no divorce that could escape a self-indicted charge of failure. If the husband were cruel, or drunk, or professionally feckless, it would connote a failure of original judgment; if he were unhappy, or unfaithful, or simply bored, her failure would be of effort or competence. She would not fail at such a thing, or any thing.

At the reception Raj had looked more suited to throwing an American football around than to any Indian idea of marriage. He had changed out of the wedding sherwani and into a navy suit from which his shoulders kept threatening to pop. A suit of Italian rather than American cut. I had never seen a man so broad in a suit so slim.

But the broadness was American rather than Punjabi. He had no belly to speak of, and his square neck was firm enough for use as a percussive instrument. Wojciech might say: Too chunky for my taste, a Hummer not a McLaren, but at least the chunks are of muscle. The Punjabiyat was announced a little higher up, in the nose and chin. He'd have been thought good-looking in any Punjabi family from Vancouver to Singapore, at any point in history. I remember thinking, What does Lila want with this block of tandoori beefcake?

Today's Raj didn't look fit for the football field, but his unfit-ness didn't fit the usual pattern of male aging: he had none of the gunny-sack heaviness of the athlete who has let himself go. Everything but the hair had receded. The shoulders and calves had narrowed; the neck looked as if it had been bullied into weak-ness by some brace or girdle. There was still no belly to speak of, but there is more than one genre of flatness. He had been married eight years and he seemed to have spent very little of that time eating. How much of this was down to Lila? Honey, I shrunk my husband.

We sat on an accustomed bench while shrunken-Raj chased Kabir around, his polyester T-shirt darkening with each step. The weather had turned. Maybe a more accurate way of putting it is that it had stepped down: to a deeper, even more gruelling level. If Delhi's human-fucked seasons were a set of tests of the viability of life in conditions of escalating horror, then July was the point at which you had to ask at what cost life itself was worth preserving.

Kabir didn't seem to mind being pressure-cooked. Lila looked at my face and neck and said, 'I'm sorry for doing this to you. I may be taking this too far.'

Raj was dangling Kabir by the legs with an enthusiasm that was painfully effortful.

'We're just sitting here. Raj is the heroic one.'

'Heroic?' She gave me a different smile, one I hadn't seen before. 'I won't tell him you said that. He'll think you were being serious.'

I only just stopped myself from saying, quite truthfully, I am. Father and son jogged over to the other side of the park. Kabir looked back at us a couple of times on the way. Not for the first time, I regretted the difficulty of asking a friend, How often do you fuck your husband? How often do you still want to? Deepti was the only friend whom I could ask, and in her case there was no need.

'You were going to tell me what you thought of Woj. I didn't know you knew him.'

'Everyone knew him. He made it his business to be known, didn't he?'

'He was doing his job. Him being known was an achievement. Whoever went to an event at the Polish embassy before Woj?' And then, before she could answer: 'You think I'm defending him, defending my dating him. I'm just stating a fact.'

'I never understood what you saw in him. He was just so thoroughly . . . average. Which is fine. Most people are. But he didn't wear average particularly well. Average that thinks itself special, yuck.'

'What are you basing this on? You met him, what, a couple of times? Did you actually speak?' If we had to have this conversation, why couldn't it be in the air-conditioned indoors?

'Twice was enough. One of those times I was stuck next to him at a dinner. Two hours of him trying to impress and charm me with one side of his mouth, and shame me for working in PE with the other. Oh, and the usual clichés about the cultural superiority of Europe to the US. At the end of it I told him, "I hope you know more about French poetry than you do about economics, because you speak about them with equal omniscience," and I tapped my bump and said, "This foetus of mine knows more about economics than you do. It knows nothing, but you have negative knowledge, anti-knowledge."' Woj's reply she did not quote. 'You never heard about this dinner? I'd have thought he came home and crowed all night about how he rattled the hell out of some banker chick.'

Maybe he had crowed, who knows. There had been a lot of dinners. At least three nights a week I'd be eating Maggi noodles in the office while he was at a dinner and, afterwards, when I was too tired to listen to his account he'd do his best to cloak annoyance with sympathy.

'So when I heard he was with you, I wondered. It can't have been the white thing, Tara—?'

'What do you think?'

'You couldn't call him good-looking. Not ugly. Just average, like the rest of him.'

I didn't say: facially, Woj was about as good-looking as I am. Facially we're both in the happy middle of the distribution. No one would fall for us on the basis of looks – no question of love at first *sight* – but if they liked us in other ways, we were good-looking enough. I'd always thought this much the best place to be. No need to ask, Does he only want me for my looks, and no need to worry overmuch about aging. No walking into a bar or party and thinking, Is that girl prettier than me? No walking into a bar or party and thinking, Do I still have it? When you tot them up, the privileges and burdens of conventional prettiness don't really appeal. Woj's case was more complicated – he had his body.

'You've never seen Woj naked, clearly.'

'You of all people, falling for a set of abs.' Her face softened into a kind of contrition. 'I'm being unfair, I know. It's just – it's you. I'd always want the best for you, the very best. In the end I rationalised your choice by saying, Delhi men are such a useless lot, she wants someone she can talk to, someone who *reads*.'

Later she would tell me that I was made vulnerable by my lack of a Western education – that Woj's Cambridge degree had conferred false glamour. Had I studied abroad I'd have seen through him.

'Tell me,' said Lila, 'did you ever hear him saying anything funny? Actually funny, not just snide.'

Had I? We had laughed a lot – but always, I now realised, at someone or something that Woj thought stupid.

'You've got me there. No.'

'That's what made me think of him. Ashwin.'

'The guy you want me to meet.'

'He's everything Delhi men aren't – he's from the south – and he's what you might have mistaken Woj for. He's *actually* smart, *seriously* well-read. And he is. So. Hilarious. We get a drink every few months and people are looking at me wondering what the hell is so funny while Ashwin sits there poker-faced. And he's single. And really keen to meet you.'

I didn't ask, Is Raj friends with Ashwin too? Raj, who stood before us panting and clutching his side. On his T-shirt the work of his sweat was complete. He invited me home for a drink; I said no, and went back to the office.

I was late to see Ashwin, although not by Delhi standards. Based on Lila's description I expected to find him reading a book while he waited. But there was no book, only AirPods. He smiled and indicated the vacant chair, but he didn't get up. '*Desert Island Discs*,' he said. 'With Billie Jean King. She's about to choose her luxury.'

Ashwin too was in the Wojciech-Tara happy facial middle. As I sat down, I revised this judgment: he had better raw materials than either of us. He had a straight nose, lips as red and swollen as some overripe fruit, and a shockingly perfect pair of eyebrows. His eyes shone with a mischief that could, I was to discover, flow all the way down to his teeth.

But – of course there was a but – Ashwin was soft and round. I don't mean big or fat. Not the type you usually see in Delhi – let's say, Kunal if he didn't work out for three months – the accumulated buttery dal and chhole bhature parading themselves on back and thighs and belly, the whole thing an assertion of the God-given male right to be unattractive, thrown into proper relief by the carefully dressed and painted skinny wife across the table. None of that here. Ashwin was unintimidating. His roundness was gentle. He had a face like a fresh idli, and cheeks that demanded to be squeezed, like a toddler's. When he rose to go to the bathroom he showed the hips of a 1960s Indian film star. I'm not even sure Ashwin was technically overweight. He just looked lazy. Later, Lila would tell me that I ought to touch his hands. 'The softest palms on earth. It's like shaking hands with a shahtoosh shawl.' The inherited softness of sedentary generations.

I admired the laziness. In a way I envied it. But the idea of tumbling around with this man was ridiculous.

But the idea of him and me tumbling hadn't seemed ridiculous, to Lila. Attempts at matchmaking tend to reveal one of two things about the matchmaker – their own taste, or where they think their friend sits in the sexual food chain. Was this really where Lila thought my place was?

Ashwin worked in publishing. He was a senior editor at the Indian branch of a famous global house. He described his role at work as essentially decorative. The house made its money from foreign books that the Indian office was required only to print and distribute. 'Publishing is one of the last pre-neoliberal industries, in that it's accepted that you keep some people around even though they produce nothing. They don't pay us much, and every few years I get a new title, since titles, like all free things, are highly inflationary. But I get along with authors and my presence is held to sustain the fiction that we are engaged in the *literary* trade. Decorative functions are never the first to be automated.'

Lawyers tapped my shoulder from time to time. He too was interrupted by greetings. So it went at Perch, which achieved in its own fluent way the Circadian versatility of a Viennese coffee house. It was cafe by morning and afternoon, cocktail bar at night. You were equally likely to run into someone you knew at any hour.

Ashwin had grown up in Calcutta, the son of Tamil parents, and had spent many years at Cambridge. He had secured 'at least two' degrees in English, but left unwilling or unable to finish a PhD. Hence publishing.

Had he known Wojciech Zielinski there? 'Everyone knew him. He made himself unpopular with the Indian and Pakistani men, because he was always after our women.'

'*Your* women?'

'"Our women" in a certain sense, but rather too rarely in the sense that matters.'

'Surely,' I said, 'if you put aside the difficulty of keeping hold of your women, Cambridge, Britain, must have suited you better than here? Why did you come back? Visa issues?'

'Patriotism.'

'Rubbish.'

'That's what I said at the time. People weren't as grubbily cynical as you.'

'They weren't as honest, you mean.'

'Have you ever lived or studied abroad? No? You may not fully relate, then. These things go in waves. In the fifties, people really did stay back or come back out of patriotism. Then Nehru becomes Indira and Five-Year Plans move from blueprint to black joke and universities become "democratised". Patriotism, like anything else, has a half-life and it decays faster under Hindu rates of growth. So by the seventies, if you could leave, you didn't come back unless you were a lunatic. That lasted until, what, the early 2000s?'

'That's the collective story. But what about you?'

A theatrical sigh. 'You demand the truth.'

'I demand the truth, or at least a more convincing lie.'

'Not patriotism, but a theory of my comparative advantage. An evolutionary theory.'

As so often in this conversation, I didn't have to say things like 'Go on' or 'Say more.' I smiled in a way I knew he understood. Talker and listener in smooth alignment.

'One of the traditional arguments offered for returning to India,' he said, 'or from the West to any India-like country, is that at home you'll be a big fish in a small pond. Cambridge degrees are a scarcer commodity here, et cetera. I thought this was in fact underselling the case. I didn't think I was coming back to be a big fish in a small pond: India wasn't a pond, it was an ocean, just one with more primitive forms of life. England was a pond, at most a lake, but it was full of fish, some of them highly evolved. I was coming back, I thought, to be the first fish in an ocean where everything else was pre-fish. The first fish in a world of plankton.' He stopped abruptly. Had this really been how he had thought a decade prior, or was this a theory developed on the fly for my benefit?

'And? What is it like, being the first fish?'

'Tragic. Not that anyone will sympathise. As in the Greek tragedies, I was led astray by hubris.'

'So you weren't actually the first fish? There were other fish here too?'

'On the contrary. I was right, and that was the tragedy. I didn't foresee what being right *meant*. I can't enjoy being a life-form at a higher stage of evolution. I'm not a fish lording it over plankton,

I'm a fish transplanted to an ocean where there's nothing for a fish to eat. And it's miserable being the only fish. You can't talk to plankton. You can't fuck plankton.'

I was at the point of asking, What am I, plankton or fish? But I didn't want to flirt. Instead I asked, 'How do the plankton feel about the fish?'

'Some of them are honoured by the presence of the fish. Most think I illustrate the unappeal of evolution; the superiority of being a plankton.'

'Or maybe they just don't like the way you look down at them from your higher rung of the evolutionary ladder.'

He looked sharply at me with curiosity that shaded into suspicion. 'Am I to take it that you are one of those who thinks our new ways of doing things are just the true ways, reclaimed? Who thinks it's fine to live in a sea of happy plankton?'

'You tell me. What do I look like?'

'You and I are members of the same class. I don't know about your background but I can see and hear you well enough.'

'What class is that?' But he fell silent. Then he was back, and he glowed with new interest.

'Your last name is Saxena. Kayasth. UP Kayasth? Delhi? What does your father do?'

'He's retired.'

'Kayasths are too few to be politically significant. What did he retire from? Business? Civil service?'

'He was a CA with his own practice for around thirty years.'

'Of course. Silly of me to not think of that. A Saxena *should* be an accountant. Upper-caste Hindu, male, CA, sixty-something, Hindi-speaking—'

'Is there a point to this?'

'Demographically your family fits the profile of enthusiastic cheerleader of the New India. Out with the Macaulayputras and all that. But you read as something quite different. You *read*, for one thing.'

'So does my father.'

'Novels? Or "Lessons from the Life of Pandit Madan Mohan Malviya"?'

'Neither.' Baba had never read a novel in his life. To my knowledge. 'I don't know what you're hoping to get at, but I am my father's daughter. Ever since I can remember, when someone asked me, "What do you want to be when you grow up?" I thought, I want to be my father. I didn't say it out loud, I knew to say something appropriate, meaning conventional, but I thought it and I still think it.'

'I can see that I'm irritating you,' he said.

He was. 'I just don't see what our caste has to do with anything. Why you need to caste profile me or anyone.'

'Good God, you south Delhi "liberals" with your squeamishness! You're wrapped in privilege quilts as snug and thick as a minor maharaja's, and when someone says the word *caste* you act like they've farted in public.'

'I've never thought about myself or the people I know on the basis of caste and I don't intend to start now.'

'And you don't recognise that for privilege? You take it for virtue?'

'Right now it may be privilege,' I said, 'but it's a privilege everyone ought to have. A privilege *you* could have, if you only took it.'

'Is your mother Kayasth? Of course she is, you don't want to answer. Exactly five per cent of Hindus marry outside caste and that number has barely budged in fifty years. Oh, if you restrict it to people who eat at Perch, it's maybe fifty per cent, but that's because they've formed new castes – they care about whether someone has an iPhone and where they last went on holiday. If anything, this new post-caste privilege is far more insidious. At least old Thakur landlord giving his servant a kick in the groin every morning wasn't a hypocrite. He didn't deny his privilege, he matter-of-factly owned it.'

'To answer your earlier question: look, I don't love the way things are. But life goes on. I don't know what else you want me to say. Institute a democracy and you're going to eventually see outcomes the people who did the instituting don't like. I don't believe in a new India or a true India. This is the one we have, and we each do what we can to live in it.'

'And you think this India has room for you? A woman, English-speaking, book-loving, a barrister who presumably *believes*, holds faith, in the Constitution, court, rule of law?'

'I've been a practising lawyer for fifteen years. You're talking to me as if I'm a seventeen-year-old first-year law student who thinks she's going to grow up and change the world.'

'Things are getting worse in the courts. You obviously don't need me to tell you that. Often what happens in there bears no visible resemblance to law. You could be disillusioned. You *should* be, if you were principled to begin with.'

'I didn't realise disillusion meant the loss of principles. I thought it meant the loss of illusions. But I should defer to the Cambridge scholar and editor here, I guess.'

'Ha! Touché.'

I'm not sure if either of us had tried to make this work as a date, or even given it a chance to. The shared realisation that it hadn't worked wasn't disappointing: it was liberating. With none of the dately weights or pressures, we could simply enjoy or not enjoy ourselves.

'What about you?' I asked. 'Whether or not there's much room in this country for the law, there's plenty of room for lawyers. We've never been in greater demand. But the ascendant India is no habitat for books. Not the sort of books I'd imagine you want to publish.'

He began to look genuinely sad. But I couldn't take back the question. And he was more than sporting. Within seconds he had worked up a sheet of irony that covered his face, like sweat. 'We'll publish ever worse books for ever fewer people. But we'll live. We already publish Dear Leader, we'll begin to publish some leading cronies. As Larkin said, no one actually starves.'

'Have you ever thought about writing fiction yourself? Isn't that a consolation or rather a way of taking advantage of dark times? Unpleasant to live in but interesting to write about.'

'Who would read what I'd write about? If I write about us – elites – you can't write about Eastern elites. If your characters are eating good food, they either need to be Western, or dead. I could write a novel set in a slum, with a token hijra, but I don't know anything about those things.'

'Never stopped anybody before.'

'It has stopped me. Did you know that the Chinese don't in fact say, "May you live in interesting times"? They say, "Better to be a dog in a time of peace than a human in a time of chaos."'

'What about *Crazy Rich Asians*? Those are Eastern elites.'

'You raise a good point. Maybe I could write something set at a really blingy Gujju or Marwari wedding in Abu Dhabi. I've been to one or two. Let's say the groom tells the bride on the wedding night that he's gay. The lower chick-lit. It could work.'

'I smell a Netflix deal. *Made in Hell*.' I thought this would please him. It didn't land at all. He had moved on – or backwards.

'I'm a fool. *Of course* it's different for you.'

'What's different?'

'India. Being here. It isn't that you never left. It's that you're a lawyer. You read, you're probably some sort of liberal, but you spend your days not as a reader or as a liberal but as a lawyer and, as you said, lawyers are thriving.'

'I'm happy in India because I'm making money?'

'Not as crude as that. You'd make money anywhere. But, yes, at root I suppose it is a question of money. I wonder if you lawyers are even aware of this – of how different things are for you than for the rest of us.'

'If you're talking about money, you should know that many people have more of it than lawyers. Our clients, to begin with.'

'Oh, I don't doubt that plutocrats don't find India insalubrious. It's something else. Law is the only field in which India doesn't systematically lose its best talent. Where people with other options actually *choose to stay*. Where you can go to work and, no matter your feelings about the client or the judge or the system, you can look across to the opposing counsel and think, "I actually respect that man, I am not ashamed to be his peer." Why do you think I came back?' He was about to give me his third answer to that question. Three whisky cocktails, a bean salad and two plates of gnocchi had come and gone. 'My PhD was going nowhere. I applied to every publishing house and agency in London. No one wanted me.'

'What about Lila? She's not a lawyer. She chose to come back. Presumably you don't think she didn't have a choice.' I was willing to bet that he didn't know about the traffic jam on the green card pathway.

'She's the exception that proves the rule.' And then he started, rapid-fire, to ask my opinion of various authors he published.

We were asked if we wanted dessert. I said no right away, and he looked regretful, not because it meant we'd leave sooner, but because he did want some. But the imminence of the bill posed another question: should I pay? Keeping only our respective salaries in mind, it might seem obvious. But you never knew whether someone like him actually lived on his salary, or whether they worked in publishing because they could afford to.

When I took the bill and said, 'I've got this,' he just smiled, in the way of someone who is used to being taken out to dinner. Only downstairs, as he lit a cigarette and we said goodbye, did he thank me.

8
Lions and Tigers

On her first Friday at Adhimukta Bharat, Jahnavi messaged me from the toilet. She had been due back at my chambers at 7 p.m. to deliver her report, but now she'd been asked to stay late and didn't think it appropriate to refuse. I congratulated her on her good judgment and said that, if she didn't mind, we could reschedule her reports to Sundays. We could start Sunday week, by when she'd have ten days' worth of material.

Later she would explain the terror of that first Friday. The structure of the office meant that the toilet was the only place where she could pass seven seconds unobserved. Her desk was in the middle of a row of five, snug as the central slice of cheese in a crowded sandwich. The men seated on either side watched her. With shy sincerity she told me that she didn't think they did so out of distrust. These weren't men who were used to women. They had none of the Delhi man's air of generalised ownership. 'They don't even make me feel uncomfortable,' she said. 'They make me feel embarrassed, because *they* seem uncomfortable. I think they both feel like they should say something, ask me out, but each is waiting for the other to go first.'

'What would happen if one of them wasn't there? Would the other ask?'

'I don't know, we'll see.' We did see, but not for some weeks.

'Aside from the men next to you, is there a general air of surveillance? Is no one faffing about?'

'It's pretty strict. People don't really chat. You can't block social media, because they have to use it for work, but you can't be logged in on a personal account.'

I said that she messaged me from the toilet, but that's not strictly accurate. There was no wi-fi in the toilet, and no phone signal anywhere in the building, so she had to type the message in the toilet – all in one text – and press 'send' on her way back, a few steps before taking her seat. Toilet breaks were logged. Smoke breaks – more than work or even lunch, in a Delhi office they gave the day its shape – were banned. Kunal was zero-tolerance when it came to smoking.

'And people are OK with this shakha-style workplace?'

'I think they really like it.'

We were in my office, which I'd opened on a Sunday because I thought she'd be more awkward in my home, or anywhere there were other people. She was at the age where they don't do hot drinks. Maybe she drank kombucha, or something else I didn't quite know – is that drunk hot or cold? I had stocked the fridge with Cokes regular and diet, and apple juice, and Limca, but all she agreed to was water, and she just looked at the glass the whole time, as if even one sip might incriminate. The next time, I decided, I would call her home, and I'd be damned if I didn't get her drunk.

'So what do they actually do?'

Two evenings later, Lila and I were back in the park. The benches and grass were slick with new rain. The shower had lasted twenty-seven minutes: long enough to make swamps of roads and give us two hours – just about – of a break from the heat. It took me forty minutes of that time to drive the three kilometres from my office to Lila's park.

This rain was a prologue. It started again at midnight and kept going until lunch the next day. On my way back from the Supreme Court I would pass trees fallen over Lutyens' avenues. Planted while the roads were being laid out a century ago, they had grown tall enough to cover from end to end, in death, the roads they had been designed to ennoble. This time it took a whole day for the heat to recover.

That was to come. In the park, I summarised for Lila Jahnavi's report.

Jahnavi had been at Adhimukta five days before she laid eyes on Chairman sir, let alone speak to him. When she first arrived, she was taken to meet a man called Sridhar, who occupied one of the two smaller private offices next to Kunal's. The sign outside his door, which I'd missed on my visit, read: SRIDHAR VENKAT, DIRECTOR OF EDUCATION. She'd taken him for mid-thirties, but LinkedIn suggested he was at most twenty-eight. She'd been misled by his hair, which was thick but substantially grey.

Sridhar told her nothing general about the organisation or himself, and asked her no questions. LinkedIn told us that he was from Bangalore, had studied to be a chartered accountant (no word on whether he passed the exam), then done an MBA, then worked three years at a large start up in Gurgaon. That was his most recent listed job. After that, presumably, he'd joined Adhimukta.

Adhimukta wasn't on his LinkedIn, however, or on anyone else's. There was no trace of it on the internet. It wasn't yet clear if it took corporate legal form, whether as company or trust. Zauba Corp listed Kunal as a director of three companies, all founded by Mr Chawla. Mr Chawla was still listed as an active director – not an unusual honour for a dead man.

Lila explained the companies: one was the AC dealership; one was used for miscellaneous investments; the last was the old AC manufacturer, now in effect a real-estate portfolio.

'How come you weren't, aren't, a director of any of them?'

'We're not allowed external directorships. No exceptions, barring charities. But Papa and I discussed his work, constantly. I didn't need to formally be a director.'

'So you knew Kunal was one?'

'It made sense. It wasn't like he had anything else to do. The idea was always that he would work in the business. Papa and I often spoke about how to structure stuff so that he could tell himself and the world that he worked there without actually having any power or real responsibilities. We knew he'd fuck it all up if given half a chance. Like so many boys do.'

All Sridhar did was give Jahnavi her first assignment. She had to go through history, science and social studies textbooks, curricula and teaching materials, for standards 6 through 8, from seven states – Gujarat, Karnataka, Tamil Nadu, Madhya Pradesh, Uttarakhand, Odisha and Punjab – and make notes on the following:

1) Positive depictions of individual Indians past and present – anyone that the textbook presented as a hero.
2) Negative descriptions of individual Indians.
3) Blanket positive or negative statements about India as a country or society ('India is poor', 'India is diverse', and so on).
4) Characterisations of Indian society or social values (caste, family, religion).
5) Achievements by India or Indians.
6) Predictions or speculations about India's future.

Jahnavi wouldn't need to track down the source material. A previous intern had done that. Her job was simply to gather what was relevant and then:

'Then you can make a PPT with all your key findings. And – if it's good – you will be given the chance to present it to our chairman, Shri Kunal Chawla.' Then he dismissed her, and as she opened his door to leave, said only, 'We work fast here. We don't believe in wasting time. We're working for 1.4 billion Indians.'

'He actually said that?' said Lila. 'Where does Kunal find these people?'

I supplied the name of Sridhar's start up alma mater.

'So he used to work in sales for a bogus fintech app, and now he's *Director of Education*? I hope someone will hire him when Kunal's thing blows up.' Not once, not even in mockery, did I ever hear Lila say the words, Adhimukta Bharat.

On Jahnavi's first Friday, Kunal returned to Adhimukta from wherever he'd been, and she was called in to see Sridhar. Chairman sir would like her to report on her work that evening. But she didn't have the PPT ready, she was still gathering the information. No matter.

At the time Jahnavi was scheduled to deliver a report to me, in Jangpura, she delivered one instead to Kunal in Defence Colony. All the other men had gone home, even Sridhar. The robot receptionist came to Jahnavi and said, 'He will see you now.' He didn't greet her as she entered. He didn't even look up. First he was texting, then he was writing a line or two in a notebook. Finally he told her to sit.

At one or two points in my narrative Lila gave me an articulate look. Hurry the fuck up or, Do we need this? I ignored her.

Begin, Kunal said to Jahnavi. She chose to start with her inventory of Indian achievements. Not just the usual stuff – the invention of zero and Rakesh Sharma and Kalpana Chawla in space. She talked about the glories of Indian botany, Indian weaponry. She seemed to have a perfect memory for what was in which textbook. It wasn't as simple as each state valorising its own local heroes. Some states were more patriotic than others. Some talked only of the pre-Islamic past; others were up to date on nanotech and vaccines and Paralympic medals.

Kunal was pleased with Jahnavi. The key thing was her understanding of priorities. Had Sridhar told her to start with achievements? No? Well. You have done very well. Now, he said, I am going to let you into a secret. Do you understand that when I say secret I mean secret?

What did she feel when he asked her this, I had asked her: fear or excitement? At first she looked at me as if she didn't understand the question, and I felt briefly idiotic. Then she said, 'Actually, the only thing I remember feeling was . . . no, this isn't even a feeling, it was a thought – was he legit letting me in on a secret, or was he just saying that to make me feel . . . valued? Was it some kind of motivation strategy?'

Something about this broke Lila's courtesy. 'Couldn't you have just led with the secret? Do judges put up with this much waffle?'

'If you want to hear the story, you're going to hear it my way.'

I'm sure you may have heard, Kunal had said, that the Delhi government recently announced that they are going to implement a desh-bhakti curriculum in government schools. Jahnavi hadn't heard this, and nor did she, a fine specimen of Westernisation, know what desh-bhakti meant, but she knew better than to speak. Now the question is, he said, where are they going to get this curriculum? They could make it themselves, but that'll take years. It's government. So we are going to make it for them. No, they don't know that yet. But we have many friends in the party. We're going to make it here, and then I'm going to rock up at the deputy chief minister's office – he's also the education minister – and say, Deputy CM ji, here it is, you can have it for free. And you don't need to mention me or my organisation once in public. What can he say? I'll be presenting him a full curriculum while his staff are still debating what desh-bhakti means. I won't take public credit. My name won't be in any paper. But we'll ensure the right people come to know. Then there'll be pressure on the private schools to implement it – they'll come to us to modify it to suit their needs. Then other states. I want you to know how important your work here is.

Jahnavi went home and looked up the phrase. Desh-bhakti just meant patriotism, right? 'Sure,' I said, 'but everything depends on what *that* means. Do you know what Kunal thinks it means?' She shook her head and half bit her lip in what looked like the fear of having disappointed me.

'So that was all last week,' said Lila. 'What's happened since then?'

'She's just been chugging along with those state textbooks. They've given her some more states to deal with. But she did make one discovery, if you can call confirming the obvious a discovery. She saw a colleague editing Rohit's next video.'

There was only one material thing that I didn't share with Lila, because she wouldn't understand, and incomprehension would manifest as irritation with me. I didn't give her my sense of how Kunal had made Jahnavi feel. There were many things Jahnavi didn't like about Adhimukta Bharat. By the second week the novel thrill of Stakhanovite productivity began to give way to a more familiar sense of oppression. She started to resent the men beside her. *They* could WhatsApp friends or, God knows, wives; *they* could look away from their screen and daydream, but not her. And Sridhar gave her the creeps.

But Kunal, I could tell, she had liked; she had been delighted to have pleased, and wanted to please further.

Thus far none of this had run up against her fidelity to me and to the task I'd given her. But what would happen if it did, when it did?

Kabir was at a friend's house. Lila and I made slow circles of the park. We were frequently overtaken by a pair of octogenarians. They were exercising; we were enjoying the weather. Not far from here the heat was getting dressed to return, but for now the air was useably fresh, like a banana that is only one-third rotten. We could eat the rest. The day after tomorrow, we knew, the city would smell like dengue fever.

'What do you make of Kunal's strategy of making this curriculum and then giving it away for free?' I asked. 'Let's assume it works and the Delhi government says yes. Will he give it to others for free, too? Who will own the copyright?'

'You think he thinks in terms of stuff like "copyright"?'

'No, and he probably says that's a non-Indian way of looking at all of this. But we do need to understand his motivations. He's definitely got a longer-term plan here. Does he want to make money, eventually?'

These were all what I think of as 'smoking-out questions'. You wanted a particular piece of information and you didn't feel you could ask for it directly. It was a genre I'd worked in for years.

'He doesn't need to make money.'

'What if he only gets half of everything?'

'Half,' she said, 'even factoring in that Delhi real estate, whether commercial or residential, has been stagnant for a decade – maybe even worse than that – and it's never been a more illiquid category, and Papa was overinvested in real estate – he'd done so well out of it that no matter how many times I tried to "educate" him he wouldn't listen . . . you know, if it ever came to having to negotiate with that brother of mine, our best strategy might be giving him what looks like sixty per cent on paper, maybe even sixty-five, maybe even seventy, but we load him with the most overvalued and most illiquid stuff while I get the bulk of the shares. He'll fall for it, too. Thinking with his gut like a good Punjabi man. Real estate has an emotional significance to these guys that equities can't touch. It *exists*, people can see you have it. You can tell yourself it was your daddy's and it will be your son's.'

'Even factoring all that in . . .'

'If he gets half, even the wrong half, he's insanely, indecently, stupidly rich.'

'You left out "undeservedly".'

'Normally I hate that one so much. Who's to say who deserves to be rich and who doesn't? But he's so obviously undeserving that he almost makes Marxism look like it accurately describes the world.'

'And if he gets all of it?'

'If he gets all, and he has a competent family office, then he's private-jet rich.'

'Buy his way into politics rich?'

'Easily. And, actually, that's another reason he'll want the real estate. Best place to generate black money, best place to get rid of it.'

The unaskable questions. What would she do with her half? Would she assign to her own wealth the same adverbs? 'If Rohit got everything, he'd be fine, but not rich or what he'd think of as rich. Well short of the life he wants.'

'Realistically, even if I absolutely kill it the rest of the way, I can't make as much money as Kunal can inherit. Whereas if you kill it, your story vis-à-vis Rohit is totally different.'

'So with Adhimukta Bharat, is the obvious interpretation the right one? The long-term game is politics. The reason for doing it quietly, for now, is that he wants to keep his party options open.'

'Let's sit.'

We were at the far end of the park, whose full length now revealed itself, like an accordion. From some cranny of Lila's Lululemons a piece of green cloth appeared, and a bench was wiped.

'What I'm trying to get at,' I said, 'is whether there's some material reason for him to fight for everything. Something beyond "I'm-the-chosen-one". The chosen one thing sounds like a story he's made up to justify his claim, rather than the motivation for the claim itself.' I could have gone on, but I stopped because Lila wasn't looking at me.

She was looking across the park, chewing on a new thought. 'For the first time in my fucking *life*, I think that I might actually have things easier than Kunal. That I might be luckier.'

'You have never once thought that the biological child might have it easier than the adopted?'

'Something about being in the park without Kabir for a change, brought it home. I found myself actually thinking – I know this sounds asinine – about the things that actually live in this park.'

I certainly wasn't going to say, Are you beginning to sound like my father?

'The birds and the bees, the squirrels and trees?'

'I was thinking, whether plant or insect or animal, of the creatures that live their entire life in here. Birth to death. That are local, native, adapted. The weather doesn't bother them; this is where they're meant to be, how they're meant to live.'

'You think they're meant to breathe the air that we impose on them?'

'You're right. Actually, that only sharpens the point.' And then she emitted a loud animal call, not a laugh or snort or sigh, but something closer to the noises babies make, something pre- rather than non-verbal. 'You're wondering, who is this and what have you done with Lila?'

'I'm not not wondering that.'

'OK, I've got myself back now. *Here's the thing*. Imagine an x and y axis.' I nodded along, imagining nothing. 'The x axis indicates whether you think the world is fundamentally fair or unfair. The y axis shows how you feel about *your* place in the world. Get it? We're each in one of four quadrants. Top right quadrant – people who think the world is fair, and are happy with their place in it. Top left – those who know it isn't fair, but are resigned to or comfortable with their place in it. Bottom left – those who know it isn't fair, but are willing to fight to make it less unfair, at least for themselves. Bottom right – those brought up to think it was fair, or to think that it would at least be fair to *them*, who have now discovered otherwise.'

'Kunal and Rohit. But have they discovered that? Isn't the world more than fair to them?'

'You'd think so. But where you stand depends on where you sit. Most Delhi boys in their position are happy. But Kunal and Rohit don't compare themselves to other Delhi boys. *They compare themselves to us.*'

'And they see not that the world has changed, but that we have changed it. We've scrambled the order of things.'

'Yup.'

'Where are we on this' – what was the word? Graph? Matrix? – 'map?'

We were sitting closer together than I could remember. In a male way, my left arm had snaked across the top of the bench behind her. Sometimes she sat forward, sometimes she leaned back against my arm. 'We move between the top left and bottom left. We've always known the world isn't fair, and we know that sometimes we benefit from the unfairness and sometimes we lose out. But we don't sit around and whine or blame someone else. We get on with it.'

'So why feel bad for Kunal now?'

'Because of how unsettling it must feel. To grow up thinking the world is essentially perfect, and that it is yours. And then – not everyone becomes a grown-up, but everyone grows up in some way or the other – to suddenly discover you were wrong.'

'Has he discovered that?'

'In a funny way, even with his ash-smoothies, the easier bit is adjusting to the knowledge that he'll never measure up to Papa. Most biological sons don't measure up, either. No, it's me that has perverted the world. Not just the fact that I was the one Papa consulted on every business matter. Everything about me.'

Nineteen hours since my last drink, I felt an untraceable surge of liquid courage. 'Including, for instance, your dynamic with Raj.' And I had my reward, as I watched her face start to glow with the thrill of mutual understanding.

'*Exactly.*'

'And Kunal and Rohit don't think they've just been unlucky in the allocation of sisters? They think the whole world has changed?'

'This is how I want us to see it. Patriarchy-wise, do you know the difference between lions and tigers?'

'Other than one not having a mane?'

'Lions are social. The lionesses provide the food and sex and, presumably, the back-rubs and ego-rubs while the males sit around feeling pleased with themselves, yawning, and occasionally there'll be a roar, for the benefit of some tourist's Instagram story. And they should be pleased – being born a male lion is pretty high up there in the Universal lottery.'

'So the answer to the question of, "What would you like to be reborn as?" is "male lion"?'

'Kunal and Rohit thought that's what they *had* been born as. That's the north Indian idea of what a male life should look like. Like a lion's. Sit on your ass while the women feed and exalt you. Obviously the Sikhs take it one step further by literally adding "lion" to every boy's name.'

'But instead they find . . .?'

'Tigers are very different. They're not just solitary. They live in Hobbes' state of nature. Everything is zero-sum. Land is scarce. Prey is scarce. Water is scarce. A tiger needs his own territory. For that he has to first fight off his siblings, then possibly his father. Then when he wants a mate he has to fight the other suitors. When you go to Ranthambore and you see an alpha male in mating season, you don't see the trail of blood that led him to that spot. His mother fed him until he was maybe two, but after that he's on his own. Do you know what the mother tigress does when she thinks a cub isn't going to cut it in the big bad world? She eats it.'

'The way you're describing it, Kunal and Rohit sound like they're living a life much closer to the lion's than the tiger's.'

'Again, you're not seeing it from where they sit. You see them, they see us. And through us they see a world in which every woman is a potential threat rather than an obedient lioness. Then there's other men. Rohit couldn't cut it in the US, could he? I'm sure he applied for jobs, hoped for an H1-B. And even here they worry about all the men with more hunger and talent. Right now their lives are pretty lionish, but what about the future?'

'So making sure they inherit everything isn't just literally claiming the lion's share, it's a way of asserting that the world is as it should be? That still doesn't explain what Kunal's up to, though. He has ambitions that go beyond his rivalry with you.'

'That's what we have your spy for, isn't it?'

It wasn't that Lila wasn't taking me seriously. She didn't take Kunal seriously, and couldn't see that she didn't.

Her analogy certainly fit Rohit. Poor Rohit – no one could be more suited to gently accepting the lion's share, no one less to fighting for the tiger's. But what about Kunal?

My friend Deepti, who now lived in Bangalore, was in town for the weekend. Of all my friends, only Deepti had ever been, in the standard Delhi way, 'part of the family'. This was her doing. Before her first Delhi summer, between our second and third years of law school, she announced that she'd be sharing my bed: 'My parents will only let me do this internship if I stay with you.' That was the first of three summers she spent with us.

With each new year Deepti and I had less in common. We'd chosen each other as friends on the basis of our personalities at eighteen, and I felt that only one of us had stayed substantially true to the self that entered the friendship. But I chose not to notice the fatiguing journey she'd made from eccentricity to blandness. When she pressed on me the new Elizabeth Gilbert I didn't say, Remember when you used to read Elizabeth Bowen? I chose not to lament what the eighteen-year-old *pataka* who came from, of all places, *Kanpur,* could have been.

Deepti's status meant that when she came to Delhi she had to see my parents. I counted on disequilibrium taking a holiday for the length of her visit.

We found the front door open and two sets of unfamiliar men's shoes in the foyer. One – a fresh-out-the-box pair of doubtless in-fashion blue sneakers – must be New York's parting gift to Rohit. Its neighbours were black, open-toed Peshawari sandals, polished to within an inch of their life.

Voices came towards us and it took me a second to trace them to the living room, usually a hall of silence. The first was my mother's. The second belonged to the owner of the black sandals.

'Rohit's friend is here,' I said to Deepti. 'Kunal Chawla. Lila's brother.'

'Do we want to meet him?'

'We don't have a choice.'

Before Rohit or Kunal could register our arrival, Deepti had both hands on my mother's shoulders, then she ran an index finger down her face. 'Aunty, what's your secret and can you please share it with your poor daughter? You look younger than she does! And how do you stay so fit! I need to send my mom to you for life coaching.'

Kunal, whom we had interrupted, pretended as if Deepti wasn't there. While she praised Ma's hair he said to me: 'Your father's out.'

I said to Rohit: 'Welcome home. Nice shoes. When did you get back?'

Kunal replied: 'He's back to stay.'

'Did he leave his voice on the plane?'

Kunal stood up. I was surprised by the effort it took him. He *looked* powerful – in a still photo he could intimidate – but there was a stiff difficulty to his movements. As he'd stood he'd only two-thirds succeeded in concealing a grimace. Sedentary sloth that I am, I thought I could take him over a hundred metres.

'Aunty, we'll continue our conversation soon. Namashkaar.'

'Later,' said Rohit, his first word since our arrival. From Kunal he got only a nod. The chairman of Adhimukta Bharat left the flat without ever having acknowledged Deepti's presence in it.

My mother had vanished. Deepti moved over to sit by Rohit.

'It's so good to see you, Ro-Ro.' A name only she had ever called him. 'It's been at least two years—? Last time you were just about to start your master's in film.'

At the best of times my brother was easily confused. Now he looked distressed. He was prepared for me, not for Deepti.

The first Rohit Deepti had known was pimply and malodorous – in other words, fourteen. Since then, through every new dilettantism, every fresh proof of his want of substance, she kept massaging him with sweet attention. In this regard Deepti had always been just another north Indian girl. With no brother of her own to fuss over and spoil, she reached for mine.

Deepti now had a husband, and she had chucked in the corporate law partner track to go in-house at an IT firm – the most boring job in the world, and a sensible option for an aspiring mother. Once she was pregnant, maybe Rohit would look at her differently. For now he was stalled. He had come up against the limitations of disequilibrium as a guide to action. You knew there was a disequilibrium: you looked at your sister and that was all you saw; but what the fuck did that mean for how you should act when her friend whom you had always adored, had honoured for years in masturbatory thought and deed, was holding your hand and calling you Ro-Ro?

By sisterly standards I was hopeless at reading my brother's mind. I'd never made the effort. But even I could hear him now: Why did you bring her? Why are you doing this to me?

'Three years,' he said, eventually.

'Well, it won't be so long again if you're back to stay.'

He wouldn't look at her.

Even in her blandness this Deepti was still sharp. Maybe she'd tell herself that it was just the sight of her, that over the years Rohit's crush had swollen into something heavy and painful, and now he had to look at her *married*. Whatever Deepti had or hadn't noticed, she kept going in the old way.

'Come on, Ro-Ro, tell me more. Tell me properly. How was it to leave New York? What are your plans here?'

'It's all good, all good. I'm . . . figuring stuff out.'

By the time Rohit was four and I was ten, certain things were already known. At four I was a confident and autonomous reader and silent in company, my book a screen that shielded me from the world. Rohit at four had yet to learn the distinction between talking and shouting. Before he was five, Vikram chacha's wife, Anita alias Manju, would say to Ma as they stood chopping onions, Rohit's head attentively by my mother's chest: 'Tara was fully reading by this age, no? Vikram used to fire all those maths problems at her and she solved every one. This one is such a sweet child, but not such a clever one.' It would be two years before Rohit would acknowledge Manju chachi. Books he took much longer to forgive. When he did, in college, it was either because he needed to appear a reader to secure some girl, or that he'd seen an interview with some Hollywood director who said that all filmmakers had to be readers.

Poor Rohit spent five years being told by each successive class teacher that he was not his sister. Out of stoicism or embarrassment it took him five years to report this to Ma, who had him moved to a different school.

If we had got past all this, it was mostly by staying out of each other's way. Deepti was the best thing, maybe the only affirmatively *good* thing, to have ever come between us. In Deepti's company Rohit had actually felt grateful for the possession of a sister. If Deepti didn't look the way she did, of course, he might have thought, I wish she were my sister.

The three of us were now locked in a silence. What if I went to the kitchen, officially in search of my mother? With me out of the room, Rohit might at least talk to Deepti. If I did that, I wouldn't be sparing Rohit. I'd be running away, only for my own sake. I could not, in any conscience, hand so easy a victory to my own fear of unpleasantness.

This is the best I can offer in defence of what I did next. It is also the truth.

'D,' I said, 'have you seen Rohit's videos?'

'His what? Ro! Videos, as in films? Stuff you made on your course?'

Rohit, who still hadn't looked at Deepti, got up. 'I don't have time for your crap today. Bye, Deepti. Sorry . . . but . . .'

'What the hell, Rohit? I just wanted her to see your videos. Rohit has a YouTube series that has gone properly viral. I mean hundreds of thousands of views. Even *I've* heard of them.'

'Just fuck off, Tara. Please.'

Rohit hadn't looked at Deepti; he hadn't, exactly, looked at me. But he'd swung his head between us, several times. We'd both seen his eyes. They gleamed with heat, as if emerging from a dishwasher.

'I'm serious. You know she'd like to see them. Isn't it a good thing that they went viral? I really don't get what the issue is.'

'God, Aunty. What's this!'

My mother stood with a tray. Four glasses of her world-class chaach. Two large bowls of namkeen. Deepti only had to show up at our house for the chaach to appear.

I wasn't looking at my mother as she spoke. By the time I'd realised whom she was addressing, it was too late. So I missed, or hid from, her face. I couldn't miss her tone. I had heard it exactly once before. To my father, at the summit. 'What's the need for this? Why do you have to make him show or not show?'

Rohit collected his glass and left the living room without saying bye to Deepti. No, he'd already said it.

My mother was not going to follow him. Not with Deepti here. Deepti was part of the family, but not, so far as my mother was concerned, subject to its loss of equilibrium. Maybe this is just a difference between what a man and a woman can afford. And so my mother sat where Rohit had, and smiled at Deepti with all the world's warmth. 'How much we miss seeing you here. So far away you are. How are you enjoying married life, beta? Are you planning to have kids? You can't wait too long – as it is, you kids get married so late.'

And I found myself watching Deepti, between tiny sips, tell my mother about her baby production schedule. They were trying the normal way, and everything pointed to them both being normal, gynaecologically or whatever the male equivalent was. But they were also the wrong side of thirty-five. If normal didn't work, then IUI, maybe, then God forbid, IVF . . .

On this subject the women of my mother's generation can only ever supply one response: sympathy adulterated with smugness. They had their children in their twenties, with no need of clinical acronyms. They gave birth without epidurals. They look at us, with our careers and our freedoms and our refusal to 'adjust' to husbands – the Indian euphemism for 'obey' – and they need something to push back against a narrative of emancipation that is all the more galling for being so obviously true. This is all they have.

But my mother could not really be smug. She gave Deepti no condescension. Deepti had always thought my mother perfect. 'All parents should be like your parents.' When she said 'your parents', she meant 'your mother'.

Deepti was talking about Bangalore, about her new job, about the rain-water harvesting apparatus her husband had added to their home. Ma took it all in, or took none of it in, nobody could have told which. Ma had never been south, had never worked, never mind attempted water conservation. My mother only bothered with what was in front of her.

Deepti talked to and at Ma and while I sat with them I could feel myself, my *self*, floating out of the room, through the foyer, into the empty dining room and kitchen. Then to Rohit's room, where I saw him at his laptop, not typing, because his palms were clenched in anger and confusion, just staring at the screen – a screen with basketball scores on it, or an Instagram model's page. He was waiting for a text from Kunal that did not come. Then past my father's door, which I would not, could not, pass through.

By the time I had re-entered what was known as my body, Deepti was on to her own parents, in Kanpur, who were living under sentence of house arrest courtesy of a tyrannical and bed-ridden childless aunt. It didn't look as if they'd noticed me leave and come back.

'Yo, Deepti, is this aunt rich? Will she at least remember them in her will?'

'As always, Aunty, your daughter can only think about money.'

I had plenty of experience of watching Deepti and my mother. I was always the silent point in this particular triangle. I'd half work or read while they talked, and yet it *was* a triangle. The talking part was theirs; but that was only really the tip. The unspoken rest of the iceberg was mine too. Call it love, call it understanding.

Now my mother wouldn't look at me, and if in not looking at Deepti Rohit punished himself, my mother was not punished. She was all punisher.

Deepti saw this, and did nothing. Deepti wanted to punish me, too. Hadn't I earned it, by telling her nothing? Her response to my comment about her aunt was, I'm almost certain, the only time that either referred to my presence in the room. I say either, I mean Deepti. In this way they continued for a few more minutes, and then it was time for Deepti to go. She hugged my mother and soundly kissed her cheek.

As we came out and closed the front door, a young white cat flashed past us down the stairs. Hauz Khas was becoming as crowded cat-wise as dog-wise.

132

'This place needs a paint job,' I said, looking around the landing. 'I've never seen it even slightly dirty before. Ma's finally getting old, I guess.'

'Dude. Fuck that. What was up with Rohit? What haven't you been telling me?'

I didn't want to have this conversation. Eventually I'd have to, but now was not eventually. And yet I couldn't deny Deepti; I couldn't lose her, too.

'I'm coming to see you soon, no, for the reunion? I'll tell you all then. Over an outdoor beer.'

'Are you nuts? You're making this sound like something trivial, which it pretty fucking clearly isn't.'

'I just . . . can't talk about it right now. Next month, I promise.' Deepti, I told myself, could forgive me anything. I was family.

As she walked down I stood by the door, as if pretending to her and myself that I might go back in to my mother. I waited until I was sure that she'd left our street altogether, and then I walked down myself.

133

9
Career Opportunities

With Rohit at home, it was no longer really viable for me to visit my father.

In equilibrium, our family for thirty years had four people. In disequilibrium it had five. Kunal hadn't gone over to talk about his marital prospects or Adhimukta Bharat. I'm sure there was some introductory hype about Rohit's future, the great work he was going to do. But Kunal's real business with my mother was my father, and me.

He wouldn't have said to my mother, as he'd said to me, 'Brahm Saxena is clinically insane.' He might say it later, if he needed to. He would have said only that my father was betraying Rohit, betraying him not only as a son but as a young man who could do so much for the country. And here was Tara, who should be standing up for her brother, and instead she's choosing to be an accessory to the betrayal.

By now Kunal was likely to have instructed, that is to say contracted, the security guard at my parents' building to record my visits.

Only now did I see that, in the months before the summit, Kunal hadn't just been my brother's final ambassador. Those ambassadors hadn't been sent by Rohit in the first place. They'd been sent by Kunal.

Not that I needed to visit to know how things stood. Baba's room, fourteen feet by twelve, was now both prison and sanctuary. When inside the flat he was only safe in that room, safe from their eyes, safe from what he, they, we have done. Ma and Rohit kept him imprisoned, but to the prison itself they had no access. Only I did.

And if I knock on the door and go in, I'm doing something worse than subterfuge. I'm gloating. I'm not just conspiring with Baba and his five properties, I'm parading my complicity.

If I went when they were out – even if the security guard hadn't been bought – even if my visit went genuinely undetected – I'd spend the whole time trying to hear Baba over the hideous soundtrack of my anxiety. Am I about to be found out? Did the guard see me? What if Ma and Rohit are already back? Fuck, what if Kunal has set up CCTV in here, or had the place bugged? Maybe the Chawla siblings share a taste for surveillance.

Each of these thoughts would come with a sickening annexure, like the nausea that attaches itself to a headache. First the detection anxiety, then the awareness that *by* my fear, I was proving Rohit right, Ma right, Kunal right.

What I didn't know, and did my best not to think about, was the practical business of how Baba was actually living through each day. With my own flat and office, possessed of a family but no longer trapped in one, I didn't *live* disequilibrium. Not as he must have. Did he really eat, now, with his wife and son? When Baba made my room his study, he took the bed out to make room for yoga, and put in a narrow divan. Was he now sleeping on it at night?

Could my father pretend that there had been no change in his family? Or did he, now that his son was at home, now that his wife thought him no husband, did he lock the door to the study every time he left the flat?

For three weeks I didn't go home. Like all Indians of any age with two parents and no children, I could not fully grow up. The flat I'd been raised in was still *home* if they lived in it. My flat was home, too, but depending on which one was meant, the word in my head always carried an unvoiceable shift of intonation.

In my hour of greatest need, the world had granted me a work well so deep that I could spend three whole weeks submerged. I could tell Jahnavi that I was too busy to hear her latest report.

I could ignore Lila's texts for days and when she sent me a series of ???? I could say, *Sorry, I'm fucking swamped.*

It happened like this. An American streaming service, barred from the Chinese market by the Great Firewall, had sold its shareholders on the dream of a billion screen-addled Indians. But after three decades of ready access to world culture, our country was more checked out than ever before, more complacently concerned only with itself. If you prefer, you could say we had finally become self-confident. Every country seemed to be going this way: we had never been less interested in the world, and the world had never been less interested in India. Maybe it was not so paradoxical that access to everything, everywhere bred only parochialism. Maybe the difficulty of getting to foreign countries, or getting hold of their books and films and music, the beyond-impossibility of copulating with their men, had been the source of our lost interest. The curiosity had really been longing.

Either way, for the Americans to make it in India, they couldn't flog their own stuff, as they had in the 1950s. They had to sell us *our* own. Their success would come down to the nature of their Indian content.

Their India strategy rested on buying an old family business that held the distribution rights to hundreds of Hindi films produced between the 1960s and the 1990s. When the cable TV rights to these films had been sold, the internet was still largely theoretical, and streaming services the stuff of science fiction. Right now the company made its money leasing out the streaming rights year by year. The Americans hoped that by waving a sufficiently large cheque at the family, they could get hold of the whole library.

Lila had said that if Kunal inherited everything he'd be private-jet rich. If this deal went through, the Sindhi film family could build themselves a university, or a yacht in the shape of the Palace of Versailles. If it didn't, then the Americans were well and truly fucked. Back home they were losing thirty thousand subscribers a week to Disney.

The acquisition made the front page of every English-language daily, not just the business papers. Three days later, I got a call from my second and final boss, a senior counsel now in semi-retirement. The following day I was interviewed by two corporate legal teams, one from the Asia office in Singapore, the other from the global HQ in Menlo Park.

I got this call because the day the papers carried the announcement (the press release had said, 'subject to the completion of regulatory processes'), the Americans began to hear from the lawyers of people whose existence they really ought to have been warned of.

These troublemakers could be classified three ways. The first group were cable TV networks who argued that the satellite rights they'd bought in the 1990s and 2000s implicitly extended to streaming; that streaming was simply a new form of television. This lot were merely a nuisance. Their legal claims were so weak that I was confident they lacked even the power to delay.

The second set was a pair of small-time operators, without the TV networks' legal resources but, potentially, with some actual facts on their side. One was a business that in the early 2000s had sold cheap, low-definition versions of Bollywood classics on DVD, priced low enough to lure people habituated to online piracy. DVDs long finished, the company was about to collapse. But some of their contracts with the distributors had been for 'digital rights'; the technology was not always specified. Also in this category was a lingerie and dental floss manufacturer in the grand tradition of men that in middle age decide to flush their fortune down the glamorous sink of movie production. He claimed to have a contract that gave him a right to first refusal over the entire collection.

The Americans were not convinced that the Sindhis were not incompetent enough to have signed such a contract. These two weren't a matter for a lawyer, not at any rate my kind of lawyer. They would have to be bought off.

Finally, there was the cadet branch. Two great-grandsons of the company's founder. Their grandfather had been thrown out of the business in 1956 for keeping a Burmese mistress. He'd been disinherited, too, but his descendants lived on in an Arabian Sea-facing flat whose last unambiguous owner had been their great-grandfather, who had died in 1977. After his death there had been some half-assed attempts to contest the will. These seem to have just been a blocking mechanism against the other side's designs of eviction. The two parties had long since settled into their own equilibrium: maintain your claim in theory, but do nothing.

No equilibrium is going to survive when there's this kind of money involved. It had been years since the cadet branch had bothered with the expense of a functioning lawyer. Now their phones were going off nonstop as lawyer after lawyer called to pitch their services, like suitors battling over a rich young widow. Four different lawyers already claimed to represent them. Each came with more or less the same story: by rights the cadet branch owned fifty per cent of the company.

None of this was in any area of law that I could truly call my own. I got the job because the Americans were – and you couldn't say unjustly – done with their Indian legal team. And it so happened that their deputy general counsel in Menlo Park had, in an earlier life, worked for my old boss in Delhi.

At the interview he said, 'I've been told that you are, and I quote, "Extremely thorough, reliable and, above all, honest." Would you agree with that description?'

'Who am I to disagree?'

'Any final questions?'

'Just the one. The Burmese mistress. Did he have any children by her?'

'Yikes. That's a great point. We'll look into that.'

Two days later he called back. 'You were right to ask. He does. It's a sad story, really. He had a son by her whom he never acknowledged. That son now works as a cook-cum-driver to the boys.'

'His half-nephews.'

'Yup. And apparently he is the spitting image of their dadaji.'

So that was my case; that was where I could go to avoid my family, and Lila's. Here too there was a family in disequilibrium; but one that I could watch with detachment, like an entomologist observing the mating of cockroaches.

In a procession of seventeen-hour days, I learned the grammar and syntax of film rights contracts and their associated case law, and became the Sindhis' unofficial family historian. These were matters that called for industry, not creativity; for sheer unrelenting work that only my hourly rate prevented being called manual, or menial. I had no current capacity for creativity. But only I seemed to know that.

Four months later, when all was settled without a day in court, the deputy general counsel in California wrote my old boss, BCCing me, to say that I was certain to be the leading advocate of my generation, and in the fresh throes of relief, which can be more intense than any joy, I think he may have meant it.

This case was an inflexion point. It was the staircase that took me from established to successful: from survival to thrival. It wouldn't really change how I was seen in court. But it would lead to a new channel of clients – American, meaning both lucrative and, for a woman lawyer, at least this woman lawyer, more pleasant to deal with. And in Delhi a certain kind of person – a Lila kind of person – would look at me differently.

After three weeks Baba messaged. Without precedent, at least in my knowledge, this wasn't a text but a voice note.

It came out, like all his speech, in formed sentences. And it was soft. You could hear every word without straining, but only by a single decibel. Volume al dente.

Beta, he said, **I haven't seen you in quite some time. You must be busy. Can you come home this Sunday around three?**

I didn't ask whether Ma or Rohit would be around. I assumed they wouldn't be. It was interesting, if that's the right word, that Ma – it couldn't be Rohit – still made him aware of her plans.

I was to emerge from my three weeks underwater into a socially packed Sunday. Jahnavi's long-delayed second report in the morning; Baba at 3 p.m. In between, lunch with Ashwin. Not, I hardly need clarify, a second date. Lunch with Ashwin and his friend. Of this friend I was given no name, only an address, and a single line of context. **He's a dear friend and he needs your help.**

But first, Jahnavi. Meeting in the morning meant I had to adjourn my scheme for getting her drunk. We met instead at Sunder Nursery. Newly refurbished and still something like a secret, it might have been the best thing about Delhi.

I said secret, but what I really mean is that for the first year or so after it re-opened, Sunder Nursery was the last refuge of our class – of the Anglophone liberal elite, more privileged than ever but also more alienated. It was lately fashionable to call us the Khan Market Gang, but anyone with money could go to Khan Market. Sunder Nursery, that first year, was the one public place in Delhi, maybe in India, where we might actually be in the majority.

On Sunday mornings one corner of the nursery hosted a market that sold artisanal cheese and sourdough and organic this and organic that. Young embassy types took to that market like the Dutch to tulips. That was the usual mix, in those days: white and wannabe white.

I met Jahnavi at the ticket counter a few minutes before nine o'clock. At first I thought she looked nervous, but she was only hot. Poor girl – live long enough air-conditioned and you grow as vulnerable as ice cream to the outside world.

'Sorry for foisting this on you. I didn't know it would be this hot this early.'

'No! No! It's nice.'

As we walked diagonally across the front garden she remarked, quite appropriately, on how beautiful and how empty it all was. And then: 'It's so . . .'

'Restrained?'

'It doesn't feel like India.'

'Enjoy it while it lasts. India usually gets to India before long.'

Until we had our flat whites and a table – in those days you could still get a table – I didn't take us beyond small talk. Mostly we were quiet. I would need two centuries of American clients to be as rich as she was, but I was also Old, which meant we had to enact the routine of my asking if I could buy her anything and her saying no.

As we sat, a squat pug rubbed against her leg in a plea for help. Its tormentors were two pink blonde toddlers. Then their mother turned up, sweaty and embarrassed.

I was about to ask her if she liked dogs when she asked me if I did.

'I wish I did. It's not that I don't. I just don't know how to be with them.'

She looked at me in a new way. I felt the newness of it on my face like a scald.

'Kunal loves them, I know. He and Lila always had golden retrievers at home.'

'Lila?'

'His sister. A dear friend of mine.'

'You know Kunal personally?'

'I've known him since I was younger than you. Did you know he had a sister?'

She shook her head.

In that new look I'd seen more than the dog-lover's familiar unregard for the non-dog-lover – sometimes contempt and sometimes pity, two sides of the same coin. I had placed her in Adhimukta; I had gamed out all the ways it might be a dumb idea, and the one thing I hadn't bargained for was her falling for Kunal. Not in the crush sense, but falling for his shtick. Taking him seriously. Being taken in. But if she had, and that new way she'd looked at me sure suggested it, then I was losing or had lost my claim on her reverence. Even her shoulders and legs, I now saw, looked loose with irreverence.

What I did next I can explain only in terms of the inevitable

141

tendency of the Old and the Young to conceive of each other as monoliths. To someone Jahnavi's age there must be some point – maybe thirty-three – where you crossed definitively from one stage to the other. Kunal was on her side of the line. I wasn't.

'I never told you, Jahnavi, exactly why I was sending you to Adhimukta. You may have thought I wasn't saying because I didn't fully trust you. But if I didn't trust you, I wouldn't have sent you.'

'You don't have to tell me.'

'I wanted you to go in with as unclouded a mind as possible. To be able to feel like you really were an intern at Adhimukta. I'm guessing here but I think you have felt like that. You don't' – and now I smiled – 'have to say whether or not I'm right. So now I think you . . . deserve to know.'

I started with the fact of Kunal's adoption. I outlined the Chawlas' family and business history. I described, with encyclo-paedic neutrality, the siblings' professional trajectories. And then I moved from fact to interpretation; but I didn't declare this move. Every sentence I produced before and after the move I believed to be true to the last syllable. But there is a difference between, 'He was born on the sixteenth of July, 1987' and, 'He hates his grand-mother', never mind 'He's a sexist.' I left it to her to intuit the difference. That is to say, I counted on her not intuiting it.

Kunal, I said, wanted it all. Inheritance-wise. Every piece of real estate, every share, every gemstone. And he wanted it, I said, not out of personal greed but on principle. He believes the man should get everything. He believes that, having married, Lila is no longer a Chawla, no longer his sister, no longer his mother's daughter. She is now her husband's property, her husband's responsibility. And I am her friend and her lawyer. I placed you in Adhimukta because I wanted to know what he's up to, what he's capable of.

'Whether he has the connections to intimidate his way to getting everything?'

'That's right.'

This is how I won Jahnavi back; or saved her, just in time, from defection. I entered her age and accent and appearance and educational history into the algorithm and it reported that this was a girl who told herself, every day, I am a feminist.

I didn't tell her about Kunal's 'chosen one' theory. I didn't say that I too had a brother, the man whose videos she'd seen her neighbour editing.

We had been sitting there an hour. Technically we were under a tree, but shade in Delhi is not much more use than an umbrella in a cyclone. In periods of celibacy I can go days without noticing my own body. But I looked at her and thought that I needn't feel bad for bringing her here. Being this sweaty suited her. Didn't Western women conceive of make-up as armour? *This* was armour; a liquid layer between her and the world. This was how I'd always imagined her, healthy.

And then I saw, at the Gruyère stall diagonally behind Jahnavi, a Punjabi man buying cheese for his white date. Each of the pieces of him – the white tight T-shirt, the salmon shorts, the Birkenstocks, the belly, the beard, the shades – were anonymising, like all cliché. But still I recognised Pavit. The first of Rohit's ambassadors, or Kunal's.

'Fuck, fuck. Holy mother of god. Fuck. I am such an idiot.'

'Is everything OK?'

'Jahnavi, you're supposed to be my spy! Who has coffee with their spy in the middle of fucking Sunder Nursery! We could have been seen by three or four of Kunal's friends already.'

'But none of them would recognise me. It's totally fine!'

'It's not the odds. It's the principle. Ugh. OK, I'm going to sit here while you wander into the stalls and then I'm going to leave. And . . . you can give me your update next weekend—? Now get lost.'

Three hours later, after the day's second shower, I stood in a white shirt and jeans on Aurangzeb Road, waiting for a gate you could drive an aeroplane through to open. The road had recently been renamed Dr APJ Abdul Kalam Road, after the government's notion of a good Muslim. But the residents were grumpy. Good Muslim or bad, Aurangzeb had at least been an emperor and Aurangzeb *sounded* right for a street on which houses came up for sale once or twice a decade, and never for less than twenty million dollars.

In his booth a young security guard was napping. I knocked, first politely then not, always unprofitably. Eventually I called Ashwin. I could hear him before the gate opened. He was panting.

'You didn't have to run.'

'Sorry, sorry, everyone's away, at a wedding.'

'A wedding at this time of year?'

'A staff wedding.'

I indicated the security guard's booth. 'I couldn't wake him.'

'He's a stand-in. Some sort of nephew. I'll tell Vicky.'

'Vicky?'

'Vikramaditya Rai. Whom you'll meet in, I think, twenty-seven seconds.'

The gate and walls were so high that when you walked through you entered a world of which nothing was revealed to the street. Unlike with a locked London garden or a window display at Prada, you couldn't look longingly at what was not yours. You had to imagine.

You might imagine: a fleet of Bentleys, each with its own designated chauffeur in white livery and gold-rimmed cap. Or a party at which champagne flutes seem to refill themselves automatically and it is difficult to know what language is being spoken, for all you hear everywhere is the laughter of young women. Or a quartet of St Bernards lounging in a room that is climate-controlled so that, every day of the year, its temperature and humidity are identical to that of Gstaad.

No class has special powers or deficiencies of sympathy. The unrich are as incapable of accurately imagining the rich as the other way round, and claims to the contrary are humbug.

The twenty-seven seconds that separated me from Vicky contained a road lined with ashoka trees on both sides, less a driveway than a private avenue. The spaces between the trees revealed, on one side, formal gardens and a nursery with a greenhouse; on the other, more gardens, a little amphitheatre and, beyond, two tennis courts, one grass, one clay.

'How large is this place? Three acres?'

'Closer to six.'

'No swimming pool?'

'Yuck. Of course not.'

The avenue curved and the house came into view. A straight-lined monument to the good taste of the 1950s, ascetic and modernist, the worldviews of Nehru and Gandhi fused in brick and cement.

A fat golden retriever slept on the veranda and served as a foot-rest. My eyes were drawn upwards from the resting feet to the man who must be Vikramaditya Rai, reclining in a planter's chair with eyes closed, wearing shorts and a T-shirt and a pair of clock-sized headphones.

'That's Vicky,' said Ashwin. 'And that's the toilet.'

'What's the toilet?'

'You see that building over to the side, like an outhouse?'

'I see it now.'

'Have you read *In Praise of Shadows*? Tanizaki? No?' His face fell, whether from pity or because what he was about to say had just lost half its grandeur. 'In the opening chapter Tanizaki describes his perfect toilet. *The* perfect toilet. When he was build-ing his own house he had to compromise, he couldn't afford to execute his toilet dream in every detail. Well, Vicky didn't have to compromise.'

'Why does it need to be outside the house?'

'Once you've used this toilet, you'll realise how barbaric it is to have a toilet inside the house. Inside the house a toilet is a thing of tiles and pipes, a room we only associate with dirt. A toilet should be a temple of contemplation. Vicky went all over Japan visiting toilets, finding the best manufacturers. It's *exactly* as Tanizaki wanted: camphor-wood floors, not a tile in sight, a view of trees from every window, the company of birds. Modern sanitation with Japanese aesthetics. The world's only perfect toilet, and it's in *India*, not Japan. The only pity is that Tanizaki himself isn't alive to use it.'

'Is that what you wanted my help with? Bringing Tanizaki back to life to shit in this toilet?'

'You and Vicky will really get along. Don't tell him I told you about the toilet, though. He doesn't like me showing off about it.'

'How does Vicky feel about the name change from Aurangzeb to Abdul Kalam?'

'Please don't bring that up with him, it's far too soon.'

We walked up into the veranda. Now, I may have only met Ashwin once previously and Vicky never, but I can say with certainty that left to himself Ashwin would have waited for Vicky to open his eyes. He'd have waited six hours if that was what it took.

We were rescued from this range of possibilities by the dog. The dog swung perpendicularly up and Vicky's feet were cruelly unseated. He turned out to have been awake. He kept the head-phones on as he extended a hand.

It is impossible to judge what volume to speak at when some-one is headphoned.

'So you are the famous Tara,' he said, not loudly.

'Ashwin has met me exactly once. Whatever he may have said to you should be taken in that context.'

'Oh, he's said very little. Nothing much. Lila, on the other hand, she talks about you a lot.'

Ashwin had disappeared. Only minutes later did he return, panting once again, a cane chair in each hand. I couldn't stop myself from saying: 'This staff wedding has practically sent you to the gym.'

What did Vicky and I say to each other while Ashwin was away? Nothing much. Mostly he looked in the general direction of the tennis courts, and I looked at him. At some point the headphones moved down to his neck.

Vicky's face did not require lengthy study. What it had to give it gave at once. You saw Vicky and your first thought wasn't a word but a whistle, a catcall. He was preposterously good-looking. When he got up I'd see that he was within half an inch one side or the other of six foot, willowy, more dancer than athlete. Whether this was luck or achievement I can't say. The face was pure luck. It reminded you of the line that will always separate natural from created beauty. Looking at his eyes, which were perfect as egg-yolks, and his cheekbones, and, above all, the distances between nose and mouth, left eye and right, nostril and ear, was like look-ing at a tiger, or a sunset. You can't look at a woman in this way, not any more; she's going to be wearing make-up, or hair dye, or at minimum she's given too much thought to her clothes.

Not all of Vicky was to my taste. He had those engorged lips – Deepti called them 'dick-sucking lips' – that young girls would soon be buying like lattes in Delhi as they already were in Dubai and Düsseldorf. Since his were not bought, he didn't look as if he'd been repeatedly punched in the mouth. I don't like lips that size of any provenance. I mistrust hair that thick. Of course I admired Vicky's face. I am not an imbecile. But the admiration was specifically nonsexual.

I sat on one of the chairs Ashwin had supplied, and then he was off again.

'Do you always use Ashwin when you have a staff shortage?'

Vicky didn't reply. His feet were back on the dog.

He didn't say Thanks for coming, or Would you like anything? But he didn't seem knowingly perverse; just unknowing, at least when it came to etiquette. The rich Delhi man is more likely to know no etiquette than too much. In that sense, you can really tell the Mughals are long gone.

Ashwin returned, not panting, with a tray the size of a carrom board. Mixed nuts, a water jug, an ice bucket, a bottle of gin (Tanqueray), four Schweppes cans (two soda, two tonic), six glasses.

'Thanks, Ash,' said Vicky, in the way that one says, Good dog.

'Let me pour for everyone—?' I said.

Ashwin didn't look as if he wanted me to, but I started anyway.

'Vicky will have half soda, half tonic.'

'Gin sonic,' said Vicky.

'Isn't that what the Japanese call it?'

'Yeah, how did you know?!'

'A bartender told me. In Rome. Are you a Japanophile? Nipponophile?'

He shook his head, meaning yes not no. 'That country. It's the only country.'

The drinks poured, I looked at Ashwin. 'Shall we?'

Vicky signalled yes.

'We wanted to talk to you,' said Ashwin, 'because Vicky has been the victim of a monstrous crime.'

'I'm not a criminal lawyer. You know that much.'

'If I need a criminal lawyer,' said Vicky, 'do you think I can't find one?'

'It's not as if you have *no* experience of criminal work.' Ashwin, again. 'And when you hear about his case, you'll see why we came to you.' Or asked you to come to us.

'I'm guessing you've already been to the police?'

'He didn't go to them. They came here. It was appalling. Thank God Vicky's mother was in Sardinia. What the sight of them would have done to her!'

Vicky liked to have Ashwin do his talking for him, but didn't always like how he did it. '*Ash.*'

'The point is,' said Ashwin, 'that when I said he's been the victim of a crime, the crime is that two policemen showed up here and before we'd so much as asked them to sit down or offered them tea, they handed us a complaint accusing Vicky of rape.'

'You,' I said to Ashwin, 'were there too?' Yes, he had been.

On our singular date Ashwin had said he rented a 'tiny hole' in a decaying building off Hawley Road. Maybe he used it as a warehouse for his books while actually living here.

'Even by Delhi cop standards they were a gruesome twosome. One looked six months pregnant, the other seven. Fattened less on fried food than by their accumulated resentments. They kept *staring* – at Vicky, the garden, the carpets, the art – and you could hear the hatred churning in their bitter little brains. It all came out in the open when we spoke to them in English.'

'Why didn't you speak to them in Hindi?' Ashwin might be Tamil, but what excuse did Vicky have?

'The last thing we were going to do was cede authority to them in that way.' Poor Ashwin the fish, all at sea in this new world of plankton.

'And all this came as a total shock.'

'I take it you're not trying to ask, "Did he do it?"'

'That,' I said to Vicky, 'is presumably what you meant by your reference to not needing a criminal lawyer. That if you'd done it, you'd need one.'

Vicky ignored me as completely as if he were still wearing head-phones. And Ashwin told us the story.

The complaint had been filed by a young woman whom Vicky had last seen two or three years prior, when she had come to say goodbye before leaving for a master's in the UK. Goodbye, and thank you: for Vicky had paid for the master's, transferring to her a sum sufficient to cover her fees and living costs in full, so as to ensure her student visa was approved. He'd thought nothing of doing it; he couldn't even remember if she'd asked or he'd offered. For eighteen months before that, the young woman had been Vicky's assistant. Assistant at what? Oh, this and that. She had, for instance, accompanied him on his travels. Not on holiday, of course. Just work trips. At that time Vicky had been particularly busy. Trips to the family estate in Kumaon, where Vicky had been thinking of establishing a Himalayan branch of a Californian clinic for the relief of chronic prostate pain – two friends, presum-ably neither of them Ashwin, suffered; a trip to the clinic itself, in Palo Alto; trips to Karnataka and South Africa's Eastern Cape, where people were trying to sell him vineyards; and to Shekhawati, where they wanted him to fund the restoration of a ruined haveli. Vicky's work seemed to consist almost entirely of trips to very pleasant places with some sort of business proposition as a pretext.

None of the projects ever got anywhere, except one. And it was that one that the young woman's complaint referred to. The Tanizaki toilet. In her time working for Vicky they had made four separate trips to Japan, visiting all the major islands. The third of those trips had taken them to the onsen town of Atami, where Tanizaki had spent most of the war. They had had a perfect day there: breakfast with a panorama of the Izu Peninsula; a productive tea with an expert on Tanizaki's aesthetics; before dinner, a restorative open-air bath, just the two of them. Dinner itself had one Michelin star but deserved at least two.

All these details were missing from the police complaint, which said only that they had been in Japan 'to research design of toilet', and that on the evening in question, the accused had invited the complainant to his room and taken from her her virginity; that he had invited her again the next night; that, back in Delhi, he had indicated that he would eventually marry her; that they had gone back to Atami two months later, and had sex on each of the three nights they spent there. After which – the complaint said 'Whereupon' – he had dismissed her from her position, and his life. It was admitted that he had paid for the master's, and implied that this was compensation.

We were dealing with the subcategory of rape known as breach of promise. Sexual intercourse obtained by a false prospectus: with the promise of marriage, later withdrawn. Even I, no criminal lawyer, knew that breach of promise claims were involved in a large percentage of rape cases. Section 375 of the Indian Penal Code, which defined rape, did not mention breach of promise; so all such claims also invoked Section 90, which dealt in a broader way with consent 'given under fear or misconception'. This was rape with no suggestion of physical violence. In theory, everything turned on two questions: whether the promise of marriage had in fact been made prior to sex, and whether it had been made in bad faith. In practice, in the only fitfully legal world in which we Delhi lawyers made our living, the case was eventually dropped, after an exchange of money, or threats, or both.

'How much of what's in this complaint is accurate?'

We went through it, point by point. The dates checked out. Vicky couldn't deny that she had come to his room after dinner each of the five nights they'd spent in Atami, and yes, they'd had sex each time.

'And each time you invited her?'

'Come on,' said Ashwin. 'She could hardly have invited herself.'

'An invitation from your employer isn't something a girl in her position necessarily has the power to turn down.'

'Your implication is offensive.' The diction was pure Ashwin, but the tone was new. 'Her employer was not some standard-issue Delhi brute, it was Vicky.'

Whether Vicky was or wasn't a brute was beside the point. The point was the asymmetry of power. That was, or ought to be, obvious.

'The first time. And the subsequent times. When you invited her, how did she respond? Was she visibly enthusiastic? Or merely acquiescent?'

Ashwin fell silent. I had hit upon a gap in his preparation. So I stared at Vicky long and hard enough that he had to speak.

'Am I supposed to remember a thing like that?'

'How does it matter, legally?' Ashwin had recovered himself. 'She doesn't say she was forced. She says she did it because he was going to marry her.'

'And he wasn't?'

'Tara, are you being deliberately obtuse?'

'The complaint says that at dawn that first time, in bed but fully awake, he patted her head and said, "I will marry you." And that he made similar remarks the next time. And the next. Now, given that Vicky doesn't seem to think he is supposed to remember how a woman responds to his invitation to come back to his room, how sure can we be that he remembers what he said to her?'

'Tara, I really can't make out what you're trying to get at. In what world was Vicky ever going to marry this girl?'

'Everyone is agreed on the fact that he didn't marry her. The question is whether he said he would.'

'In what world was Vicky ever going to tell her something like that?'

Even if I couldn't force him to speak, I resolved to keep looking at Vicky, never at Ashwin, as if the latter were not a spokesman but a ventriloquist's dummy.

'Why did you need to take her along?' I asked Vicky. 'What were her duties on the trip?'

'You know what assistants do,' said Ashwin, too quickly. 'Note-taking. Making sure everything is as planned. Logistics.'

'Was sex with you one of her duties? Why did you invite her in, the first time?' I watched Vicky look at Ashwin and because I wasn't going to look at Ashwin, I had to guess at what they said to each other without words. Could Ashwin really have said, This one I refuse to answer on your behalf? For it was Vicky that spoke.

'It made sense,' he said. 'It was the right ending to that day.'

'Are you saying that each of the five times you had sex it was because it made for the right ending to that particular day?' He nodded. 'Why is it specifically and exclusively in one particular Japanese spa town that sex with your assistant is the right way to end the day?'

'You know what Japan means to Vicky.' Usual service restored. 'And he's never felt what Japan has to offer more deeply than in Atami.'

'Have you been back to Atami, since she left your employment? With another assistant? And you didn't have sex with them? So it wasn't sex in general that you needed to complete the day, but sex with her?'

'Look,' said Ashwin. 'The way you ask these questions. They're so clinical. You erase Vicky's humanity.' Ashwin, who not for one sentence had spoken of this girl as if she were a living human. 'She's quite attractive, you know. Or was. What you might call swadeshi-sexy. What our parents called dusky. Cheekbones. Great eyelashes.'

'And the contrast between earthy Indian village girl and pristine Japanese spa was irresistible?'

'You mock, but why shouldn't it be irresistible?'

We were going nowhere, or nowhere good. On this track we would soon come to the sex itself. What it had been like. Vicky might actually reveal some human feelings for the girl. I could do without knowing if he possessed any. I needed to find my door out of all this, but there was one question I had to ask first.

'The complaint states that you took her virginity. Did she tell you she was a virgin?'

'She wasn't.' Said Vicky, in his own voice.

'She told you she wasn't?'

'You really think I can't tell?'

'That's exactly it,' said Ashwin. 'The diseased heart of the matter. The girl wasn't a virgin – God knows how many men she'd fucked before Vicky. And now presumably her parents have found her a husband, she's failed the test of hymeneal purity, and cried rape-by-boss. That's all this is about.'

'So now,' I said, 'let's talk about why you wanted me. You don't want a criminal lawyer because you think they exist to get guilty people off, and you regard yourself as innocent.'

'You've met these fellows,' said Ashwin. 'Are any of them fit to be invited into a decent home? Not to mention the message it sends to a judge. He sees the lawyer you've got and concludes, This man is very rich and very guilty.'

I didn't say: Boy, for a book editor you seem to know a lot about trial court judges. I said, 'That doesn't explain why you want me. I have no expertise in matters like this, guilty client or otherwise. I'd be no use in court or outside.' Surely even Ashwin the fish knew what I meant by 'outside'.

'We don't want "outside". Vicky isn't going to pay a ransom to get rid of an invented crime. We want it resolved legally, that is by going to court and getting it speedily dismissed. What we want is someone who can, with crisp precision, explain to a judge that this is a ridiculous case with no basis in fact or law. You'd do that better than any so-called criminal lawyer. Unlike them, you actually believe in the law half of the word *lawyer*.'

For an hour Ashwin had been saying Vicky this, Vicky that; now he was saying We. And in that We I saw why Vicky needed an assistant, and why Ashwin lived here. Vicky could bear anything but his aloneness. Sex was the least of it. Yes, in Atami the girl had been made to provide or receive it, and Ashwin . . . there was some part of Ashwin, which a Western mind in its earnest commitment to authenticity might call the truest part, that found the idea of sex with Vicky too beautiful for words, or even for nonverbal fantasy. Ashwin was in the long and thriving tradition of elite Indian men who reserve their love for other men, but are happy or at any rate resolved not to want that love to be physical. If Lila had set me up with him, it wasn't because she didn't know all this; it must be because she thought that, at our age, sex and love and companionship had no necessary relation.

If Lila was the reason I was here today, she must be absolutely certain that Vicky was innocent, and she must want to spare Vicky and Ashwin's tender sensitivities an encounter with an actual Delhi criminal lawyer. I'm sorry to let you down, I said to Lila, and then I stood up. My gin seemed to have drunk itself. Theirs lay untouched, and by now undrinkably warm.

'If that's what you want,' I said, 'I can suggest some names, but I'm not at all what you're looking for. Thanks for the gin. You have a beautiful house. Don't bother, Ashwin, I know my way out.'

How early had I known I couldn't do it? The first mention of the word rape? Certainly by the time we entered his bedroom in Atami. It was, as Lila might say, overdetermined. I shrank from moral thickets. Vicky was, surely, only a thoughtless asshole, not a rapist; that didn't mean *I* was obliged to defend him. Whatever Ashwin might think, this matter would eventually have to be dealt with 'outside', by nonlegal means, and those had never yet been my means.

Whether I acted for Vicky or – not that this was on offer – the girl, I wouldn't be a lawyer. I'd be a woman lawyer. Lila might have recommended me for my presumed competence, but with Vicky and Ashwin my sex would have borne the greater weight. And I knew, too well, what sort of lawyer took up the cause of girls like this. Some of them were dowdy, and genuine, and fearless, and made slightly insufferable by their chosen line of work. Some were elegant frauds whose highest ambition was a *New York Times* profile about a lone warrior in a sari saving Delhi's women. Whatever they looked like, they had this in common: on the legal rather than moral scale, no one took them seriously. None of the really big commercial or constitutional matters ever went their way. For eighteen years I had fought to avoid becoming one of them and I was closer than ever to winning.

On my way out I found myself thinking, These guys could learn a thing or two from Kunal. Kunal was capable of getting himself into a situation like this – unlike Vicky, he might actually be guilty – but he wouldn't ask someone else to help him get out of it. And Kunal, in his own way, knew which country he lived in. Before he bribed or bullied the cops, he'd have put them at ease. In Hindi.

If I ran with Lila's analogy, and the Delhi men we knew now had to fight for the tiger's share, not simply enjoy the lion's, then Kunal, at least, would fight.

IO

Please, God, Not In Our Family

My favourite way to look at Delhi is from the back seat of a car around noon on a sunny day between May and August. It can be any car – Maruti Alto or Maybach – so long as the windscreen is clean and the air-conditioning works, and the Delhi Edwin Lutyens', obviously. Each time the car turns into one of those roundabouts then exits into a new road, the tree-lined red carpet is rolled out again. In summer, when the air lets the light through, you can see that Lutyens was hired as a set designer, not an urban planner. A city is for living in; a capital is for the impressing of visiting dignitaries. For seventy years we had trimmed and watered the plants, swept the streets, and managed to avoid fouling up the Lutyens plan with Stalinism or bling. Our new rulers were beginning to chafe against this legacy of restraint. But all that was to come. For now, when I found myself in a back seat on a Lutyens avenue in summer, I could spread my arms either side of me like eaves and gawk at our governmental Disneyland. On a sunny day, no capital comes close: not even Vienna.

I drove myself to court every day. But to Vicky's I'd taken a taxi, because I'd expected or hoped to drink. I'd spent the Lutyens leg of the journey in the usual stupefaction. On the way home this was not an option. Three minutes into the journey home I saw that my feet were stuck together, my left hand a clenched fist, and I thought, Wow, I'm angry.

I don't get angry. This isn't some freak of heredity. It's an achieved deformity. Not trusting myself to not act on anger, I had decided not to feel it.

Fifteen years of not being angry and now you fall to the insipid challenge of Vicky and Ashwin. Vicky and Ashwin who, even if only for a moment, made you think better of Kunal.

What was it with this generation of Indian men? What was it about men like my father and Mr Chawla that had flung their XY apples so far from the tree? Sure, Kunal was adopted, but we were dealing here with a matter of nurture. Vicky's father, I knew, was dead, and I would never meet Ashwin's. But surely they couldn't be half as feckless as their sons. Why couldn't fathers raise sons?

By leaving Vicky's when I did, I'd rendered myself both unfed and an hour early to meet Baba. But I didn't go to my flat. I went home. I did this because Baba was the desperately needed antidote to Vicky and Ashwin, and because I'd made a bet with myself that Ma and Rohit were gone all day.

Every time I saw a lift these days I heard Lila in my head, in that tone of robotic authority used by air hostesses telling you to fasten your seatbelt. Two months of this and the stairs no longer squeezed my pollution-patched lungs or sent hot fluid up my legs. Why hadn't Wojciech ever told me to take the stairs? Why was Woj, with his temple of a body, so unconcerned with mine, which like an old sofa bore all the marks of life and none of care?

I guess Woj was one of those men who actually prefers things this way. Looking at my body, which he did plenty of, only intensified his pleasure in his own.

When my father answered the door I said: 'Were you afraid Ma and Rohit were back early? Maybe they'd come back to get something? Did I scare you?'

'I was confused.'

I closed the door and made the first move in the direction of his study. With all the flat to ourselves, I wanted to make sure that was where we sat. The door to my old room stood open, but now I stopped to let Baba go in first.

'You can sit on the divan,' said Baba, who took the swivel chair, Guangdong's finest imitation Herman Miller, that I'd bought him for his sixtieth birthday.

On the desk stood his TV-sized Mac and keyboard, his retirement presents from me. On either side of the monitor he had

157

placed a framed photograph. In the one on the right, two children stood arm in arm outside what I believed, although I wouldn't say it in conversation for fear of revealing ignorance or racism, was called a yurt. A brother and sister. She was about a head taller.

On the left was the famous photo, the only one I've ever seen, of Bhagat Singh, with his calligraphic moustache and his hat aimed north-east at the angle they call jaunty. He must have been twenty-one when it was taken. Awaiting trial for his bombing of the Central Legislative Assembly. No boy ever looked more a man; few men have. In 1929 they had passed that photo around Punjab like a bootleg of the next instalment of *Harry Potter*. In March 1931 he was hanged.

'Bhagat Singh,' I said. 'I've never even heard you mention him, Baba. Was he interested in the environment?'

He looked slowly at Bhagat Singh as if waiting for him to speak for himself. 'None of them were.'

'Gandhi was.'

'Don't talk to me about Gandhi.' I put a pin on Gandhi. I wanted to know why I wasn't to talk about him.

'And the children? They're brother and sister?'

'They were.'

'They're dead?'

'He is dead.'

Hansel and Gretel of the Central Asian steppe. Gretel and Hansel. Steppe siblings. Not once did I ask myself, What the hell are they doing on Baba's desk? To know Baba was to know there was always a reason, a good reason, and he would in time tell you.

He was looking at Bhagat Singh again. 'Vikram says there's a saying. Everyone has a picture of Bhagat Singh in their house, but no one wants their son to be Bhagat Singh. Let India have a million Bhagat Singhs, but please, God, not in our family.'

'Do you feel that way too?'

'Recently I have been thinking about when I was his age. All I thought about was getting on. Acquisitions. Acquiring English,

CA, a wife, a house. I never gave one thought to the country, never mind the world, never mind life.'

'You and every other young man, Baba. That's why people don't have to worry about their sons turning into Bhagat Singh.'

'But what if those thoughts had crossed my mind? What if someone had told me the story of Bhagat Singh. For five minutes even, I would have asked myself, "Will you do it?"'

'When did those thoughts first cross your mind?'

'You must have been four years old. It was the first time we left you with your nana-nani and I took your mother on a holiday.'

'To Ranthambore.' This was the closest thing I had to a solid pre-Rohit memory. I'd been left in Meerut while Baba took Ma to see tigers. It was something he'd promised to do when her family accepted his suit. All I remembered of those five days in Meerut was rolling around Ma's childhood bed, hard as iron, repeating out loud my one incantatory question: Have they seen it? Have they seen it? Have they seen it? By repetition I intended to establish a live telepathic link between my bed and their safari jeep. When they saw it, I would *feel* the answer, Yes, electric and everywhere.

When they came back I asked Baba to tell me the exact time they'd seen their first tiger. Not first, he said, we only saw one. He gave me the time, to the minute, like the record of a birth, and I knew in my heart that at the moment they saw it I wasn't on my bed, I was having breakfast.

'Yes, Ranthambore. But even then I dismissed the thought. I placed it under lock and key for almost thirty years. At first when the thought came back—'

'It came back after your retirement?'

'Just before. In my last year of work it came back and then I could think of nothing else. Vikram thought I was retiring because I was bored. Your mother thought I was scared of not serving clients well enough, and so I left before that could happen. Nothing of the sort. The thought had come back, it had broken out of the jail I had put it in and it said, You have kept me there long enough, now I won't let you think about anything else. So I retired. At first I felt guilty. Ashamed. As if I had been a coward all these years, instead of being a Bhagat Singh.'

While my father spoke I didn't look at him. I couldn't.

'But then, Baba,' I said, 'you realised that what you'd done was right. You'd had your duties to us. Even before that, even when you were Bhagat Singh's age, you had Vikram chacha. You were never free. And now you are, and it's never too late.'

And now I looked at him, because I wanted to see that I'd given the right answer unprompted. I wanted to see my reward on his face as I did with Lila. But Baba did not give so easily. I looked at him and his face was just his face, gentle and calm and bright as the full moon.

'Only God can say about too late or not too late. But you are right. I came to understand that it's not a question of wanting a Bhagat Singh in my family or not. I keep Bhagat Singh here because he gave his life. If I look at him enough I might learn fearlessness. But it is not for the young to be like Bhagat Singh. You have other business first. At my age, what does it matter?'

'Is it also,' I asked, indicating the steppe siblings with my head, 'a question of what the old owe the young? I don't mean people like me. I mean children, future generations.' I felt imbecilic and wanted to correct myself rather than be corrected, by him. 'No, I don't mean that.'

'You are only saying what you hear. Maybe from the youngsters in the office?'

'Not so much from them. Young lawyers are mostly just ambitious in the usual Delhi ways. So they want to make money or they want to save the Constitution.'

He gave me three nods of affirmative lament. 'Lawyers aren't going to save anything.'

'I hear it more from my friends. The ones with kids. From the age of about six they're already on it. Insisting on being "plant-based", no plastic. By eight they're asking how far the food on the table has travelled. You old people ruined the world for us. And it's always Greta, Greta, Greta. I guess she's to them as Bhagat Singh was to children in 1930. But Baba, when Rohit mentioned Greta back in . . . March, you made a face. You don't like her.'

'It's not for me to like or not like. Who am I next to her?'

'Still, there is something you don't agree with. There's a reason she isn't on your desk. The girl there – the older sister. What's her name?'

He said something that began with a G but that I won't attempt to reproduce in sound or letter. It emerged later that his very possession of this name was unusual. 'Everyone calls her Sister.'

'And you look to her the way others look to Greta?'

'She is my leader. We shouldn't get – please don't think ill of Greta or anyone. Each of us has to make our own way.'

'But at least tell me this – your way, your leader's way, is different from Greta's. How?'

'When people say the old have ruined the world for the young, or that we need to look after it for future generations, it's just a version of what Rohit is saying. They are saying, "Don't just think about yourself, think about all humans. The ones you haven't met and the ones who aren't yet born." Sometimes they sound like my old clients. You know, I used to ask them, when they had a good year: "Why not give a bit more to charity? We can find you the tax benefit." Always the same answer. "It is not my money, Brahmji, I am just the custodian. It belongs to my children, their children, their children's children . . ." Of course, not all are like that. Some of them, especially the younger ones, they really care about other species too. About preventing extinction. But even they are stuck in this same place with humans as the centre of everything. Humans have to protect others. Humans will lose out if other species go extinct. You see what I'm saying?'

'Have you watched Rohit's other videos?'

'I've watched them all. He is not less wrong than others. In a way he is right. What is "conservation" but man trying to play God? At least Rohit knows that man is not God. No more or less God than a bush or a squirrel is. When a tiger goes for a deer, that's all he is doing. Tigers don't think it is their role to eliminate all deer or protect all deer. Only humans think we are better than others. Instead of trying to be better, let us stop being worse.'

'I think I get your philosophical disagreement with, forgive me for using this shorthand, people who follow Greta. But in practice does it matter? Aren't you working towards the same things?'

'I am working towards a world in which we don't place ourselves at the centre. I don't think that's what those you are referring to are working for. And unless we understand why we are where we are, nothing will change. In the short term we might reduce air pollution or carbon emissions, but that will be the work of engineers, not activists. And then we'll think the problem is solved and we'll fall back again. So long as we think the problem is with how the world is for us – the air, the weather, the scenery, the prices of things – and we don't want to see the true problem, we can't do anything that will last.'

'And that's what your Sister believes?'

'That's what I believe. I won't speak for her.'

'You call her your leader.'

'So far I have told you what I think is wrong. The question is, what do I do about it. There, she leads me.'

'And others like you.'

'Yes, and there must be others. Few things can be done truly alone.'

'And the things that you can do, or that others can do. That she leads you towards. They're different from the things that, um, those you disagree with philosophically are already doing?'

'Maybe it is better if I explain in terms of what I won't do.'

'Just say it, Baba. You're only saying it to me. Where are they going wrong?' I wasn't helping. 'Sorry. What won't you do?'

'I can't tell others what to do. I am no one to do that. I . . . I . . .'

The day comes when we look at our parents and say in our heads, You are old. What follows is harder to universalise. It might be, I'm responsible for you, the great irrevocable inversion, like the instant in which you see that there's more sand in the lower bulb of the hourglass. Or it might be, God, you're old and I will be, too. With my mother it hadn't yet come; the neglect of the landing outside the flat could be put down as easily to disequilibrium as to age. Her face remained as smooth as the jacket of a new hardback. With my father I had thought, always, that it wouldn't come, ever. Not because he wouldn't grow old, but because he'd do it at a pace so even that you'd never notice. No *thing* could age him, no event jolt his regularity.

Now this father of mine was unable to find the rest of his sentence. He had disappeared into himself. His hands were at his belly, the fingers of the right digging into the left so that I saw only the knuckles, the body firm as ever, as firm with unease as I was used to seeing it with assurance. He reached into himself and returned with his sentence, or another.

'The point is not to make anyone a hero or villain. Not to say the old are villains, the rich countries are villains, the companies are villains. Nor, Greta is a hero, Sister is a hero. Let alone,' and now he grinned, 'Brahm Saxena is a hero. The point is not to scare people, bully people, annoy them. What is annoying them going to achieve? The point is not to lecture, to say, "I am right, Do this, do that."'

'It's always easier to say what the point is not, than what it is.'

'The point – *my* point, only mine – I know what I think it is. I can't tell others what to do. That is my only sacred rule.'

'Does Sister tell people what to do?'

'Never. She helps. She guides. But she never tells. Never.'

'So what you are going to do, looking to do, is something that involves you only?'

'When I ask, what I can do that does not involve telling others, forcing others, then I look at Bhagat Singh. You could say he achieved nothing. Forget whether killing for revenge can ever be right. The man he killed wasn't even the right man. He couldn't tell one Britisher from another and shot the wrong fellow. But what he did was make people think, My country is worth giving my life for.'

163

'You can't tell them what to do, but you can inspire by example?'

'It's not that I know I can. But I ask the question, what if I can? What if I can make them pay attention. If only for a few minutes, stop whatever they are doing and pay attention to what I'm doing and why. If I can do that, anything is worth it.'

'And do you know how?'

A pause the length of a traffic signal. 'Not yet.'

'Baba, how did Sister's brother die?'

'He was run over by a bus. That will be four years ago soon.'

'So she's quite a bit older now than in that photo.' Unlike Bhagat Singh who, thanks to a photographer and a hangman, will be forever twenty-one.

'I had asked her for a photo that I could keep on my desk, to give me daily courage.' He looked searchingly down his body, as if scanning himself for signs of bragging.

Who the hell *is* Sister? How did you come into contact with her? Did you meet her on the 'dark web' (whatever that is)? Who and where are her other followers? It isn't that these questions didn't occur to me. Or, rather – I was aware of them, but not as questions I might want to ask, much less choose to.

'And Baba, one last thing.'

From the day my father announced the summit to the morning I last saw him, I never wavered. I would not come between my father and his aspirations for himself. The price for sustaining this would vary. Today, the price was that I had to leave. I was already on my feet when I asked: 'What's your problem with Gandhi? He gave his life for his country, didn't he? And wasn't he the only one who saw the dangers of putting human greed at the centre?'

'He was the world champion in telling others what to do. Do you know that he denied his own wife antibiotics when she was dying? And you say he saw the dangers. Why then did he make Nehru the prime minister? A man who believed in no god and thus, of course, only in material questions with material answers.

Either Gandhi couldn't see the dangers of Nehru, or he didn't care.'

My own views on Nehru I was better off not declaring. As for Gandhi: like most people my age I knew little about him. Gandhi and my father were actually alive at the same time, but still he felt like Kabir or Joan of Arc, something half-fictional and imaginatively remote. Nehru was different. Nehru, the self-hating lawyer ('If you examine its words like lawyers you will produce only a lifeless thing'), had come, for some tiny minority of Indians that happened to include my friends, to imaginatively embody goodness and greatness and glamour *in this world*.

The difference is not difficult to locate. Gandhi was holy, Nehru secular. Gandhi sleeping naked next to his nieces to test his powers of self-denial; Nehru finding his match in love and friendship in the viceroy's wife. Yet I couldn't shake the notion that there was something too willed about my father's dislike of Gandhi.

At the door Baba said, 'I was not fully honest with you.'

'That's not possible.'

'I said I don't know yet what I want to do.'

'At most you implied it.'

'I have known for thirty-three years. But I am not yet ready.'

I went home and it was only thirty-six hours and two-thirds of a bottle of mezcal later that I did the maths and worked out that thirty-three years ago my father had taken my mother to see a tiger.

II
Our Place

Two or three times a year I'd find myself in a properly large group of contemporaries. Rarely more than three, these days; between twenty-five and thirty-five marriages had served this function, but that well was almost dry. One in ten were now divorced or divorcing – in India divorce, when it comes, typically comes quick – but remarriages were smaller affairs. Now we were down to maybe one wedding a year, and a couple of large parties. Soon we'd be at that stage where the first members of our cohort made senior counsel, and each senior-designation would bring us together just as the marriages had.

At these congregations the childless among us inevitably found each other. We didn't talk about being childless – we were not that boring – but of the things that attend childlessness, childfreeness. Like the ways our hangovers were changing. In my early twenties a hangover was nasty, brutish and blessedly short – a memory more or less by lunchtime. Now they lasted all day, but were muted. I just went through the day at sixty to seventy per cent. Ninety per cent of the time, sixty per cent was plenty.

My nightly gin-and-soda could become a nightly trilogy, and no one would notice.

That first week after Baba told me about Sister, I'd come home from work between nine and ten and watch the hours before me like a lake whose other shore cannot be seen. Lawyers can't afford to wait until *after* work to drink. If you want to drink, you need to be able to drink while working. Whenever a hole appeared in the fog I'd built with work and drink, through it I saw my father, and of course I wondered.

Technically a millennial, I was somehow someone who still expected answers to be found in books, or life. The oldest of my juniors was only eight years younger than me. How long must those eight years feel to him, whenever he watched me with technology? Into eight years, I felt like telling him, you could comfortably fit a world war.

When I finally turned to Google in search of Sister, I turned up nothing. Later, when journalists and governments went looking for Sister, Google didn't help them, either.

Well before I'd even thought of Google, I'd thought of the only place, other than Baba himself, where anything my father knew about Sister might be found. A place where journalists and governments wouldn't know to go, and would find nothing if they did.

Whether the question was, Who knows Brahm Saxena best? or, Who really knows Brahm Saxena? there had only ever been one answer.

As a child I thought of Vikram as *my* chacha, but never as Baba's brother. Vikram was always taller, and starting age thirty he grew sideways too, at the standard Delhi pace of an inch a year. He projected as actors and politicians did before the invention of the microphone. When he came home he'd announce himself from the stairwell: 'Brahm! Keep the beer ready!'

My mother never seemed to give much weight to where, to *what* Vikram had come from. Most of the difference between the brothers she put down to Vikram's choice of wife. Unlike my father he had married for love, not through the classifieds. Married a Punjabi air force brat. Manju, my mother said, had made a Punju of Vikram. Manju played mah-jong. They belonged to the Rotary Club. Vikram dyed his hair, using first Godrej and then, courtesy of a son-in-law in Ottawa, Just for Men.

Above all there was the beer. He was Delhi's happiest drunk. Mug after mug made him louder, warmer, ever more avuncular. But the beer didn't go down any better with my mother than Manju did. By my teens, Baba was mostly meeting his brother one-on-one.

It wasn't just that Vikram had known Baba longest, known Brahm unformed, Brahm forming. Their closeness would hold through anything. It had held not just out of mutual duty, but because Vikram was much more like Baba than even he knew. The beer and the Rotary Club and the hair were only manifestations of a chosen coarsening, a way of being in the world that relaxed him, that made up in ease what it might lack in nobility.

Vikram chacha will have watched Baba form his new resolve, week by week. He'd have been the first to hear of Sister. He was something I knew I would never be – my father's confidant.

But it wasn't just that I couldn't go to Vikram behind my father's back – a matter of Vikram's principles as much as my own. I couldn't want to. I couldn't want something of my father that he didn't choose to give. Nor could Vikram.

When it came to Sister, I would have to wait.

My parents were not the kind to reminisce about their preparental life together. I knew something about the circumstances of the marriage itself. Baba had arranged his own marriage. He had never really known his mother's relations. His father's he was resolved at all costs never to know again. A man without a family, without evident roots, is no one's idea of a son-in-law, whatever his achievements. Baba had been lucky. The Meerut family who advertised their daughter in the Kayasth section of the matrimonial page could hardly afford to choose. A year before he placed that ad, my mother's father had lost, in court, his claim to the ancestral land that he believed his brothers had diddled him out of. Losing it had taken two decades. I once tried to calculate what he had paid out in legal fees. At any estimate it was more than his putative share of the land could be worth.

My nana placed that ad at a time when he knew that he was never likely to stand a wedding or dowry. One might hope, however implausibly, to find a family opposed in principle to the latter. The toothless grin of the law was on his side there. But how did you get out of a wedding?

My grandfather paid for a matrimonial ad, and felt the bite of even that expense. But he was resigned to keep housing a daughter who would grow more spinsterish with each year.

And then my father arrived. No family, but immaculate references (not just Mr Asthana, but four other Kayasth CAs, all known in the community). My father, who insisted on no dowry, and no public wedding. The only suspicion of him was emitted by my mother's brother, who was caught between his fear of having to pay off my grandfather's debts (if he borrowed to fund a wedding) and his fear of being held responsible for my mother if my father turned out to be a dud. All his life my mother's brother worried about the prospect of other people's claims on his money. That might be why he never made any.

My father did provide a honeymoon – Shimla, three days. And the promise, kept like all his promises, of a tiger safari. My father 'provided for' my mother far beyond any conceivable son-in-law. The year after the Ranthambore trip, it was he, not my uncle, who settled her father's remaining debts. My father was incapable of violence, or harshness, or jealousy; incapable of raising his voice or of wounding quietness. He was as likely to be unfaithful as the sun is to rise in the west.

Still, he had his quirks. When my mother arrived in her marital home, she was told – she must have been – that, however well he did, she could not expect to keep servants. Not in the usual way.

It is not that no one was ever hired to cook or clean in our home. There was almost always a woman who came to clean for a couple of hours every few days. In some years there was also a hired cook on similar terms, five or six hours a week across three shifts. But my mother can have known no other woman at a similar level of income who did half as much unassisted housework as she did. Statistically, my family was an outlier.

There were other departures from the usual form. The cleaner and cook dealt with my father, not my mother. I was going to say 'answered to', but he would have deplored the suggestions of that expression. He changed cleaners nearly every year, even when their work was good.

This last point is crucial. My father's attitude to domestic staff was transactional: always cold and always fair. My father was not a cold man. But here his fear of warmth made coldness an obligation. In other homes, warmth was an optional but common part of the arrangement. The arrangement itself, call it feudalism. You were warm, or at least told yourself you were warm. People worked for you for decades and your children regarded them as part of the family. Warmth, my father knew, was how families launder cruelty.

My father was not going to allow feudalism into his home. Our family would not contain servants. Where there was a cook or cleaner, Rohit and I hardly got to know them – they usually came on weekday mornings, when we were at school.

Ever since I left home at eighteen I had worked on being able to speak to absolutely anyone on equal terms, and I could – except for servants. With my inherited and nurtured anxiety that warmth = feudalism, I became self-conscious in their presence. Even my thank yous were barely audible.

No subject is more potent at making people boring. Sometimes merely boring, like the diaspora writer who visits India and thinks that he is the first person to conceive the relationship between middle-class Indians and their servants in terms of power. Servants are how political columnists and anthropology professors know how the other half lives and what's going to happen in the Bihar election. 'Everyone in my maid's village is voting Lalu this time.' Sometimes worse. One of the many fates my father had saved my mother from was that of the women who, for decades, had spoken at parties about servants in the tone of inhuman generalisation that it had more recently become acceptable to extend to Muslims ('However sweet they seem, you can't trust them').

My mother had never given a sign of protest or resentment. She had done most of the cooking and cleaning and ironing for forty years. Female friends, or a sister, might have supplied an external source of dissatisfaction.

But my mother, like my father, had no sister and no friends.

The question of servants had freshly risen because Lila was late. She had wanted for some time to return the favour of a post-dinner drink at hers. I had a Jahnavi report to share. Raj was in the US.

Kabir was asleep. Lila had put him to bed, of course. When he was born she had vowed that until he was four, if she was not travelling on work, she would put him to bed though the heavens fall or a buyout be in its closing stage. This day that meant rushing back to work. I was searching for parking when I saw her text, **I'll be at least an hour late. Sorry. They've been instructed to keep the gins out and make sure you eat dessert.**

The doorbell was answered by a stout woman with a yellow kurta and a sceptical mien. She didn't say anything, and neither did I. Then she was gone, and I was left facing a rack full of toddler shoes – an uninformed observer would think this flat housed three children at least – and a semi-abstract painting of what might be a tanpura the colour of blood. It was the sort of painting that, at a party, guests would stand around trying to 'guess' – a grown-up version of Pin the Tail on the Donkey. I could see what was presumably the living room to my north-west, and there I went.

Presently another woman arrived, slim and distractingly pretty and as apologetic as her colleague had been sceptical. She directed me to a bar in the corner of the living room. Lila had put out six different brands of gin. Bombay Sapphire plus five 'craft'. All five, I knew, were unavailable in India and must have been brought back from trips abroad. I could name the imported gin brands sold in Delhi and Gurgaon by heart. The woman returned with soda, craft tonic, an ice-bucket, and then again with olives, hummus, cheese, crackers.

'Would you like some music?'

I was curious: what music had she been trained to put on? It turned out to be one of those devices that plays old Hindi film tunes at random. A safe bet, the musical equivalent of offering someone a glass of prosecco as they enter a party.

Men like Mr Chawla only employed men at home. Men who spent their lives in service in Delhi, with families back home in a village in Bihar or UP or Uttarakhand or Himachal ('Servants from the hills are more honest, or less dishonest. The only problem is they drink like fish! Make sure to keep the booze cupboard locked. An old-fashioned lock, not a combination – you'll forget to scramble the code and they'll memorise it.'). They'd go home at best twice a year, and if they were lucky they'd find an unpregnant wife and sons who remembered their father. Drivers excepted, Lila seemed to only employ women. Did they, too, have husbands and children?

The only non-elite people Lila interacted with were those she or her mother employed. If Lila were to come to my office and meet Lallan Singh, my clerk, she would take him for a servant and speak to him accordingly, in her Hindi that was so bad that it crossed the line from embarrassing to enviable – if you were from Delhi and spoke like that, you'd grown up *rich*. If she saw me speaking to him, she would confuse my respect for this man, whose practical grasp of the courts comfortably exceeded my own, for a case of *noblesse oblige*. Servants aside, her knowledge of the other half, the ninety-nine per cent, was theoretical.

This was the story of a class, and a city. In Rome, said Juvenal, you had better make a will before you go out to dinner. Not in Delhi. Delhi, with its weirdly low crime rate, its gated colonies, was a city of many countries. As lawyers we saw people from all these countries in court, especially trial court; but after court we went back to our own.

Lila found me half attentively turning the pages of a coffee-table book of Indian tiles. 'Didn't think you were interested in that kind of thing.'

I put the book down, saying nothing.

'Did they take good care of you? Which gin did you choose?'

'Excellent care, thanks.'

I surveyed Lila's face and upper body for signs of tiredness or stress. A fruitless quest, as ever. 'Everything OK at work?'

'Mhm.'

I took my empty highball to the bar. 'What will you have?'

'Whatever you'll make me.'

Jahnavi, good girl, had given me plenty of new information. She had been granted only one further audience with Kunal. But in it he had offered to extend her internship, and to pay her. And my Jahnavi had done something astonishing. She told Kunal that she'd hoped to spend some time at a dog-rescue NGO her family supported. If he wanted her to stay for months, she'd love to know more about Adhimukta Bharat. What was its broader point, its *vision*?

Kunal seemed to welcome Jahnavi's temerity. He took it for enthusiasm, for engagement.

For Adhimukta Bharat, he had said, the desh-bhakti curriculum was a trial balloon. A way of showing what they could do and of building ties with political parties. You see, in India things have to go through governments. Only they have the power to change things at scale. But if you join one party, support one party, what if that party loses an election? You're out. So what we do has to be with different parties, all parties. We should work with anyone.

Did Jahnavi know about the ed-tech boom? All over India people now had smartphones. Down to the remotest village. Give a poor man a phone and what do you think he'll do with it – watch videos of monkeys dancing? Rubbish. They want to better themselves. Raise their families. So there are a hundred apps promising to teach your son to code or get him into IIT. There are apps for high school, middle school, all the way down to teaching maths to babies.

But it's all science. Science or English. What about everything else? What about India – our history, our geography, our culture, our values? No one is thinking about that. And yet – does every-one need to know science? How many people are going to get into IIT and become engineers? Even if they do, they'll just go off to America. For nine hundred and ninety-nine out of one thousand, this is all useless. India doesn't benefit.

But would parents actually want this India content for their children? asked Jahnavi. Isn't the ed-tech thing driven by demand? People think these science apps will get their children better jobs.

You have a point, he said. But first, let me ask you: what is the one thing that unites nine hundred and ninety-nine out of every thousand Indians? You don't know? I'll tell you. That they love India. They cry with joy when an Indian wins an Olympic medal. They cry with sorrow and rage when Indian jawans die in a terror-ist blast. No one loves their country like Indians. The thousandth person is embarrassed by India. She wishes she lived in America. But the other nine hundred and ninety-nine love their country like no one on earth. Now to your point. At first parents may not see the value. So we go through governments, through schools. Soon they'll see it. And when they see our videos they'll cry with love for their India.

In any case, said Jahnavi, the last thing you're doing this for is money. Jahnavi reported that when she'd said this, Kunal had said: 'Your parents should be proud of you.' No, he didn't need money. He was doing this for his country.

This time I told the story straight and quick. I left out stuff that to me might be interesting texture, but not to Lila . . . not that any of it was that interesting to Lila. She didn't see any strategic value in Jahnavi. To Lila, the value of these reports was that they gave us a pretext to hang out.

'So,' I said, 'are you impressed with your brother? Surprised?'

'He's an idiot with delusions of grandeur. What's there to be surprised about?'

I was about to ask some obvious follow-up, like, 'But surely you agree this isn't standard behaviour for an obscenely rich Delhi boy? He could spend his time collecting Jags and golf clubs.' But then I saw a way into something different. I hadn't told Lila about my trip to Dr APJ Abdul Kalam Road.

'Would you call Vicky Rai's Japanese toilet a delusion of grandeur?'

Lila's features formed a new configuration – new on her, but all too familiar in Delhi. It was the look of indulgent fondness, the look Punjabi women reserve for their sons and younger brothers and sons-in-law, the look that she had always denied Kunal and, in a different way, Kabir.

'Oh, don't be so harsh. Vicky's the farthest thing in the world from a dilettante. That was a genuine passion project for him. You didn't go inside, did you?'

So she'd had a proper report of her own, from Vicky or Ashwin or both.

'I'm sorry I couldn't help Vicky.'

'No, *I'm* sorry. He just asked me, "Do you know a lawyer?" and I said, "I know the best." I didn't get into what he needed one for.'

Could she really not have known?

'He needs a very different kind of lawyer. But after meeting him,' I said, 'which was also the second time I met Ashwin, I thought a lot more about what you said. About the lion's share and the tiger's.'

'I'm flattered you pay so much attention to me. Everyone needs a Tara.'

'Even Kunal?'

'I said everyone needs one, not everyone deserves one.'

'Wouldn't you say that your point about these guys who have been raised to expect the lion's share being unequipped to fight for the tiger's applies just as much to Vicky and Ashwin?'

'Vicky? He doesn't need to fight for anything.'

'Does he have siblings?'

'He was a late child. His mom was over forty. They'd thought they couldn't have kids.'

'Well, what if he did? What if he had a sister like you?'

175

'Look, things like my lion-tiger analogy, they're meant as a general point, general not universal. This stuff doesn't apply when you're that rich. Also, Vicky is just *different*. He's sort of above this stuff.' Above, meaning too rich: so rich that oddness is elevated to distinction.

'Ashwin, though. Would you agree that he isn't any kind of tiger?'

'Is that why you two didn't hit it off – you thought he was lazy? Not manly like your Polish electrician?'

'Unlike my Polish *diplomat*, I struggle to think of him in a sexual way. You'd struggle, too, don't deny it.'

'I grant you that Ashwin isn't some go-getter. But it's fine, because he knows it. He's not bitter. And he doesn't resent women.'

'You wouldn't agree that Kunal shows a much greater capacity to adapt to this new world than Ashwin? At the very least, that he's trying to?'

'What evidence do we have for that? Trying to bully his sister out of her place in the family? Siphoning money from the business my dad built into "creating pro-India content"?'

'He sees the world and wants to be relevant in it. And even if he thinks that for him wealth is an entitlement, relevance is something he's willing to fight for. Work for.'

'Is this what it means to be a lawyer? *Literally* "devil's advocate"? Be contrary in every situation? Even so, there are limits.'

'I'm a believer in taking people seriously. Dismissing an adversary is a risk. The only pay-off is psychological – contempt is pleasurable, but I'd rather not take my eye off the ball.'

'Do you think you take Rohit seriously?'

'You're right. I try, but not enough. Look,' I said eventually, and I wasn't sure I was emotionally equipped for some of the places this might be going, 'on Ashwin. I guess he just struck me as kind of fatalistic. About the world and his place in it. He kept going on about the eclipse of "our class". About how he wasn't good enough to hack it in the UK, so he came back to India where he'd be better than other people, and he found that in India people like him are finished. Well, he kept saying people like us, and he could see I wasn't fully buying it, and he decided that was because I'm a lawyer, and according to him lawyers are doing well.'

'Lawyers *are* doing well. You know that. There are somewhere between twenty and fifty lawyers in this city who make more than their equivalents in London, in *raw money*. Purchasing-power-wise, they probably make five to six times as much.'

'But you agree that he's fatalistic? In a slightly pathetic way?'

She was visibly forming her next sentences word by word in her head, like writers did in the age of typewriters. I couldn't tell if she was trying to conceal irritation with me or avoid being mean about Ashwin.

'Even Ashwin, much as I love him, has become one of those people – ugh, it's basically every other person now. One of the reasons I'm so grateful for you is that you are *never* one of those people. LOL, you look so confused. People who think the world is ending. This stuff was already in the air around the time I left New York. Then Trump happened and everyone actually lost their minds. And I come to Delhi and it's exactly the same. Every day fewer humans are poor than at any point in human history. They're taller. They live longer. They have better skin and teeth. Their husband is less likely to hit them. Instead of repetitive drudgery they have actual sources of entertainment. And yet you hear people talk – "Things have never been this bad". "Democracy is in peril". "This is not a nuanced time". When I came back I thought, at least in India people will be more sensible. Well, not the ones you and I know. It's actually only a few months ago that I properly worked it out. I was talking to Vicky, as it happens.'

I nodded along, concealing my scepticism that Vicky could provide or stimulate any such answer.

'What is true there, and here, is that the people who are running around like Chicken Licken saying the sky is falling are worried about *their* relative position. White liberals are scared of a world in which they aren't twenty times as rich and a hundred times as important as their equivalent in China. And over here, people like Ashwin think the country used to be run by "us" – Macaulayputras – and it isn't. But here's the thing: they'll be fine. We'll be fine. Not just fine, but, frankly, better off than anyone else.'

'Obviously I can't speak to the US', I said. 'But isn't there something to what Ashwin is saying? You can't deny the country's changed.'

'For Muslims, yes. No getting away from that. But not for us. The thing is, Tara, they can't do without us. No one else has any skills. Just basic competence. The ability to think and write in clear English, organise a workday, make a PowerPoint, be *efficient*. Be able to deal with an American VC fund. Ashwin probably gave you his spiel about how, except for lawyers, we bleed our best talent every year. If that is true, you could say it actually benefits those of us who've come back. And the guys in power get it. They don't want India to turn into Zimbabwe. They're quite badly dependent, more than you think, on the flow of American money, and they need a group of people here to bring it in. So they'll go after Muslims and NGO workers and journalists, but if what you want is to be able to spend your weekends at The Book Shop and Sunder Nursery, send your kids to a good international school, eat and drink well, they'll leave you alone. They get that they need us.'

'This sounds like a version of Ashwin's first fish theory. But he said that theory had failed him in practice.'

'He's just whining for effect.' Lila had failed to catch the sadness in Ashwin's whining – perhaps you had to look at him properly, not just listen, to catch it.

'Even so. It's not like you to want to be the first fish. You'd want to be the best – compete with the best. You can't do that here.'

'I am doing it from here. My investors are American. My fund is judged against global benchmarks. And I get to actually see my son.'

'The old argument about India being better for a professional woman, because we have cheap help?'

'Domestic help, family help, the works. All of it. And look, I'm not being sentimental, Delhi is home. What do you want me to do about it? I didn't choose to be born in this shithole. Shithole with compensations.'

My father had always had email, but except for logistical matters this was the first time I'd ever used it.

> Baba, shall we email more often from now on? It may be more convenient than meeting, although of course we'll meet whenever we can.
>
> I will also force myself to meet Ma soon. I will just have to come over when no one else is around – maybe the late morning – and force her to talk to me.
>
> Rohit is working with Kunal at Adhimukta Bharat. He hasn't made any of his own videos lately, but I hear he's working hard. Who knows – it might be the making of him. When I say that, I mean that maybe this will make him whatever it is he's going to be. Rohit has always been . . . unformed. I've never had an idea of him, a hope of what form he would eventually take. I hope formed turns out to be better than unformed.

For a whole week Baba didn't reply.

Jahnavi began to deliver her reports on the phone. This may even have been her idea. They grew more frequent, but shorter. From the standpoint of actionable intelligence, we'd hit a lull. Her reports didn't bore me, but they gave me nothing at all I could take to Lila.

In the last week of September, two months into her deployment, a long-strained levee gave way. It was a Friday, Kunal was out of the office, and Jahnavi was done early. She decided to take the metro home. She wasn't allowed to, strictly speaking, like all Delhi girls of her class. But her driver wasn't due for another two hours, and if she got home before he left, she could brazen the whole thing out.

One of her coder neighbours watched her leave, overtook her on the staircase and barred her way out of the building.

'How are you going home?'

'The metro,' she said.

'It's not safe for a girl like you. I will escort you.'

'It's totally safe.'

'Doesn't your driver come for you every day? Where is he?'

'He comes at six. I'm done early today.'

'Then we can get coffee? We have two hours until he comes. We can go to—'

'You can go to—?' Rohit, right behind her. 'Jahnavi may be done with her work, but are you? I don't think you are.'

'Was he?' I asked Jahnavi. She didn't know. Poor chap, I half thought, but didn't say. The same system that meant he wasn't done with his work if Rohit didn't think he was meant that he couldn't answer back to Rohit. He took the lift back up, leaving Jahnavi with Rohit.

'Were you really planning to take the metro?'

'Yup. Mainly because I'm not supposed to. I love riding the L, in Chicago.'

'Tell me about it. I miss the subway, even though it's such a piece of shit.'

Rohit was lingering. Was he angling for a coffee, for a drink? 'I'm sorry about that dude. You know how it is with these techies. They're basically all incels.'

He was angling for a thank you. 'And that,' said Jahnavi, 'I would not give him. I didn't need rescuing from that guy. It's exactly like you said. Kunal, Rohit, the way they see women. I don't know about Kunal, but I got the impression that when Rohit thinks of himself, he uses the word "gentleman".'

I didn't say: You only see part of it. You think he wanted to protect you because you're a girl. The other part – Rohit enforcing his social order by separating the coder from a girl of a class he was not, strictly speaking, allowed to approach – that part she wouldn't see. Probably ever.

Instead I said: 'In case you didn't know, he's my brother.'

'I know.'

'And so you know why I didn't tell you.' I hardly knew what I meant.

'Oh, I know, don't you worry about that.'

12
Delhi Airs

October. Season of smogs and mellow murderousness. A month, in Delhi, that begins in summer and ends reliably in smoke. The smoke comes in from Punjab and Haryana, where the paddy crop is being burnt to make way for wheat. When it arrives in Delhi it has a mutually stimulating encounter with our own producers of particulate matter: vehicles, factories, coal power plants, construction dust. There was a day in October when you knew it had arrived. You smelled it in the late morning like the news of your neighbour's lunch.

If the Hindu calendar dictated that Diwali was to fall in October, then we could add on top the smoke of the crackers, Diwali in practice being a festival of smoke and sound, only tertiarily of light. Lately crackers were officially banned, but only in Delhi – not in neighbouring Gurgaon and Noida and Faridabad and Ghaziabad. So Delhi could have its crackers, just not collect tax on them.

Diwali this year fell on the 27th of October. Two weeks earlier, Lila called to say her mother had decided to have their usual party the night before, despite everything, and would I come?

'Your mother is inviting me?'

'I'm inviting you.'

'What's Kunal's role in this party?'

'He never bothered much with it in years past. But this year he's guaranteed to have circled it as a chance to parade himself as Head of the Family. So I'm bringing all my friends.'

I didn't say: Isn't this ever so slightly childish? And then I thought better, or worse, and said it.

'When you're dealing with a child,' said Lila, 'sometimes you have to become one. Not the law of the jungle but the law of the playground.'

I actually didn't say: Jungle or playground, you're playing a game where he's written the rules and spent years or a lifetime practising. You should stick to keeping the New York office happy, the Californian pension funds. At that, you're the champ.

At the end of his reply to my email, Baba appended three links to articles about our air. One about the latest research on the long-term effects on not just the lungs but the brain and blood and heart; one about the social and institutional pathologies that meant it was likely to get worse rather than better; a third about India's indigenous Air Quality Index, custom-built to certify the terrifying as adequate and the apocalyptic as unsatis-factory.

This was the full text of his reply:

Yes, we can email. Of course. Please don't feel that you should not come here.

Then the links, and:

I have sent these to Rohit as well.

Two minutes later, a follow-up.

You may note that all these articles are only concerned with the effect on human lives, human bodies.

This one, I bet, went to me alone.

On the 18th of October the smoke came in. We could no longer see the sky. Other cities whine when the clouds deprive them of the stars. They talk about the scourge of light pollution. To us light pollution would have come as a blessing, a luxury. We lived in smoke.

On the tongue it was a chaat of dust and gravel, as if you'd rolled your shoe over a cigarette stub and then proceeded to rub the stub along your tongue. On the skin it was the malevolent scratching of uncut nails. One sense alone was spared. The smoke had no sound. But it was only silent because the air was still – when we needed it to be anything but.

If you prayed, the most practical thing to pray for was wind, to take the smoke somewhere else, to choke some other city.

For those who claimed not to notice the smoke, or not to mind it, for those who kept their windows open at night, it's not for me to speak. But even I – who felt it on my tongue, and in my hair, whose eyes watered within ten minutes when outdoors, whose breathing passages from late October until early March housed a rent-free cough, who grew sleepy by noon each day and on Sundays found walking from bed to kitchen a struggle – even I, who noticed all these things, was guilty of moving on from them, living with them. I felt the air but I didn't think about it for more than a few minutes each day. I had air purifiers running in every room, but I was flaky when it came to replacing the HEPA filters. I didn't have my doors and windows appropriately sealed.

The smoke was appalling, but it grew familiarly appalling, appallingly familiar.

The Saturday before Diwali, I went home after breakfast. I had received no invitation, given no warning. What made me do it? My character is not marked by sudden capillary actions of courage. My attitude to the unpleasant is defer, deny, delay – the attitude of the respondent whose legal strategy is a Fibonacci sequence of adjournments. But I'd received a text from Lila:

Mamma says your whole family is coming to the party!

Whole family, no chance. Even in those decades when Baba was a working accountant and a man of outward social conformity, he didn't do festivals, not even Diwali. He sent boxes of sweets to his clients and he let us burst crackers with the neighbours. But he himself observed nothing, celebrated nothing. Most years he actually went to the office on Diwali itself. It gave him a day of work that the rest of white-collar Delhi didn't have. Baba would not go to the Chawla Diwali party. But Ma might. And if I was going to see her there, even I knew I had to go home and talk to her first.

Rohit answered the door, just as he had on the morning of the summit. But this time he was dressed for the day, for the world: a Lacoste polo, green as a gummy bear, loose white trousers, tight white shoes. The shoes were technically sneakers, but their relationship to sports was one of homage, not usability. They looked as new as the blue ones I'd seen with Deepti.

He was dressed for an outdoor social event. In this air. 'What are you doing here?'

I ran through thirteen or fourteen different attempts at a snide comeback and every one made me wince. Unlike Lila, I knew which games I could beat my brother at, and which I couldn't, and which I'd rather not be able to.

'I'm here to see Ma.' I was happy with this, in the moment. It wasn't untrue, even if it might confuse him, make him wonder if behind Ma's front of loyalty there lay a traitorous back-channel.

'Bullshit.'

'OK, let me rephrase. I was hoping to see Ma.'

'Well, you hoped in vain. She's out.'

Rohit's one surprising quality was that he couldn't lie. In this, if in nothing else, he was his father's son. If you aren't from Delhi, you may not see the measure of Rohit's honesty, its strangeness. It isn't just that Delhi is a city of liars. Lying in Delhi is rarely an act of hypocrisy. Ours was not a city that reckoned in virtuous terms. If we had norms, truth-telling was not reckoned one of them. You did what you had to do, and sometimes, quite often, lying was what you had to do.

If I knew Rohit, I had got him just as he was leaving. Rohit didn't sit around once he was dressed to go. He'd lose his shit at anyone who was holding him up.

If Baba was in his study, thought Rohit, then if I leave now, she goes in and I've basically left them to their conspiracy planning. But at least I caught her in time.

'Oho,' I said. 'Achcha, where are you off to looking so swish?' If Deepti was wrong, and I knew Rohit, he was incapable of saying the words, 'None of your business.'

'Friend's birthday.'

'Farmhouse party?'

'Uh-huh.'

I could watch it all on his face, in montage: the irritation at me for holding him up, the anxiety about my impending session with Baba, the conviction that every word that came out of my mouth was either conniving or condescending, the three decades of accrued resentment. I watched it all and I saw that though he was looking straight at me he didn't see me, he didn't see that all I did was keep myself from crying, that all I felt was a helplessness beyond words.

Every feeling passes. In refusing to cry, in working my face into false coldness, I made it pass quicker.

'Crazy for them to have an outdoor party in this air. You at least have always been careful when it comes to the air. I mean sensible. Most people don't get it.' And then I did what I now knew to be the only decent thing I could, and released him. 'Anyway, will you tell Ma I came by? Have fun at your thing.'

As I went back down the stairs I sensed him lingering in the doorway. At the bottom of the stairs I stopped and waited to see how long he'd wait to make sure I was gone. Finally he closed the door.

The next morning I flew to Bangalore. That year marked fifteen since our batch graduated law school. The party that I attended called itself a reunion, and it was, with qualifications. Our law school, like other Indian public universities, didn't really know what to do with its reservoir of alumni. The standard Indian verb for graduate – pass out – got the sense of it. Your lot passed *out*, and someone else passed in. And so our attachments were to the people, not the place.

This reunion was being thrown by Sanam. Sanam would describe me as a dear friend, but then we were all her dear friends. Socially, she was our batch's vital centre; people who still despised each other, whether or not they could remember why, could not refuse her. Despisal was as common as love with us. It couldn't be otherwise. Four hundred of us; just eighty a year, living out our late adolescence together, and what united us? Only ambition. It was only on my first Italian holiday, reading *The Magic Mountain*, that I saw our law school for what it was: an inverse sanatorium, a place where you were injected with anxieties, not cured of them. Later we'd all say we were grateful, and mean it.

No one had yet seen Sanam anxious. Irritable, yes, vicious, occasionally, violent, when it came to golf balls. Uneasy, never. At eighteen she already wore her wide shoulders and town crier contralto as if there were *no such things* as masculinity and femininity. Immoderation in food and drink had thickened every part of her since, but no one carried their weight lighter. Soon after graduation she'd acquired a Goan husband, addressed always by last name – Mendonca – and two sons. The sons were Mendoncas too, with Rizvi as a middle name.

They lived in Whitefield, in a California-themed gated community called something like Vivek Pacific Palisades, densely studded with Beemers and swimming pools. If you came in from California you could laugh, or cringe; but not if you came in from Delhi. In Sanam's garden, the Sunday before Diwali, it was 24 degrees Celsius, and if the air was terrible by WHO standards, if you were coming from Delhi those were not your standards. If you came in from Delhi you breathed in and your first thought was, This isn't smoke, this is air.

Mendonca, whom no one really knew – the inevitable consequence of being married to Sanam – welcomed me in, and went off to get me a drink. I found Sanam at a table under a jacaranda tree, with Deepti and two others. Defiantly not at the table, but leaning against the tree by a slender elbow, was our classmate, Iftikhar. Ifti, like my mother, did not believe in sitting.

I liked to tell him that he'd chosen teaching at our alma mater over actual lawyering precisely for this reason.

'She's here!' The usual Sanam greeting, a compactor of a hug. 'Why hasn't that useless Mendonca got you a drink? Mendonca!'

'They can hear you in Tamil Nadu.'

Poor Mendonca appeared with a cocktail of urinary yellow.

'Thanks so much.'

The two others did not like me. When Sanam drove off to another table they followed her. Telling themselves, perhaps, that they were doing Deepti and me the kindness of leaving us alone together. Deepti and Tara, the forever double act.

Until now I'd been protected by them, by Sanam, by small talk. Now Deepti looked at me and I was naked in the worst of all ways: morally. Every day since I last saw Deepti, I'd done everything I could to avoid preparing for this.

No one was saying anything. Could I use Ifti, still behind me against the tree, as an excuse to keep deferring? We weren't close to Ifti, any of us. We were all a little too scared of him.

Deepti broke first. She indicated Ifti and said, 'If you're waiting for him to leave, you know him, he won't leave. So you might as well start.'

Maybe Deepti wasn't scared of Ifti, or of anything. I needed to learn from my father, and speak only for myself.

'D . . .' I heard Ifti adjust his position, like a seated man recrossing his legs. And I began. 'Six months ago, Baba convened a family summit.'

In my telling, on that day, it was the straightest story in the world. Not one digressive clause or footnote or backwards loop. If there was a person who needed no context for any of this story, it was Deepti. My test for what to include was simple. If Rohit knew it, so could Deepti. So I offered most of what I knew of my father's worldview, his diagnosis. I mentioned the trip to the trash mountain. But no Sister; no Gandhi or Bhagat Singh; no revelation at

188

Ranthambore, thirty-three years ago. Not even the suggestion of speculation as to what Baba might do. Only what he had done.

People kept coming in to the party, including some I hadn't seen in years, and some who genuinely loved me. But no one approached us.

'I have a question.' Ifti.

I turned my chair so I could see him.

'What are your father's politics? I mean his party politics.'

'None declared.'

'Fascinating.'

'Fascinating because?'

'Your father is an upper-caste, bourgeois, elderly Hindu man. Now, our country is engaged in two *principal* projects of collective sadism. One, merely sadist – what we're doing to the Muslims.' That deployment of pronouns was classic Ifti – what *we*'re doing to *the* Muslims, not what *they*'re doing to *us* Muslims. 'The other, I suppose, sadomasochistic – what we're doing to our ecology. And by rights your father should be like others of his kind, and see neither. But he sees one of these things with appalling clarity. And the other – does he see it at all?'

The most natural urge in the world – to want to defend your father – and yet, after only a second the urge reveals itself not as loyalty but as betrayal. I looked to the truth for refuge, and found it. 'I don't know.'

'Well, one out of two is better than none,' said Ifti, who went off to choose new company.

Ifti had protected me from having to truly look at Deepti. Deepti's face is ceaselessly penetrable. I looked at her and in the warm tightening of her eyes and cheekbones – if, like Lila, Deepti was thirty-seven and had never looked better, you could thank the late emergence of those cheekbones – I saw many things, but most of all I saw a hug.

'I'm so, so sorry, D. All I can say is that you know me better than anyone, and while I'm not asking you to be OK with my taking so long to tell you, I bet you're not surprised.'

189

The eye-hug had done its work, and was gone. What she gave me now was concern. A look only a step or slip away from pity.

'I'm a little surprised. Maybe I shouldn't be. Not with you not telling me.'

'Then?'

'With the way you tell it. You've chosen – maybe that's unfair, but anyway – you let yourself sound helpless. This is what's happened to the family. This is what my father has done. And now what? You just accept it, watch it?'

'What else can I do?'

'*Talk* to your father. Push him. See how far you can. If not now, then when? If you don't want to alienate Aunty and Rohit, then fight for them.'

I shook my head as if to say, Deepti, you are so far from understanding.

'I've never seen you allow yourself to be helpless,' she said.

'If it were my money, D, different story. But it's not. My father has already done more for us than should be asked of any father. His duties are discharged. And besides – why should we expect anything of him at all? He worked, he invested, Rohit and I had nothing to do with it. None of it is ours. It's all his. And it's pretty clear that he can find better uses for his money. We've been given an education. You really think the world would be better off if it all went to us instead? You think *Rohit* would be better off? Or do you think if, instead of trying to be an entitled Delhi boy, he knows he has to make his own life, might that not be the making of him?'

'God, listen to you. Maybe it's not you. Maybe this is how it is with siblings. *I* wouldn't know. This is why we only want one. A sibling is absolutely guaranteed to bring out the worst in a person.'

'What do you mean by how it is?'

'Listen to yourself. *Who am I to tell my father. Won't this actually be for Rohit's good.*' She knew, Deepti, how I feel about my own words being misquoted back to me. 'Forget all the hypocrisy. All the stuff about how no one should tell anyone what to do.

Remember how proud you were of yourself when you, at least according to you, convinced your dad to pay for Rohit's master's? You probably think I'm asking you to do something like that, again. No. I'm asking . . .' and she held back, and then said, 'Remember when . . .' and braked again.

Deepti, for the first time in her life, thinking better of saying something?

'Remember when what?'

'Nothing. I'm not asking you to do anything. I'm asking you, no, I'm *telling* you what you may think isn't a hard thing to hear but, believe me, may be the hardest thing in the world for you to understand. You don't know Rohit. You don't understand him. You don't know the first thing about him. And because he's your brother you assume you know everything. And because you are, let's face it, extremely smart, hyper-aware, on some level you know that you don't know very much about him at all. And what do you tell yourself? If *I* don't know much, it means there isn't much to know. You never say, "If I don't know much, it's because I've never tried to find out, never actually been curious, because when it comes to him I'm smug and condescending and my mind is *shut*, because there is nothing I can learn from him or about him, ever."'

Deepti knew what she would get from me. She knew I'd say nothing.

'If you hadn't written him off, if you had any capacity for actual curiosity about him, you wouldn't come here today and plead helplessness.'

I didn't say, Deepti, these remarks of yours are vaporously general, you're not giving me the slightest concrete sense of whom this Rohit is that you say I don't know. She wasn't, after all, talking about him. She was trying to talk about me.

'So what do you want me to do?'

'Nothing. It's probably years too late. It sounds like your family is well and truly fucked. Always was fucked, finally come out in the open. You thought you saw through your mom and Rohit, you

thought that was because you and your dad were superior intel-
lects. You never thought, What if they see through me? They
always have. Nothing for you to do but accept it.'

She didn't mean this. Not Deepti – she was ultimately too opti-
mistic, too committed to a world in which families worked. Given
how hard she was trying to get pregnant, she must be more
committed than ever.

'You don't mean it,' I said. 'The last part, about us being
fucked. You're saying this to make sure the earlier stuff gets
through to me. I get it.'

'Enough,' she said, waving a feudal palm in the direction of
Mendonca, who had taken up the role of waiter with Strasbergian
ardour. 'Enough of being unpaid family therapist to the Saxenas.
Now I want to be allowed to actually have fun at this party.'

Sometimes Baba merely sent links, unannotated. Usually there
was a line or two of commentary. What agitated him most at this
time was a project at Harvard, led by a man who looked like a
face-morph of Charles Darwin and George R. R. Martin, which
hoped to create living woolly mammoths and 'reintroduce' them
to the Russian steppes so as to restore the natural balance and
ecological diversity of the biome. The original mammoths had
been foolishly hunted to extinction; enlightened by hindsight, we
could redeem our ancestors.

I see no reason why my father should have heard of either
Frankenstein or *Jurassic Park*. He wasn't one of those afraid of
what could go wrong with such PhD-playing-God science
projects. He was afraid of them going right. Let's say it worked
perfectly. Let's say the mammoths restored the Siberian steppe to
the glory from whence it had fallen. Let's say that by 2100 AD we
succeed, fauna-wise, in making large parts of the world look as
they did in 6000 BC. To Baba, the men behind such schemes were
if anything more dangerous than governments who built new
coal power plants, or mining companies that ravaged hillsides.
Even Rohit's video series had taken humanity for just one species

in competition with others. The mammoth-makers, said Baba, would tell you that humans were a species, but they didn't believe it. If they succeeded, then by the start of the twenty-second century most humans would regard the puppetisation of nature not merely as a necessity for human thrival, but as an expression of our true identity. Man in the image of God, Man as God, Man as curator, Man as creator.

He never wrote to me about the melting of ice shelfs and glaciers, or the proliferation of 'extreme weather events', or even the inaction of governments. My father was not interested in the symptoms. Or at least no longer interested. But even at the time I wondered why Baba sent me what he did. Did he simply hope to prepare me for whatever was to come – explanation preceding action as always, if a touch indirectly? Or did he want me to join him?

Baba had Sister on his desk and he said she was there to give him courage. Bhagat Singh was there to . . . had he said what? He had said that he could not tell other people what to do, that he hoped or aimed only to provoke, to stimulate. I had said, Do you hope to inspire, and he had replied, I hope to make them pay attention. Was Bhagat Singh there as an example of someone who had made them pay attention? Bhagat Singh had provoked rather than instructed, but only because he'd been jailed and then hanged. As a free man he'd have been like Bose or Gandhi, with obedient followers. Or was he there as an illustration of the worthiness of giving up one's life, of how little the private *possession* of life, of a life, really mattered?

Which was my own version of the Golden Rule – Do as Baba would do, or Do as Baba would have you do?

Every time I asked Baba about Sister, about his network of comrades, I put my question to a pre-emptive test. I wouldn't ask him anything that could be construed as investigative. No questions about the movement's origins, or funding, or location, or even if there was a movement at all. Everything I asked was really about Baba himself: Baba, do you get these links from Sister and the others? Some of them, not most. Do they share your broad view, or are they more focused on the symptoms? They agree with me about the root causes, but if they're focused on symptoms too, I can hardly blame them. They're younger than me. They have to live with the symptoms. In any case, I can't speak for or about them in general terms. Everyone has their own approach. I didn't, couldn't, ask: Have you told them what you're going to do?

What my father offered in the realm of information he gave unprompted. Once he said that almost everyone in Sister's network lived in Asia or Africa, plus a few in Australia. And once he said that his or any of their getting to know Sister, finding Sister, had involved an amazing piece of luck. Sister and her family were refugees, although she disclaimed the word. They'd escaped from western Xinjiang into Kazakhstan.

From Xinjiang, even if she was spared the worst, she'd never have been able to reach us.

13
From Each According to His Ability

I had never been to the Chawlas' family home. Back in our maths tuition days, where Lila and I first met, I knew little and thought less about class differences and the significance of an address. I knew Lila was rich, but I'm not sure *how* I knew it. She didn't dress rich. It was the late 1990s and what was to happen in London and New York had already happened in Delhi: the rich could no longer be distinguished from the merely bourgeois by their accents. It wasn't just a question of declining Anglophilia. You heard it in Hindi too, and presumably in other languages. What happened in India, and would happen everywhere, was this: the rich grew comfortable in their philistinism. They were rich, not classy; fancy, not posh. Where they'd once held Hindustani classical concerts at home of a Saturday, they now listened to the same Punjabi folk-disco that their drivers did.

Lila would become different, but at seventeen she wasn't that different, yet. How did I know she was rich? Was it the white Merc – in 1990s Delhi still the first and last word in luxury – that came to pick her up after class? Was it that she was applying to American colleges? To do that wasn't *that* rare, even then. What was rare was to go without a scholarship.

Every afternoon we lingered after class, for fifteen minutes to an hour, chatting about anything and everything, her driver waiting in the car. Then she'd go and I'd take an auto home.

I had no other friends in Golf Links. But I knew that, judged by the 'objective' measure of average sale price per square yard, it was the fanciest of all Delhi colonies. Partly this was a function of location. As the name implies, it stands next to the Delhi Golf Club, a preposterous theme park of sand-traps and Mughal tombs. Step out of Golf Links, walk north-west, and you find yourself in Khan Market. Walk west and you're soon in Lodhi Gardens. Partly it was that the plots were larger than in Jor Bagh. But, as usual in Delhi, there was a bureaucratic angle. Golf Links was still subject to the old height restrictions. Its homeowners were barred from replacing their bungalows with four floors of flats. Supply was thus artificially suppressed.

My chief Golf Links client, Manoj Vaswani, was a leather goods magnate who had recently bought himself a seat in Parliament. He was insufferably pleased with this acquisition. He paraded it like a car, or a wife. He called everyone he knew and subjected us to disquisitions about the nobility of the institution of Parliament, the architectural subtleties of Central Hall, the value for money of the food in the canteen (is it only a Delhi thing that the more money a man makes, the more excited he is by a bargain?).

Manoj-ji lived three doors down from the Chawlas. For years he and Mr Chawla had taken their evening walk together. Mr Chawla, he once told me, would have made an excellent MP. In the taxi over to the party I totted up the people I might know. Manoj – Mr Vaswani to me – would presumably 'put in an appearance' rather than linger. A man like him, even before his ascension to the Upper House, would have more parties to go to than days in the week. But I wanted to catch him. It's not for me to say, I know, but Mr Vaswani was fond of me, and I liked the idea of Kunal bearing witness to how fond.

Kunal's ambitions, whatever they were, were on a different scale from Manoj Vaswani's. For Mr Vaswani a seat in Parliament was a Veblen good. But for now, he was in Parliament, and Kunal had an NGO no one had heard of preparing a curriculum for the Delhi government, except the government didn't know it yet. Mr Vaswani might be of use to him. More to the point, he wanted Mr Vaswani to recognise him as the new head of the family.

I had the driver drop me around the corner. The houses of Golf Links stand in semi-circles around small parks. On the night of a party the semi-circle is part parking lot, part catwalk. Cars built for the autobahn – Audis and Porsches and Beemers and Maybachs – are forced into painful ashtanga contortions as they find their way in and, eventually, out. The guests go into the party and the driver commences the long search for parking. Three hours later he's asleep in his seat as his phone rings. 'You go home, someone else will drop us.' My Uber driver, in his sensible Swift Dzire, was on the whole better off.

The Chawla house seemed to take up two full plots. I walked into a long driveway that looped around the house, ending, I would later find, in the servant quarters. Diyas lined the driveway, like bollards. To my left was a hedge and beyond that the front garden. I was early.

A few guests, geriatric and thus earlier even than me, stood with whiskies at round tables, with long white tablecloths that reached for the ground. Look underneath and you might find a hiding child. For all their aesthetic crimes, their fraudulent warmth, for how demented it was to hold an outdoor gathering in this air, for all that and more, Delhi parties were made wonderful by their disregard for generations. You could count on meeting growing children and shrinking grandparents and all those in between whose ongoing expansion was horizontal, meeting all of them on terms of ease and generosity.

Liveried waiters moved to and fro, fixing lights and drinks. To go into the garden you had to first enter the house. The front door was open. The doorway was graced, not guarded, by two golden retrievers, who ignored me. The next guest cooed and yelped, as if in foreplay. The dogs sprung up in eager reception.

I was in an oddly empty hallway the size of my flat. French windows opened out into the garden. On the opposite wall hung a piece of contemporary art on a mythological subject obscure to me. It ticked both the boxes that matter in Delhi, namely sheer girth and the prominent signature of a known surname.

Lila had grown up in this house and outgrown it.

'Tara.' She wore a salwar kameez in a sort of pink. Did it suit her?

'Have I seen you in desi clothes before?'

'When in Rome.' A hug, vice-like and lingering, and then a second. 'You've never come home before. It's crazy.'

'I just remembered that I have to be on my guard, throughout. Anything I do here is recorded on one of your hidden cameras and beamed straight to your phone.'

'Anything, and anyone.'

'I shouldn't have come so early. Can I help with anything?'

From time to time I'd thought about my place in the hierarchy of Lila's friends. Weddings and parties are the places where these things manifest: who sits where, who gives a speech, but also who comes early to help, who is intimate with every aunt and every servant, who knows exactly where the single malts are kept and where the dogs like to be scratched.

I was an old friend, and a new one. A friend for twenty years, a friend who had never been to this house. A friend with whom Lila seemingly shared everything, even unto CCTV footage, and quite possibly a friend of whose existence her mother was unaware.

'Don't be silly. And it's good you've come early – you can meet Mamma before all the world claims her.'

'Where's Kunal?'

'Excellent question. And long may it remain a question.'

She led me to the garden. Two waiters passed us, carrying a ladder. Their uniforms bore the logo of their employer, a hotel. It was always going to be that hotel, or the Golf Club.

'You do this every year, so it runs like clockwork?'

'Mamma's birthday is next week. Kunal's the week after. So this is usually our big annual party. Just happens to fall near Diwali this year.'

Mrs Chawla stood with her back to us and a man to either side. Lila grabbed her mother's plump right arm, without acknowledging – much less apologising – to either man.

'Mamma, this is my friend Tara Saxena, whom you've heard so much about. The brilliant lawyer.'

I extended both hands. I thought, Mrs Chawla, and said, 'Aunty.'

'You're Rohit's sister.'

'That's the least of what she is.'

I smile-nodded, privately agreeing with them both. 'You know Rohit.'

'He is such a good friend to Kunal. A very talented boy.'

'He works with Kunal now. At Adhimukta Bharat.' If any of this was news to her, her face did not show it.

'I'll be right back.' Having brought us together, Lila was making sure her mother stayed put. It would be rude to leave me on my own.

It was impossible to look at Mrs Chawla and not think of my mother. Fair, even faces of studied opacity, hiding either the truth or an emptiness. My mother's blandness I'd always taken for the absence of thought and feeling; not stupidity, but a kind of unsurprised acceptance of the world, all rooted in a radical self-acceptance that no one of my generation seemed to possess. I looked at my mother and thought, Inner life is optional, and we might be better off without it. My mother's warmth was shallow, but genuine. Mrs Chawla's face, I speculated, was more likely to be the conventional Delhi kind of opaque: that is, fake. Polite society deserves respect, said the poet. You can't hold phoniness against an individual when it is a socially validated norm.

My mother was not slim, but that was a business of build, not lifestyle. Mrs Chawla was unembarrassedly fat. Unlike my mother, she'd never been encumbered or liberated by housework. In a few years, you could tell, she'd be too fat to walk.

'How are you getting on, Aunty? I still can't believe Uncle is gone. He was so young.' Uncle, whom I'd never met.

She looked glassily back at me. 'It has been very tough. But I'm well looked after.'

I scanned the conversation library for anything Lila had ever said about her mother or her parents' marriage. Or for anything else of use. I was avidly, ravenously curious about this woman, but also wrenchingly aware of the uselessness of this conversation as a means of feeding that curiosity. In a general way small talk is not

199

one of my skills, but I struggle specifically with women of this kind – women who have never worked, never read, never *thought*; women who have led lives of gossip and gesture. Not domestic lives – not with their platoons of chauffeurs and cooks – but lives of arid, low-stakes sociability. What the fuck are you supposed to talk to them about?

I fell pathetically upon: 'Thankfully you have your children nearby. And Kabir. He's so lucky to have you.'

'Oh, I hardly see him. His mother likes to keep him for herself.'

The way Lila told it, Kabir and Lila's father had lived joined at the hip.

She was confronting me with an almost obscene lack of interest. If I said nothing she'd just look at me with a regal indifference that I knew I could not bear. So I kept talking, praising the house, the party decorations. I said that Mr Chawla's chautha was the most elegant I'd ever attended. It was only later, in the customary exercise of ashamed review, that I realised that I ought to have had the sense to spend this time praising Lila.

Lila was getting herself or someone a drink. I took this chance. 'Lovely to finally meet you, Aunty.' I caught Lila leaving the bar.

She took one look at me and laughed. 'Sorry about that. I should have known you and Mamma might not be a natural fit.'

'Have you ever wondered,' I said, 'how you and your mom would get on if you weren't mother and daughter?'

'Ha. We wouldn't. Her appeal would be entirely lost on me.'

'That's how I feel about my own mother. So I don't expect to be an instant hit with anyone else's.'

Other people's fathers were another matter. No one's father could remind me of my own, but many fathers reminded me of my clients, or of my seniors in court.

'Get yourself a drink? I'm so sorry, Papa's friends refuse to get enough of me.'

A queue had begun to form at the bar. Not a queue – three crowded ranks, like drivers outside an airport terminal, their hands raised like placards. I was the only female and the only under-fifty.

When I reached the front the waiter reached for a poured glass of white wine and I held out a palm to say Stop, and asked for a whisky-soda. A double.

The party had filled up all at once. There was Rohit, and where there was Rohit there was Kunal. There was a gaggle of Lila's yummy-mummy friends, above my station. There was – fucking hell, there was Jahnavi, with what I suspected was her mother. Under a mango tree, and staring with shameless expectancy at me, were Ashwin and Vicky. It is not for us to come to you. It is for you to come to us.

'The way you were looking at me, you clearly expected me to bring you drinks. Leave aside that I am not your waiter, how am I supposed to read your minds and know what you want?'

'I'd be happy with what you're having. Vicky is doing dry-Diwali.'

'You can get it yourself.' He did.

Vicky, in a setting like this. Were there any single women of marriageable age about? They'd see him and think, Is he real? and that's without an inkling of his net worth – although there did appear to be diamonds in his shoes.

'Do you come to this thing every year?' I had no idea how long he'd known Lila. Had their fathers been friends?

'Do I look like the kind of person who comes to this thing every year?'

'How am I supposed to know?'

Ashwin was stuck in row three at the bar. Vicky was stuck having to use his own voice. 'Lila seemed to think it was *essential* I come.'

'Were your fathers friends?'

Unusually for him, he actually looked at me – if only to convey how cretinous he found my question.

'*Friends?* I see no reason why my father should have heard of Lila's.'

Vicky, I'd been told, had been a late child. An only son's only son. His father had died when Vicky was ten. Mr Rai had had two sisters, but they'd been sent off with dowries. Vicky's father had inherited everything.

Raj, who stood chained to some aunt or family friend, kept looking over at me in a way that could mean one of two things. Was he trying to say, Would you like me to rescue you? or, Could you please rescue me? I hadn't thought his face capable of such ambiguity. Eventually I declined his gaze and the next time I saw him, he was leading a troop of children on a treasure hunt.

I stayed standing with Vicky, but stopped talking. Kunal was being introduced to Jahnavi's mother. I thought of that cover letter I'd written Jahnavi, of how pleased I'd been with myself for that fictional account of a friendship between her grandfather and Mr Chawla. I saw no reason not to be pleased now. Even if Kunal said, 'My father and your father-in-law were dear friends', what would she say? She wouldn't deny it. You never want to risk revealing ignorance, and guests aren't allowed to be sceptical of their hosts. Polite society deserves respect.

Kunal was finished with Jahnavi's mother. Now that I knew what to look for, I could see clearly his old man's walk, stiff and over-deliberate. He walked as if his left leg were heavier than his right.

Ashwin was back. Given the options available at this party I'd have been happy to talk to him, but not with Vicky. I made an excuse, but this meant I needed somewhere to go to.

In an unpromising field I selected a pair of yummy mummies. Being neither, I could at least offer them a temporary rush of smugness. They would never guess how mutual the feeling was. That took up eleven or twelve minutes. Then I was identified by the father of a client who had 'heard such good things' about me. I offered to get his drink refilled, and mine.

He was telling me about his brother-in-law's plans to invest in Tanzanian farmland – 'Suicidal. But the bugger knows I'll be forced to bail him out when the shit hits the fan' – when he saw Jahnavi. She was laughing at a joke or story of Rohit's.

'Do you know that girl?'

'I don't think so, no,' I said.

'Sanjiv Bhalla's younger daughter.' I nodded. Whether or not he knew that I represented Sanjiv Bhalla, I'd look a twit for not recognising the name. 'He and I were in school together. Bloody hard time they've had with her. Sent her off to college in the US. She collapsed completely. Some trouble with a boy.'

If there had been trouble of that kind, I'd bet good money that it was with a girl.

'It's nice to see her here. She's looking better. You mind if I say my Hallo to her? Janu! I don't know if you remember me. I'm an old friend of your dad's.'

Kapil Uncle, she remembered. Good girl.

'And this is my friend Tara Saxena, one of Delhi's top young lawyers. You should really talk to her, beta. Have you ever considered law?'

God Almighty, how my Jahnavi rose to the occasion. Narad Muni wouldn't have been able to tell that she was acting. She looked blank, then polite, then friendly, all in perfect sync. I wasn't half as good.

Anyone could have seen the pride on my face, and the relief. But Kapil Uncle wasn't looking at me. 'Who was that boy you were talking to, Janu? He suddenly disappeared when he saw us.'

'He's a colleague, Uncle. I work with Kunal Chawla at his NGO, Adhimukta Bharat.'

'He's my brother.' I was too old to Uncle new people, unless they were the parents of friends. Where I could I avoided addressing them as anything.

'Your brother! You're joking! No? He ran away as soon as he saw you coming. As if you were a rakshasi! Ha-ha! Too good! So Janu, what's all this NGO? I never knew the Chawlas had an NGO.'

'It's new, Uncle. Kunal set it up two years ago. It's in the education space. Mainly to do with building patriotism among children.

You know how these days everyone is only focused on science, coding. We promote Indian history, culture, national pride.'

'My God! Imagine. Kunal's daddy only cared about two things: buying real estate and beating people at golf. I wonder where Kunal got all this. Hey Kunal!' For our host was twelve feet away. Standing still, one arm on a table by a glass of water, he looked intimidatingly healthy. Until, that is, answering Kapil Uncle's call, he moved towards us.

'Arre, Kunal, Atul Chawla's son running an NGO! What would your daddy think? As long as you are still bringing in more than you spend, ha? Ha-ha!'

'I don't know how well you knew Papa, Uncle, but in this, in everything, I am pursuing his dreams. Papa loved this country. He had everything taken away from him in Lahore and everything he built here he thanked India for.'

'I was just teasing, son. Your generation is so inspiring. Not like us.'

'Sorry,' I said. 'I didn't catch your name.'

'Jahnavi.'

'I once visited Kunal at his office. It's a shame we didn't get to meet then. Kunal, you employ at least one very impressive young woman. I hope we meet again. So nice to meet you, too.' I left them and within minutes I saw Jahnavi go in search of her mother, and then I saw the two of them saying their early goodbyes.

'Tara – what a wonderful surprise.'

Manoj Vaswani, MP. In his old life he'd looked like any other Golf Links businessman. Now, in politician khadi and with a held paternal smile, he looked like a father on his daughter's wedding day in one of those life insurance ads.

Where was Kunal? Right where I needed him to be. He heard what Mr Vaswani said, and he saw me hug him. Whether he could see how much Mr Vaswani would rather stay talking to me than yield to other claims, I can't say. In his old life Mr Vaswani would have stayed. In this one he had to yield.

So I had him to myself for three minutes, tops. Then I shared him, first with one person, then with a hovering set of grins. Then I went to the main hallway, where I knew there was a loo.

Outside the loo was a small sofa or wide loveseat, in pollution grey. I didn't remember it being there when I'd arrived. It must have been placed there to seat women as they waited for the loo.

At this time it seated my mother.

'Waiting for the toilet, Ma?'

'Ha.'

'How long have you been here? I saw Rohit, not you.'

My mother was not slim, but she was slim enough to make room on this loveseat. She ignored my question.

We sat together in a gruesome silence. Until the summit, my mother and I had shared silences as happily as she and Baba did, as happily as anyone. Even she and Rohit, to my knowledge, had never said all that much to each other. In a way this long habit of unspeech had allowed me to get through this year.

'Tell me, Ma. I'll do anything for this to end. Just tell me what I've done.'

She looked around for means of escape. She listened for signs from the toilet of impending release. But there was no gurgle or hiss or roar. Someone really was taking their own sweet time in there.

'Tell me, Ma. Please.'

For the first time since I'd sat down she looked straight at me. Directly she looked away. But one look had told me enough. For all I know it was the first and last time in her life she looked at anyone or anything with disgust.

Her little hands in her lap with her clutch bag, she said: 'All your life everyone says, "Tara is so clever, Tara is so smart, Tara knows everything, have you ever met a child like Tara?" And you took it to heart and you always agreed with it. And you told yourself, "Other girls may be prettier, but I'm smarter. And they'll get older and stop being pretty, I'll still be smart."'

Only later could I see the novelty of this, the sheer quantity of words emerging from my mother. But it wasn't as if a half-blocked pipe had finally been cleared; there was nothing joyful or uncontrolled in the flow. On the loveseat I just looked at her and held the look and with every pore in my cheeks and clenched hands I tried to project this: What you are saying, Ma, is the most important thing in the world, and believe me I know it.

'And now,' she continued, 'when it suits you, you decide to act like a fool who doesn't know anything?'

'Ma, whatever you think I know, I don't know. What you think I mean, I don't mean.'

A woman came up to us and said, 'Are you waiting? Both of you? Oho, I'll go find another one upstairs.' In the toilet the man – I was certain it was a man – had finally begun spraying his anus. No matter how soothing he found the spray, or how pedantic he might be about the washing and drying of his hands, my mother was stuck with me for at most three more minutes.

'Ma.'

'Who is the most important person in your life?'

'That's easy. Not one person but two. You and Baba.'

'No. Your *life*. Soon we'll be gone. Then what?'

'You want me to say Rohit. You misunderstand me, Ma. Just because Rohit and I are different, or because we're not close, doesn't mean what you might think. I don't just . . . "want the best for him" in the way people say it, while meaning nothing. I *really* want it. I think much better of him, of what he could be, than you can know.'

'You're lying. So much lying.'

'Why did you want me to say Rohit, and not you and Baba?'

'Who else will be there with you throughout your life? Who else will be there with him?' She meant *for*, she said *with*. 'When we go, only you two are left.'

'Ma, I'm not lying. You know I'm not lying.'

'Maybe you believe it, but it is lies. You only have Rohit, Rohit only has you. But there's a difference. Since birth everything has been easy for you. First in class, apple of Baba's eye, always confident. Every thing you want you get and you think, I deserved it.

206

I'm not saying you didn't. But what does "deserved" mean? It was all easy for you to get. That is deserved, and that is also luck. Has Rohit had any of your luck?'

'Ma, what Baba does with his property is none of my business. I've never asked a single rupee of him. *I have no expectations.* That's just what I think is right, and it's got nothing to do with Rohit. If Rohit needs anything, he will always be able to get it from me. If you have any doubts on that front, I'm telling you now. What's mine is his. What will be mine will be his.'

The man – no, it was a girl, somewhere between fourteen and seventeen – was coming out of the toilet. She must have been on her phone the whole time she sat on the pot. But Ma stayed put.

'You say all this because you think you're better than Rohit. "I need nothing, I expect nothing, only Rohit expects because he's a boy." Need and expect are two different things. And you have the cheek to say Rohit can always come to you to beg for money. Look how you were when he needed you!'

'Yo. Tara. Where the hell have you been? Can you come back out, right now?' Lila.

My mother rose. Before anyone could attempt an introduction she was opening the loo door. For a woman of her age, for a Delhi woman of any age, my mother could move.

'Did you,' I began to ask as I followed Lila, 'did you know who that was?'

'Malini Saxena.'

'You've met?'

'And I know I was clearly interrupting the long-delayed mother-daughter reckoning, but I had to. Look what's going on.'

We were about to be invited to eat. But for now the foil covers remained on the containers of food. An instruction was being passed like a baton, person to person, that before we could eat we were to shut up and pay attention.

'Kunal is about to give a speech.'

By instruction or collective wisdom, a presumed speaker's space had opened up in front of the chaat counter. It was clearly the optimal spot from which to address the whole garden. Word had reached the house, and those inside were stepping out. The waiters from the hotel continued with their work; the staff from the house itself were to listen to the speech.

The space had opened up, but Kunal hadn't taken it yet. He stood with Rohit, twirling a mike in one hand while going over a sheet of paper. Even in the fugged lamplight of a Delhi garden in late October I could see that the sheet was ruled and that it had been crudely torn out of a notebook.

My brother, the speechwriter.

In Sanam's garden, Deepti had said: 'Remember when . . .' and gone no further, and I'd thought nothing of it. Now I knew what she had held back from saying.

Remember when, Deepti might have said, you were in Bombay clerking for that judge, and Rohit took your room for two weeks while his was being painted? And when you got back you found all those loose sheets of paper in the bin. Twelve attempts at the first page of a novel. And you decided to call me and read *each one* out loud, and I mean loud, as if you were on stage, and every vocal effect was calibrated to one end alone: mockery. And you did all this with the door ajar, and you were so loud that you didn't hear him come home. Or hear him go into his room, which still smelled of distemper, and bawl until his throat was sore and he was all out of tears. And the next day and the next you called me and you wanted to laugh about it again; in fact you wanted to read them out again but someone had emptied the bin, which was odd because you didn't think the cleaner had come. It was only weeks or months later that I told you that he'd called me that night. At first I could barely hear him through the tear-stains. And I'd tried to comfort him, but even if I'd had the words, he was sixteen. An age where you can't receive comfort. Somehow, somehow, he never worked out whom you were on the phone with. I convinced him you must have been trying to impress a boy. He still doesn't know that you know that he heard you.

My brother, the speechwriter. Were they going over an actual prepared speech, or just a set of points? Either way, Kunal left the sheet with Rohit as he walked to his position.

'Friends, family, colleagues.' An unacceptable degree of disobedient chatter continued. Kunal went silent until it stopped. 'Friends, family, colleagues, well-wishers. I don't like to give speeches. Vaise toh I prefer not to talk if I can.' He smiled straight at Rohit, whose heart swelled up into something his ribs were not built to contain. 'But sometimes it's a question of duty. First, I want to say thank you for coming today. I know you've not come for my sake. You've come for two people. My mother, who is here, whom you all love so much. Happy early birthday, Mamma. And my Papa, who is not here.

'Some of the elders here are even elder to Papa. You knew him from the day he was born. You know how he was born with nothing. You know how he came from an old family, a big family of Faisalabad district. You know how everything was ripped away from them. I'm not just talking about land and money. His chacha and chachi, brutally murdered. Newly married. She was pregnant.

'I think about that boy in her womb who never got to be born. My uncle. I think about my father who was born with nothing. I was also born with nothing. But my father had to make everything for himself. I was born with nothing, but I was chosen by Papa. Everything was handed to me.

'So I just want to say ki I know who my papa was. What he achieved. I know what he chose me for. I know the value of what I've been given. The opportunity and the responsibility. I will not waste it. I just want to say one final thing.

'Papa cared about two things. His family and his country. For his family he had already done everything. With what was left of his life he was going to give back to the society, the country. But Bhagwan in his infinite wisdom snatched Papa early.

'Papa, you could have had a biological son. You could have gone to any orphanage in India. In my orphanage itself there were one hundred and seventy-seven boys. You said that when you saw me you knew immediately. As if in a past life we had been father and son. Papa, I will not let you down. Every day I will work to fulfil your dreams. To all of you here today, I want to say, if you want to work for the country, you know who to call. Happy Diwali. Now come and eat.'

Rohit had written some of this speech or all of it, but it was only Kunal's. It was Kunal's because he had *it*. He had whatever you call it that makes people actually stop and listen, putting away phones and drinks; that makes words themselves superfluous; that can alchemise the shoddiest knock-off emotion, the obvious manipulation, the most reckless perversion of fact, into solid rhetorical gold.

Among us that night only one person was immune. She stood next to me, and with every sentence you could see her body hum with rage.

Later, she would have chance after chance to calmly speak her rage. 'Every word he said was shit.' 'He can say whatever he likes, but he can't bring my father into it. My father whose DNA he'll be no closer to sharing by the time he drinks his way to the very bottom of that urn.' 'Everyone knew he was full of shit, but they put up with him out of politeness. Pity-politeness.' 'Mamma, I admit, is still deluded when it comes to him. He's convinced her that there was this whole side to Papa that only he knew because he was the Chosen One.'

As everyone watched Kunal, and as he said, 'Happy Diwali,' I grabbed her arm. 'I'm not going to let you do what you're about to do.'

'Fuck off, Tara. I'm sorry. I don't mean that.' And then she was off.

Before she knew it, she had a mike in her hands. Kunal had seen her approaching and far from offering what she expected, what she wanted – a conflict – he simply gave her the mike.

Lila, I projected with dismal futility, Lila, this is not the time. The time to have gone was first. Now people want their dinner. Lila, please make this quick.

'Hey guys,' she said, flashing her Manhattan-bought perfect teeth at us, teeth wasted in this light, this air. 'Well, well. How do you follow that?' The smile shifted to a sarcasm intended for me alone. Maybe also Vicky and Ashwin.

Lila hadn't gone up to 'say a few words' at a family function. She was playing for different stakes. She was there to show up Kunal; to put him in his place. Show him up to this assembled world of the Chawlas, to Mrs Chawla, most of all to himself. Now the smile was gone, and in its place stood something reassuringly or worryingly familiar. The firm self-possession of investor-Lila, mother-Lila, my friend-Lila. Winner-Lila.

'I want to talk about my father.' This was not going to be short. From three directions came the terribly audible groans of the men whose food stood delayed. They had loved Mr Chawla, or at least envied him, but they had heard enough about him for one evening.

'Not want, I *have* to talk about him. This is our first Diwali without him. Mamma's first birthday without him, in forty-one years.' The irrelevant number, thrown in because she was certain Kunal wouldn't know it.

'All of you loved Papa. But did you really know him? He kept a lot of himself hidden away. Typical of that generation.' And she looked in vain at Mr Vaswani, and at his contemporaries, for nods or smiles of grateful affirmation. 'Yet Papa was so far from being a typical man. Probably the best place to start' – to *start*? – 'is the place I know best. His approach to parenting. To daughters and sons.'

Ears can't be closed, at least not conspicuously. So I searched for other means. As if in a dentist's chair, I pressed down with the nails of my right hand onto the metacarpals of my left, until the back of my left hand was covered with masochistic diacriticals. I hummed a steady drone, inaudible to my neighbours. If I couldn't close my ears, I did everything I could do to scramble the reception.

Mostly it worked. What I heard of the rest of Lila's speech came only in words and clauses. Talent and gender are uncorrelated. Wharton. Pivoting after liberalisation. Balancing between risk and prudence. Joy and duty.

And then I slipped. I decided things might be going OK; that my strategies of drowning out might constitute disloyalty. And I heard Lila say: 'And so, after thirty years of my father guiding and advising me, I was now, although it seemed incredible to me, guiding and advising him.'

This burst the dam. For some time the food counters had stood ready. First two and then easily a dozen men walked past her and started filling their plates. Lila just kept talking, like an ineffectual air hostess who asks the passengers to please remain seated long after they've started retrieving their bags from the overhead lockers. Eventually the flow of men past her stopped. On the faces of those polite enough to stay, I saw the inattention that was palpable everywhere, like the particulate matter.

I looked for Lila's mother, and found a page on which there was no pride.

I remember thinking about Lila at work, about how many times she must have had to present to boards, investors, industry summits, Women in Leadership conferences. About how good she must be at it, and how traitorously false was the confidence all that had given her.

I remember looking around the garden for Raj. Would he, later, tell her that she'd given a brilliant speech?

I remember being grateful that Mr Chawla wasn't there.

And then, shamefully little, shamefully late, I saw Lila catch my eye and I tapped my left wrist where on other wrists you might find a watch. She looked furious, but relenting.

'I know I've kept you guys from dinner, I don't want to keep you longer. I just want to leave you with this . . .'

What 'this' was, we shall never know. The word 'dinner' acted on the remaining men, the children, even some of the women, like the releasing beep of the seatbelt sign. My beloved Lila faced those that stayed, and she shrugged. Not at her own failure, but at the inadequacy of the world. 'Never mind. Let's eat!'

In the days and years that followed – for the year of the summit really was prologue, and Lila and I would end up spending our lives in conversation – I never once referred, to Lila's face or behind her back, to the speech she gave that Diwali. I listened sympathetically to her rants about Kunal's speech. She never brought up her own.

I went home that night and in the sort of tired and emotional state in which, no doubt, Woj hoped I'd finally see my folly and beg to be taken back, I sent two emails, neither to Woj.

To my father:

Baba, what exactly happened in Ranthambore thirty-three years ago? What did you see or discover?

To Jahnavi:

Thanks so much for handling things like that today. You're a champ. Also – any idea what's up with Kunal's, I'm gonna say hip? He can barely walk.

14

An Exchange of Brahmastras

October became January. The smoke peaked in early November, then there were two merely 'very poor' weeks (average AQI between 300 and 400). There was the usual week in late November, a kind of pollution Indian summer, where you could even see the sun, fragile as a cup of Darjeeling. Most days that week the AQI was 'moderate', peaking below 200, only ten times higher than the WHO's limit for what constitutes air that is fit to live in. In that week we had picnics in Sunder Nursery and rooftop drinks and decades later couples would tell their children, We got married on the most beautiful day.

Lila missed it all. The week after Diwali she took her husband and son to Dubai, where Raj's parents still lived. In Delhi the choices were confining her son to his purified indoor prison, or watching him run around outside while mentally calculating how many of his cells were being poisoned per minute. Fifteen years from now, she said, imagine he shows up at Princeton and he's slower at everything than his American peers, all because I decided it was a good idea to bring him up in Chernobyl.

She stayed there two months. She said that it was important that Raj got to see his parents, and Kabir his other grandparents. I got the sense that being thought a good daughter-in-law mattered quite a bit to Lila. Sons-in-law never have to worry about being judged; they can lie back for a lifetime on the massage chair of adoration. In Delhi the very existence of a son-in-law is a blessed wonder. Here he is to be fed and feted. A good Delhi mother-in-law could make up for almost any wife. But being a daughter-in-law, even for Lila, meant a life spent on a different kind of chair – at a desk, writing a perpetual exam. Every day in Dubai was a chance to get another A+.

The Monday after the Chawla Diwali party I ordered an Adhimukta-style couch for my chambers. Even by my standards November and early December looked brutally, beneficently busy. I had always taken work home; increasingly, I started living at work. I began to take bottles of gin and whisky in to work, to be stashed one at a time behind my parakeet-green volumes of Constituent Assembly Debates.

What about my juniors? We'd always been known to drink together in the office, on celebratory days, but I hadn't been known to drink there alone. My juniors watched me the way dogs and children do their parents. They saw the bottles of club soda in the office mini fridge and they saw that they were used only at night, when everyone else had gone home.

After the party I'd called Jahnavi in and said she'd told me all I needed to know. She was released from spying, and free if she wanted to be a normal intern at Adhimukta. She spent another month there. In January she went back to college, and by all accounts thrived.

When the courts went into recess I could go, finally, to Italy.

Italy had become many things to me. Most of all it represented an imagined future, with none of the trappings of actuality. I had no wish to find the 'real Italy' – an Indian knows there is no real anywhere. In Italy, when I was ready, I would live just outside a medieval hill town, in an olive grove. I'd have a stone cottage next to my house which I'd rent out on Airbnb. One summer there'd be a Chilean geologist and his Greek architect wife; the next, a pair of Yemeni lesbians from Toronto. They'd ask me to plan their trip to India and six years later I'd receive a postcard from the Qutub Minar.

The Italian fortnights I'd actually lived usually involved a fling. I might meet him on a connecting flight from Doha, or a train northbound from Roma Termini, or in an Anglophone second-hand bookshop (there's at least one decent one in most Italian cities, full of paperback Chatwins and Mishimas). He was usually European, only once an Italian.

I may have given the impression that I'm not the kind of woman a man would go for on sight. In Delhi I was never that woman. But in Italy, judged by different standards, presumably awarded extra Orientalist points, I seemed to have my constituency. Not forever – custom might not stale, but age was certain to wither. But facially I looked younger than I was, and my advantage in that regard over European women would grow stronger. I had at least a decade left, maybe more.

The sex in a fling is rarely better than adequate. Mine were no different. But this didn't matter, because in a fling I never subjected sex to evaluative scrutiny. Sex in Italy was like everything in Italy – pure experience, unaccompanied by the footnotes of my running commentary.

The only time I didn't enjoy myself in Italy, I was with Wojciech. I'd made the mistake of telling him too much about past Italian flings, and he was there to keep a watch over his property. With him around, I couldn't even look. Monogamy in *thought* is an ideal that only a man could have come up with. No woman could have written, Thou shalt not covet thy neighbour's husband.

It was no accident that our relationship foundered within three months of that holiday.

This time I landed in Rome on Christmas Day, too late for mass with the Pope. I came out of the terminal into a scene of familiar crumminess. Italy, unlike Dubai, has the luxury of not having to work to seduce. In the taxi I watched Lazio reveal itself, its hills and tree-hidden villas and, at glorious last, its eternal city. I looked away only once, to text Woj Happy Christmas. Woj would always be Catholic. When someone expressed surprise at this, he'd say fiercely, I'm Polish.

That evening over my aperitivo we texted back and forth, sharing our plans for the last week of the year. I was going to Umbria, to hill towns evacuated of tourists. He was to go to Berlin, to see a friend who had just become a father. We both knew how much Woj still wanted children. **But you have no need to fret, I texted. You're a man. You have easily thirty years left for your sperm to fulfil itself.**

Three nights later, in Perugia, I drank in an American cocktail bar in a piazza to one side of the duomo. No tourists, but students from every continent, in Perugia to learn Italian at the University for Foreigners, and in this bar to speak English over four-euro negronis.

I found or was found by a pair of freckled twins from Kansas City, who had recently come down with Naipaulitis and were sincerely curious about my opinions on various Indian writers. There was a time, there might still be a time, when inquiries of this kind were opening moves. Not tonight – these boys were Jahnavi's age, and like her they inspired cautious optimism about what Rohit had called the human future.

At midnight I left them to girls their own age, and walked back to my hotel. I was about to wake the concierge, for my key.

'Tara.'

Wojciech Zielinski had not gone to Berlin. He had, with a new subtlety, extracted from me the details required to pull off this surprise (when I'd mentioned Perugia, for instance, he'd said 'I hope you're staying at the Hotel V——', and in my reply I'd named my actual hotel).

Nothing about the way I reacted to Woj that night can be put down to drink, or to pity, or the pity that calls itself generosity. I was *actually* surprised, which is a feeling whose sheer weirdness I can never quite handle. The kind of surprise I'm talking about here belongs properly to childhood, a place I never felt comfortable in. Woj being here was like an April Fool's joke. These things make me break out in self-consciousness, like hives.

He knew this, and was prepared.

'Sorry. I knew that if I told you I was coming you'd say over my dead body, and I didn't want to hear that.'

Was I happy to see him? I'd have to think in those terms first, and I didn't. But he was here, and he came upstairs. And then I really looked at Woj, as if at one of those old newspaper puzzles asking you to spot the difference between two images, and every square centimetre of him seemed unchanged. In that moment I saw before me something from a pre-summit life. A life where all was in equilibrium. A life that in this moment I felt certain I'd liked.

Some minutes later, we were largely unclothed. Woj's body was if, anything, even more perfect than I remembered. He was still more adept with mine than anyone else ever had been. He pushed the old buttons with the old matter-of-fact precision and the old results. Over time, in the usual way, I'd grown bored of his ways and later, in the usual way, remembered them with nostalgia.

He didn't put a foot wrong that night. I wish there was a way for me to make him *know* that. As much as Woj had strained to convince me that leaving him was a mistake, my mistake, the feeling truer to his nature was that he must have *done* something. He had to win me back because it could only be by some correctable failure that he'd lost me.

I can't say where his hands or tongue or penis were when it happened. It had nothing to do with any of them, with any of him. I know that I didn't pull away. I locked. I was on my back, my hands by my side, my panties at my knees, all of it locked. My breath was caught above my collarbone, half-in, half-out. Then it escaped, and I was panting for life.

Many years earlier, a friend had accused me of insensitivity to his troubles, and with reproving envy he'd said: You just can't understand, you're one of those people with perfect mental health.

'You OK? What's going on?'

Poor Woj. Convinced that whatever's going on is his *fault*, if not morally then at least tactically. Wondering what his fingers or tongue should have done, wondering whether he's got his syntax wrong, or his pacing.

I knew at least to slow and deepen my breathing. If I did that I could, if not be myself, then at least be something dignified, something unpathetic.

'It's just been a crazy month. I haven't been sleeping. And – this is so unexpected. Are we sure this is a good idea?'

'That "we" is awfully unfair, and you know it.'

'I just can't do this tonight, Woj.'

'Can we at least talk?'

I wish I could say that Woj and I had talked; that I had sat up in bed and, starting the month before the summit, told him all about my year, for Woj when he wanted to be was an extraordinary listener of the you're-the-centre-of-my-world kind, and in his own way he did really know me; that we'd had our cappuccini and cornetti the next morning and spent the day walking Perugia; that we'd parted in friendship that would sustain even when Woj truly moved on.

None of this happened. Instead, I got dressed and, using a skill honed over fifteen years in the law, willed myself to sleep. Woj didn't sleep. He waited for me to wake up and he took his leave with heart-breakingly false coldness. Shamed by what he could only see as defeat, he left Perugia and if he went to Rome or Warsaw or Berlin, I have no idea. I heard from him on average three years in every ten, on my birthday. I wished him on his, every year.

Lila and I both arrived back in Delhi the same morning, the first Sunday in January. We were only an hour away from catching each other at the airport.

If you left Delhi in early November and returned in the New Year, you'd learn the difference between apocalyptic and post-apocalyptic. Near Diwali the smoke was fresh. You had felt it come in on the wind; you followed its lashing progress down your throat and eyes and nostrils. In January it was stale, and it hung dully about the ground. Our city spent that month in a state of manmade solar eclipse. The smoke and the cold held on to each other for dear death.

Raj had come back a week earlier. Over lunch that Sunday he told Lila that the previous evening Kunal had called. They've sold the Mashobra house, he said.

'They? You mean our house?'

Mr Chawla, as befitting a man of his station, had followed the migratory pattern of a viceroy. Winter in Delhi, summer in the mountains of Himachal. By 1980, when he'd bought the house, Shimla was already on the way down. Mashobra was the thing.

Lila had spent two months there every summer until she turned sixteen. These days it was closer to two weeks, but Kabir went for longer. Last year he'd done the proper two months, with his grandfather. Life in Chernobyl was a fairer bargain if you could intersperse Mashobra between the acts.

Even as a boy Kunal had avoided the hills if he could. He'd never seen the point of leaving Delhi for a place where nothing lived, except in the biological sense. He hadn't been there in five years. Mrs Chawla tended to be mountain-sick. She'd suffered Mashobra for her husband's sake.

Lila had left the lunch table to call me. 'I'm going to fucking end him. His shitty NGO, his political ambitions, everything.'

'Lila, isn't it time you set aside your scruples about not involving your mother? I'm guessing she has no idea what's going on.'

'That's exactly what he wants me to do. Listen, T, it is time. For what we've been putting off. I'm going to set up the meeting and you're going to be there. We're fucking doing this.'

I didn't have to ask what 'this' was.

At six that evening the doorbell rang. The quietest hour of the week. Usually a doorbell ring at this time was a pizza delivery to the wrong flat. Was it Lila, come to more cathartically air her fury? Lila is more Delhi than me. She is capable of showing up unannounced.

It was my father.

In the twelve years since I'd left home, how many times had Baba visited me? Less than once a year. He hadn't needed to. It may be the one rule for living that I have not once violated: never subject anyone else to my cooking. With my previous flat and this, Ma had helped me move in. But once I was settled she didn't drop in either.

'I'm not disturbing you?'

'You know you're not, Baba. But what's happened to you?'

For the first time since Rohit came into the world, which was when my book of memory began – all else being snatched and half imagined – I looked at my father and he was changed. Magnificently slim had turned thin, and his shirt sagged longingly around the departed flesh. The fine knitted grey of his hair had gone cold, half-dead. Worst of all, half the light had gone out in his face.

Baba had never been handsome, but he had been perfect. He had taken his genetic inheritance and he hadn't worked on it like Woj, as some project of vanity or ambition; he had simply fulfilled it. In his slimness and his posture and, back when he'd had one, the moustache that was tended each day like a fairway.

When you looked at my father, if you knew to look, you would eventually see nothing but his eyes, those gas giants of omniscient calm, enveloping goodness. The eyes of truth.

Now my father sat at my dining table and his eyes looked ready for a long sleep. The longest sleep.

'Baba, you look like you've spent the last two months walking around Delhi as if trying to prove what breathing this air can do.'

'I have done too much of that. It's true.'

I went and stood by him, one hand on the back of his chair. I stood as close as I reasonably could and I did not let myself look away.

'I'm ready,' he said.

'You're ready to do what you've been preparing yourself for? Or ready to tell me about Ranthambore?'

'Please sit.'

'Baba, are you sure you're ready? You don't look it.'

'The more I delay, the worse it will get. The greater the chance I may fail to even try.'

'Baba, what happened at Ranthambore?'

When it came it was in the usual Baba way, the sentences formed and shaved, but at ten times the usual effort, or a hundred.

'The first day we saw nothing. Malini was devastated. I thought, It's not to be. Those were the early days of Project Tiger. We thought that in fifteen or twenty years there would be no tigers. They would only be in zoos, like Indus Valley sculptures in a museum. She didn't think she could ask me to take her a second time. That trip was her chance.

'The second morning was foggy. Our driver said, "Today the chances are bad. Even if the tiger is there we won't see it." For two hours there was nothing, barely even a bird. And then, right at the end of the ride, when we had given up, Malini trying not to cry, she emerged from the bushes. Right in front of our jeep.'

Up to this point, every detail was known – told to the four-year-old Tara, told again through my teens. The story had ended always in bathos, the ship of mimesis running aground.

'And what happened when you saw her?'

'At first I was just stunned by joy and relief. I hadn't been able to bear the thought of Malini's disappointment. And then I looked for myself. Malini was so giddy she could hardly look at all. And I was seized. I knew what, one day, I would have to do.

'I wanted to do it then and there. I wanted to jump out of the jeep, walk over to her – slowly, so as to not startle – and then I would offer myself. My body, which is all I can actually offer, and all that would be of use to her. She would take what she needed for herself and any cubs. And then the rest of me would be there for the jackals and vultures and, finally, the insects and the fungi.

'I am not telling this right. All that came later. I only saw her. It was her I had to offer myself to.

'I don't know how long it lasted. But I remember hearing Malini squealing, and the shutter of the camera. And she said, "I will never forget the gift you gave me." And I came home and for a long time I forgot. We can all think strange thoughts. But we have things to do. We go on feeding and clothing our children and saving for a rainy day. Of course I couldn't forget completely. Every few months I would remember. But I wouldn't think, Not yet, I would think, What a crazy feeling that was. After a certain point even our feelings are taught.

'And then I was sixty-four, and not even really thinking about retirement, until suddenly I remembered everything. And this time I couldn't forget.'

I was sitting with both hands on his knee, pressing down. 'But Baba, when we – when we had our summit, you said you'd found your way through reading. And through looking around you. You didn't say you'd known for decades.'

'I did find my way like that. Thirty-three years ago I learned *what* to do. I had to do all these other things to find out *why*.'

Again, the awareness of the questions I wouldn't ask. Baba, are you serious? Baba, have you lost your mind?

My father was always serious. As for the line that separated him from madness – it was as thin as graphene, and as strong. And easy to miss, if you didn't know.

'And Sister is helping you.'

'If – when I do it, it will all be thanks to her.'

'And why are you telling me any of this, Baba? You don't need my help.'

'In March I hoped to tell you all. Then I decided I would never tell. And would never have, had you not asked. Once you asked, I was powerless.'

In April and May, when all I had was the summit's worth of words about how my father now saw the world; in June and July, when I'd learnt to see as he did, so far as I could; in August, when I'd seen Bhagat Singh and Sister on his desk; in the months of smoke – even I, when I couldn't help it, when I couldn't find the shelter of work or drink, had looked up at the ceiling and asked what my father was going to do.

Now I knew, and I watched my body go limp, like an unfilled duvet. And I heard myself say: 'Just a minute, Baba.'

And I watched myself rush to my suitcase, which stood tall and unopened to the right of the front door. And amidst the books and toiletries and half-folded underwear and bottles of Montefalco

Sagrantino I found a long brown envelope and returned with it. 'I drafted this while I was in Italy.'

As he read my two-page document his eyes flicked thrillingly back, for the last time in his life, into accountant mode. He read contracts and balance sheets like a dog sniffing, for ganja or truffles.

'This is very well done. It is amazing how you've written it, beta.'

'You know it's not, Baba.'

'It is perfect. Everywhere there should be a blank for me to fill in, you have put one. Other than filling those in I don't have to change a word.'

'Even now, Baba, I'm going to assume that you can fill them in with access to nothing but the contents of your own head.'

Even now, he had a pen in his shirt pocket, and all the figures he'd ever need.

When he was done, he said: 'So this is your price.'

'This is my price.' For what, God only knew.

'You have mentioned two witnesses, but no names.'

'Two is all you need. For obvious reasons I shouldn't be one. I think you're best off with Vikram chacha and Manju chachi. She won't read it if he tells her not to. And if she does read it she won't see anything wrong. He'll read it, but that's fine.'

'He'll be very angry.'

'He won't. He's like me, Baba. With you we can't be angry. If you ask him to sign, he'll sign.'

Lila picked me up on her way back from the board meeting of a portfolio company, in Gurgaon.

'I know you haven't been to the Adhimukta office in its Adhimukta avatar. But I'm guessing the office itself belonged to your dad?'

'He bought it, but I don't think he ever used it much. It was just one of his typical deals. So much of what Papa did worked like that. Someone calls him and says, This property is going for a song, and so he picks it up.'

'That wasn't just him, though – wasn't that the way of doing business in those days? Everything based on hearsay, and huge returns to scale, because you have the capital to actually do the deal quickly?'

'What made Papa different was his judgment. What they call instinct, but it isn't instinct at all. He wasn't a trained investor, he didn't know how to read a P&L, much less make a model. But he never bought something because "Ravi says it's a sure thing". He might have heard about it from Ravi, but then he exercised his judgment.'

There are three or four days each January when the eclipse lifts. This was one. As we drove into Defence Colony market, with its Manhattan rents and Ghaziabad architecture, you could actually see the shadows of trees on concrete. The air was only stained by smoke.

In the car Lila rolled her window two-thirds down, and rested her elbow there.

'How are you going to show it to him?'

'We can watch it on my iPad, but I like the sound of this big TV you said he has.'

Kunal had been as easy about giving Lila an appointment as he'd been with the mike at the party. In the half-year since I'd last visited him, the stationer downstairs had gone out of business. I wondered if Kunal himself might have had a hand in that.

The stairwell had been repainted in diaper white. Along the way up you met framed photographs. They were all broadly speaking patriotic, but they started a bit UNESCO and progressively militarised. The Sun temple at Konark; the famous headless sculpture of the emperor Kanishka I, from the Mathura Museum; the Mangalyaan orbiter; Atal Bihari Vajpayee with APJ Abdul Kalam at the Pokhran nuclear tests; Lt Gen Jagjit Singh Aurora receiving the Pakistani surrender in Dhaka on 16 December 1971. Lila and I walked up in silence. She didn't notice the photos, not even in contempt.

There was a new receptionist who turned out to be, of all things, male. And unrobotic, and yielding. Chairman sir would see us at once. In fact, he was waiting for us. Would we take tea? Coffee? Juice?

The office was fuller than I remembered. Had the desktops always been Macs? The photo series continued inside.

Rohit was leaning over two young men, a coach's hand apiece on the right shoulder of one and the other's left, as they edited a video. He had his back to us, but turned at the sound.

'Don't worry,' said Lila. 'He's expecting us.'

'I never worry.' Under Kunal's umbrella, why would he?

Chairman sir had in fact been waiting. As we entered he made zero pretence of doing anything else. His computer was off. There was no phone in sight. Only the iced glass with a little left of the drink that looks like Scotch and tastes like sweet battery acid.

My eyes fell on the couch I'd been inspired to emulate. And then to two dumbbells and a kettlebell, in a corner.

'Tara,' he said, using my name for the first time I could recall, 'you can sit on the couch.' His sister's name he didn't use. His hand indicated for her the chair opposite him.

Lila had already been let down. The big TV was gone. On that wall were three photographs, not quite continuous with those outside. Three portraits. On the left, the late Mr Chawla. On the right, the man who a few days prior had been made India's first chief of defence staff. That one was signed. In the middle, the prime minister.

Lila saw me looking at them, and turned around, and then faced her brother again. 'What do you do when the AAP guys come and see you for this curriculum you're pitching them? Do you hide that photo? Substitute something more convenient?'

Her tone was excruciatingly jocular. The work she was putting into this act showed all across her face, like surgery scars.

'Kunal,' I said, 'we're here because you seem to have disregarded everything I said when I came to see you last.'

'Is that right? And did you regard what I said?'

'I said then that things didn't have to be this way. No one is against you. No one wants to stand in the way of your aspirations. But your sister is your *sister*. You're not obliged to love her. But you've made it clear you believe in family. Why not respect her stake in your family?'

'You think she,' and he pointed at her, 'respects my stake? Does she regard me as her brother?'

'Who lives in your family home, with your mother? Who is managing director of all your father's companies? At your father's funeral, at your first big party, you wanted to show you were head of the family. Did she ever come in your way?'

It was never going to take Lila long to lose patience with me. I don't know why I bothered.

'If this didn't work last time, T, this approach of yours, why do you think it'll work this time?'

Still I persisted. 'Tell me, Kunal. How did you get through your class 12 exams? And college? Did you take your sister's help? How much did she help you?'

For the first time he addressed her. 'Is there a point to this?'

'We're here,' said Lila, 'because you've gone and fucking sold the house I grew up in. The house my son was going to grow up in. And like the pathetic, disgusting coward you've always been, who used to sit on smaller kids in the playground and run away when the teacher came, you did it behind my back.'

'That house belonged to my mother. Selling or keeping it is her business.'

'We're here because this ends now, or I really do start standing in your way. And we both know exactly how ready you are to handle that.'

Kunal looked at me as if to say, Handle her, please. And when I showed no signs of doing so, he opened his desk drawer and withdrew a cell phone, non-smart. Was this really the only phone he owned? At any rate, it had been switched off, and we were involuntarily transported to a time, implausibly recent, when all our phones looked like TV remotes and many of them sang

227

themselves awake, like Japanese baby toys. Once the music stopped he copied a number out onto his notepad, tore the sheet off and gave it to Lila. 'Here is the buyer's number. If you want to buy it for yourself, feel free to call him. It's the best location in Mashobra, he says he expects the value to double in five years. But I'm sure you can find some price that is acceptable to him.'

Lila held the sheet between two fingers and for a moment she looked rattled. But then she brightened. In the manner of a woman who is holding a Brahmastra. 'By the way, you never answered my question. What *do* you do about that photo when it becomes inconvenient?'

'It's better for you not to talk when you don't know anything. I am not your husband to sit here and take it quietly.'

Lila let the sheet of paper drop to the floor, and pulled her iPad out of her bag. 'Fine. Let me spell this out for you. Given how long these things usually take, I'm pretty confident you haven't closed the deal yet in Mashobra. *You* call the buyer – don't give me that look, he doesn't even know who Mamma is – and say it's off. I don't think you have a choice here.'

'I have already said to you, it's my mother's house. And she has sold it. Aren't you supposed to be the smart one?'

All feelings, my father had said, are taught. To live in Delhi was to know the full range of siblingly feeling. Under our conditions, in our air, with our property values, the love of a brother was retractable, like a roof. Still, they shocked me; not with any human feelings, but with their absence.

The record showed that Lila and Kunal had never been deprived of love, except by each other.

She turned her iPad on. 'You should know that Tara really didn't, doesn't, want me to do this. And she'd be right, but she doesn't know you. Here you go.'

And Kunal watched himself drink his filial ash-smoothie, and when the video was done he poured the rest of the Red Bull into his glass.

'OK. What's your point?'

'My point is this. Your nightly smoothie habit obviously has its psychological compulsions. Call it deep-seated insecurity about being adopted, inadequacy when you compare yourself to Papa, inadequacy when you compare yourself to me. Whatever. Your psyche is your business. But what you're doing there is a whole other thing. It's literally a crime on multiple counts, as Tara has confirmed – and don't worry, any lawyer will agree. Of course, no one's going to come after you criminally. But what will they think? Quite a few of them are going to think you're a cannibal. The rest are at minimum going to think you're a fucking psycho. *Even* if you are, though, you seem pretty aware of the costs of being exposed as one. You know what would happen if either of the political parties you have your eye on saw it. You know what would happen if Mamma saw it.'

Somewhere between my last visit to this office and now, Kunal had made some lethal acquisitions. He had learned to listen, or at least to stay quiet. The anger, once so easily triggered, so help-lessly palpable, was controlled or hidden.

He picked up the receiver of his landline and pressed a key. 'Send Rohit in? Ask him to bring me the Abdul Kalam file.' The behaviour of a Chairman sir, in predigital times.

Rohit came in with a long thing in black leather.

'Thanks buddy.' Dismissed.

From the file Kunal took out two sets of photos, and gave one set, face down, to Lila. I could have made this man who could barely walk get up, but I didn't. I went up to the desk and collected the other set. By the time I sat back down, Lila was crying. 'What have you done, Kunal?'

'What has she done. See for yourself.'

I turned over the first one. Lovers on a garden swing, a swing loveseat, in a garden I recognised, their throats and tongues engaged in what in California they now call deep work. To coin a Hindi phrase – jeebh sammelan. Tongues in joint exercises, like navies. On the whole she was the initiating power. Her right hand pulled at his hair.

The garden was Vicky Rai's, and so was one tongue. The other was Lila's.

One photo was enough for me. Lila saw them all. How had they been taken? It took me a little while to see that they'd been taken by a drone. My own means of espionage had been positively quaint by comparison.

Lila was not done crying, but she was about to speak. 'You unbelievable bastard. You bastard.' I was standing next to her, my hand on her left shoulder. 'This', and now the tears had stopped and only their deposit could be heard in her voice, 'is way below what I'd in a million years think even you could stoop to.'

'Listen, Kunal, you've got this wrong. The two situations aren't remotely symmetrical. If you plan on showing this to Raj, then you'll find out exactly how not symmetrical.'

I said it, and in a sense it was all true; but my heart wasn't in it.

Lila, I thought, if you had to go for Vicky of all people, I hope you did it for his looks, not his money.

Lila, for months I wondered and finally I'm sure – when you sent me to Vicky's you had no idea what he needed a lawyer for. I hope you never find out.

Lila, now I know, God, how slow I am sometimes, I know why you wanted to set me up with Ashwin. Lila and Vicky, a vertex of wealth and glamour fit not for life, but for some magazine ad for the Amalfi coast – that was how they must see themselves. Why not complete the picture by setting up the sidekicks?

It wasn't that I'd thought Lila was too good for any of this. No one is too good for anything. But the best of Lila turned out to be so, so far from the rest of her. The different parts of us struggle and the question is only and always which parts will win. The best of Lila was worth fighting for, waiting for, through anything.

I'd asked the question, but Kunal's reply was for Lila. 'Raj? I showed him months ago. Remember he suddenly had to fly back from Dubai for a day, right after you got there? The week after our party. You were shameless enough to call this man to your brother's home, your mother's home? In front of your husband?

Her husband is useless, I knew he wouldn't do anything, but still, I owed it to him. Can you imagine, he just sat there quietly, went back to Dubai and stayed quiet? The person I haven't shown it to is Mamma. And Kabir, of course, but he's too young.'

Eighteen months later, at the height of the pandemic, Lila would be the subject of a 3,000-word *Bloomberg* profile. Her fund's returns would lead the firm, globally. But the profile would focus on something else – her Covid relief work. Tapping all her networks – business school, private equity, Golf Club – she would finance and organise the import and distribution of seventy thousand oxygen concentrators. One picture caption would describe her as having saved more lives than Oskar Schindler. The profile would mention, in passing, that she had a five-year-old child, and another on the way.

In Kunal's office she had lost her capacity for speech. But we all knew she was never going to sign any instrument of surrender, not now, not ever. Kunal vs Lila was going to keep playing out, until death did them part.

Some days later I heard from Jahnavi. She was settling back in. She had more friends than she'd remembered having. She was shopping for courses. Which sounded better to me: *Political Thought of the American Founding* or *Chick-Lit: Austen to Rooney?*

I'm so sorry I never got back to you about Kunal. He has a degenerative hip condition. By the time he's 45, he'll be in a wheelchair.

15
The Offering

Vikram chacha wanted to meet, and we both knew why. I said I would show him around Sunder Nursery. He could see where the cool kids hung out. He'd love the sight of all those consular women in their floor-length linen skirts.

It was February. For six weeks, until Holi, Delhi would approach non-Delhi standards of liveability. There were exactly two Sundays a year where you could take a book to Humayun's Tomb, going early enough to secure the right bench, and feel that this life was unimprovable. In Italy, of course, you could feel that way every Sunday.

I took Vikram chacha past each stall, bought him his first flat white, pretended not to have expected that as soon as we left the market, the words 'flat white' would inspire him to a tit joke. We went in the direction of couples' corner. Unlike in Lodhi Gardens, you weren't yet liable in Sunder Nursery to hear human rutting and rustling in the bushes. But in one section of the garden each bench was private, separated from the next by a copse. On any Sunday you could go there to listen to proposals, break-ups, and stay-with-me-baby pleas. I know your mother thinks I have no prospects, but just wait, have faith, just watch where I am in two years.

A private bench would suit us, too.

'Will you bring chachi here? Or just the granddaughters?'

'Ha! You know which. Manju hates exercise.'

My uncle was chuffed with his morning. When had we last been alone together? It had to be at least twenty-five years.

Soon we'd be the only people left on earth who had truly loved, truly understood, Brahm Saxena. What would we do about it? If

I ever wanted to learn more about my father, here was where I could come. But would I ever want to?

'Chacha, you want to talk about the will.'

'Yes, beta. I am very angry with you. I don't understand. Why do you want to do this?'

'I don't think "want" is the right word, chacha.'

'But why are you going against everything Brahm has done, everything he stands for?'

'Am I? I never expected anything from Baba. Anything from his will, I mean. He gave me what he wasn't given himself, what he had to fight to give you, and give us. Education. A platform.'

'Arre, don't do this lawyer nonsense. You think what you've done is consistent with what Brahm wants?'

'If he didn't agree, he wouldn't have signed.'

'Listen, I know everything. I know what all has happened in your family. Last year he told you kids that you couldn't expect him to leave you anything.'

'He could change his mind. He never said, "I won't leave you anything." He said, have no expectations. There's a huge difference.'

'Just tell me why. Why you have to do it like this.'

'If you know everything, chacha – no, no, I'm not trying to duck your question, hear me out. If you know everything, you know what Baba is going to do. So you know that, whatever he said a year ago, he didn't end up selling any of his properties. Or cashing out any of the investments. And as wisely as Baba has invested, you know that ultimately he decided that what he wanted to offer the world was not money. Offer the universe, might be a better word.'

'Offer God.'

'Offer God.'

I'd had three days to game out this conversation. But in that time all I'd ended up knowing was what I'd started out with: what I would not say.

I would not say, Chacha, I'm doing it this way because I would prefer to lose to my brother than to lose him. Deepti might say I'd

233

never had him. I'd rather still have the chance. I watched Lila and Kunal and I thought, anything, anything but this.

'Answer my question.'

'Chacha.' Four false starts. 'Chacha, two things. First, Rohit had expectations. And why shouldn't he? Baba sold a flat to pay for his foreign degrees. Implicitly Baba was saying, All this is yours. Baba didn't send me abroad, did he? How is it fair to tell him now, after all these years, Sorry? And, please don't take this the wrong way, I mean it in the most practical sense. Rohit thinks he needs the money. I don't think I need it.'

'Then why take anything at all?'

All this could be a little different a month or year from now. But at the time of signing, my father's will, at current market prices, gave seventy-three per cent of his assets to Rohit and fourteen per cent to my mother (who, additionally, had the lifetime right to stay on in our home). The remaining thirteen per cent, i.e. the second least valuable of the remaining flats, in Vasant Kunj, went to me.

'Chacha.' I had no answer to his question. But did he even want this question answered?

'Beta?'

And then it came to me. Not an answer, but a thought, one that might or might not be the truth – without my father, there might never again be such a thing as the known truth – but that had seized me. And next to me was the only other person on earth with whom I could possibly share it.

'Chacha, you and I have two really important things in common.'

'We drink too much and think others don't notice. That's one. What's the other thing?'

'One, we're the only people who have ever come close to knowing Baba. To valuing him. Two, if we have a religion, and I know that unlike me, chacha, you believe in God, but if we have a true religion, it is rooted in him. And because we know him, we know that we aren't him. Chacha, have you heard of someone called Mahadev Govind Ranade?'

Thirty feet from us, under a gulmohar tree, a nervous young woman was trying to dissuade her dalmatian from an unsuitable friendship with a stray. Within eyeshot three games of badminton were in swing. The secret of Sunder Nursery was long out.

'I have not.'

'He's a kind of hero of mine, but you couldn't find someone more obviously different from Baba. He was a hero to many people, in his lifetime. A public hero. A judge of the Bombay High Court – what we'd give to have him as a judge now – and someone who dedicated his life to improving India. His great causes were ending child marriage, and ending the inhuman societal ban on widow remarriage. This is all barely a century ago. Chacha, are you listening to me? Ranade's first wife died. His followers expected him to be true to his beliefs. They expected him to marry a widow. Do you know what he did?'

'I'm listening, in the hope that there is a point to all this.'

'His father had chosen the first wife. Now his father said, You are my son, you will marry whom I choose. If you don't, you are no longer my son. And Ranade knew he was telling the truth. And he couldn't lose his father. So he betrayed his followers. He didn't just not marry a widow. He married a child.'

'Betrayed his followers, or his principles?'

'But that's the point, chacha. Do we live for principles, or for people? You and I are not Baba. We don't always know what's right. And even if we did, we wouldn't have it in us to follow it all the way. Only so far. And Baba knows this. I wrote that will and you signed it, and not only did he let it happen, not once did he even say, Are you sure? Because, chacha, for what principle could I lose my mother?'

'Now tell me. What if one day you are in financial trouble. You have given him most of your share. Will you go to him for help?'

Never in a million years.

'It won't come to that.'

*

235

A year to the weekend after the summit, my father came to my office. It was a Friday on which we had contrived to have no hearings. We sent out for lunch from the famous local purveyor of chhole bhature. My father didn't interest my juniors. There was nothing superficially interesting about him. There never had been. Later, when each had cause to reflect on the historical weight of their having *met* this man, the need for something to say to parents and siblings and boyfriends and, in good time, grandchildren, they mined the memory of that lunch for material with which to build their fiction. It's not enough to say, I had lunch with Brahm Saxena: you were expected to have some answer to, But what was he like?

Only the youngest junior, Shambhavi, showed any power of observation rather than invention. 'Your father,' she said, 'kept asking us questions about our lives and work, and he actually listened to the answers. I'd never before met an old man in Delhi who could actually listen to someone young. Old women, sure. But old men only talk.'

From the office we drove to the airport.

'You told Ma?'

'I said we were going to MP for the weekend. I didn't say anything more.'

'And she didn't ask.'

We were flying to Jabalpur, well known to me as the home of the Madhya Pradesh High Court. We wouldn't enter the city itself: from Jabalpur airport we'd drive two hours to Manda, where we'd arrive in time for a late dinner.

The next morning, and again in the evening, my father would try to do as he'd done for my mother, and show me a tiger.

Show me a tiger, not offer himself to one? Baba had said, 'I want to show you a tiger.' That was all, unaccompanied by any warning or request. If there was another purpose to this trip, I thought it had to be preparatory.

Jabalpur had an airport, because anywhere planes landed was now an airport, with a one-room schoolhouse of a terminal.

'Do you feel like you're going back to your childhood, Baba?'

236

'In what way?'

'Don't you think this aerodrome, airfield, whatever you want to call it, is a bit of 1960s India, left behind by history?'

'My childhood was not yours. I didn't know there was such a thing as an airport.'

I'd checked in a small suitcase packed with files and bottles. Baba had only an old valise. At the baggage belt we fell silent, until I tapped him on the wrist. Seven feet away from us stood an abandoned trolley. Someone had left behind a bottle of water and a Hindi magazine. *Kayastha Samachar.*

'I thought our caste was too small to have its own magazine.'

'Apparently not.'

'Baba, if – when – you do what you're going to, will they put you on the cover? Will they treat you as a hero, or someone never to be mentioned?'

'It will be funnier if they put me on the cover.'

'Funnier?'

'If they make me a community hero. I'm as Kayasth as that trolley over there.'

'You mean because caste is made-up rubbish?'

'I made myself a Kayasth when I was twenty-two. Asthanaji suggested it. My mentor. He said, After all you have no parents, you're cut off from your family. It's just you and your brother. You're starting from nothing in Delhi. No history, no baggage. Your family starts with you. I can help you do this. Your children will benefit for generations to come.'

'Does Ma know any of this?' Of course she didn't. Only Vikram, and now me. But I didn't actually want to let Baba answer, and so I went on as if I hadn't asked. 'But Baba, do you think Mr Asthana was right? No one looks at Rohit or me and thinks, "Kayasth". Or even "upper caste". No one we know thinks in those terms. Of course that's privilege itself in action. But if we had a different surname, would it matter?'

'Asthanaji was working in the old system. In most places that is still the system. But it's true, you grew up in a different system.

The castes changed. Money became a caste. English-speaking became a caste.'

'And you achieved both. You gave us both. And they counted for much more than the surname.'

'People with English and little money resent those with money and little English, and the other way round. With both you are unassailable.'

Before Baba proposed this trip, I hadn't heard of Manda. Neither had Lila. Brandwise, it was not one of the great tiger reserves. When you said 'tiger', no one said 'Manda', in the way they did Ranthambore, Corbett, Kanha, Bandhavgarh. Baba had chosen it, he said, precisely for this reason. Its ratio of likely tigers seen to likely tourists seen was unbeatable.

We were staying at a resort that had opened only the previous year, run by a Tasmanian naturalist and her Indian husband. They grew all their own vegetables, and were leading a project to clean the local river. The naturalist, Janine, was waiting for us when we arrived. A woman of appropriate sturdiness.

She greeted Baba with what seemed more like personal reverence than generalised hospitality. She regretted that she wouldn't be able to drive us herself the next day. She was leaving for Australia in the morning.

Baba, I didn't ask, Do you know her from before? Does she know Sister?

She sat with us for a while at dinner, telling us about the history of the area. I asked a series of follow-up questions, each more desultory than the last. Baba didn't speak. He didn't look at Janine, or at me. His irises were trained somewhere above my right shoulder. His mouth kept chewing. But Brahm Saxena was elsewhere.

After Janine left, I said, 'Shall we?'

We were staying in neighbouring tents. Baba's was first. By the door I held his hand. 'I'll see you in the morning?'

He didn't let go. Eventually, I withdrew. Later I'd search, fruitlessly, hellishly, for whatever his final words that day had been. When I left him at his tent, he hadn't spoken for an hour.

238

In my tent I got down to work and gin, in that order, and then combined. I fell asleep somewhere between three and four. At 5.15 my alarm went off. One final slug of gin – a tiny one – and a few waves of the toothbrush before I went outside.

The others were already in the veranda where we'd been asked to assemble. The ranger, whom we'd missed at dinner, turned out to be, of all things, a woman. A Tamil Christian, she would tell us, from Bangalore. With eyes of swift alertness – tiger-spotting eyes – and the morning person's energetic calm. Unlike Janine, she gave no sign of knowing my father.

He sat undisturbed in a corner of the veranda, and although he took my hand when I offered it, he didn't speak.

The other couple, whom we'd seen but not met at dinner, were married dentists, from Pune. My father was dressed for the office, I, for Sunder Nursery, while these two had got themselves ready for a *National Geographic* audition, in matching hats and jackets. Both glowered with the same restlessness. Anyone could read it – not excitement at the prospect of seeing a tiger, but pre-emptive bitterness at the prospect of not seeing one. For now this bitterness was directed at me, for having held them up.

We set off in the direction of the park. The dentists took the back row of the jeep, and began to unload their binoculars and speciality lenses. My father and I were in the middle row, the ranger up front. We left the highway behind for a dirt road, and then slowed to let a jackal cross. A good omen, said the ranger.

'I've had enough of omens,' said he-dentist. His wife kept nodding. 'We've been to seven tiger reserves. Ranthambore and everything. Not one sighting. We don't want omens. We want tigers.'

'No one knows better than you, then, how difficult and precious a sighting is. You know I can't promise anything, but the last few days—'

'I know, I know, there have been so many sightings, blah blah blah. Here are fresh pug-marks from last night. We have heard it all before, OK? We are sick of it.'

We entered the reserve by sunrise. We crossed a stream, and turned right, and found ourselves in *The Jungle Book*. We watched the birds sing the sal trees awake, one by one. I asked the ranger, 'Does it feel like this every time, or does it get old?'

'How can this get old?' This was worth putting up with the dentists.

Another jackal. Schools and colleges of young spotted deer. 'Next time,' said the ranger, 'come at mating season.' Night-coloured nilgai, and sambar and barking deer. The twelve-horned barasingha.

Briefly we left the forest and entered open grassland, and something low shot past. 'A rarer sight than a tiger,' said the ranger. 'A hare. The first we've seen in months. You're a lucky bunch.'

But the dentists did not feel lucky. Whenever she slowed or stopped to point something out to us, I watched them wince.

'Our time is limited,' he said. 'Park rules say we have to leave by ten. Can you just drive, please?'

More forest, and then we came to the big river. 'Here,' said the ranger, 'if you like, we can turn left, and there are the ruins of a seventh-century temple. It's a very special place. The deity is carved into the hillside.'

The dentists groaned, and spoke together. 'Can we focus on the tigers, please?'

We drove on, but the tigers did not come. The jeep radio was silent – other jeeps had been equally unlucky, or did not want to share their spoils. 9, 9.15 – it was almost time to make for the exit. The dentists had no energy left even for sullenness.

I could not help myself. 'You know, there's an old superstition,' I said. 'She didn't say this when she offered to take us, but people say that if you go and see the temple, you will see a tiger. That's the power of the deity. I don't believe in that stuff myself, obviously. And as people of science you must—'

He-dentist leaned forward, so that his head floated devilishly between mine and Baba's, and his voice was a gasp. 'Is there time for us to turn back? There must be time!' There was no time. He was ready to grab the wheel himself. He would risk anything.

What have they told every hunter after tigers, whether they go armed with rifles or DSLRs, since the beginning of time? Do not scream. She-dentist screamed, and the tiger cared nothing. The ranger, who had seen all this before, had been the first to see her, had slowed and stopped and turned off the engine while he-dentist was still demanding the temple.

'Don't stand up,' said the ranger. 'And keep those cameras quiet. There'll be time for photos. First watch her.'

Thirty feet ahead of us, the tigress raised her tail and sprayed one tree, then the next, then the next. 'Her cubs are nearby. They're nearly a year old. A very healthy litter. She's a champ, this one. Had to fight off her mother for this prime territory.'

Now the champ turned, to face us.

'She's going to walk this way. Just stay still, and relax. Cameras down.' At best it was said in hope. This was the moment the zoom lenses had been procured for. The dentists gurgled with joy. This was what my father had said he wanted me to see; but I hadn't looked, yet, not truly. First I looked at him.

My father's spirit had returned from whatever strength-gathering journey it had made last night. His eyes shone again. They looked at her. And we watched her pad towards us, sure-footed and slow. The dentists never saw her, except through their lenses, but those lenses, let's face it, captured pretty much everything tangible about her, really did make you feel like you were there. What they couldn't capture was the dentists' struggle: the seven fruitless trips before this one, the pain and desperation that, the very moment before they saw her, had been about to overwhelm them. They captured her eyes, in high-definition close-up, but not what she was looking at. For she had stopped, she who had seen off her own mother: eight feet ahead of the jeep, just to the right. And her eyes met my father's.

'Wow,' said the ranger, as the tigress walked back into the forest. 'The best kind of sighting, a gift.' She said it for the dentists, but then she raised her eyebrows, for my benefit alone.

We made it out of the park within a minute of the deadline. Back at the resort a late breakfast awaited us. I went to the bathroom and when I returned, I was told that my father had chosen to go to his tent.

'You'd better have a nap,' said the ranger. 'Before the next drive. Although I know this one will be hard to top. We leave at four o'clock.'

I was woken by the banging of fists and palms, and cries of 'Madam!' It took longer than it should have for me to register that they banged for me. When I let the poor fellows in – two young men, both from Kerala, who worked at the resort – they couldn't speak.

'What's happened?'

'Madam,' said one.

'Is everything OK?'

'Madam,' said the other.

And then my eyes caught my phone, on silent but ringing. Deepti. Missed calls from Lila, my clerk, from every friend I'd ever had.

In the years to come the young men at the resort would tell their friends, their wives, We came to tell her what had happened and she didn't even pretend to seem surprised.

There are sixteen billion videos on YouTube, and only sixteen that have been viewed more than the only one to ever feature my father. All sixteen are songs, many Korean, a few nursery rhymes.

The Sister network arranged for it to be livestreamed. Manda was chosen because, almost alone among national parks, there was excellent data connectivity throughout.

The title was designed to evade algorithmic censorship.

BRAHM SAXENA OFFERS HIS BODY TO THE TIGER

Once it went viral, YouTube wasn't going to take it down unless legally compelled – unless, for instance, the family requested. I did not request it. Neither did Rohit.

Rohit didn't exactly recant his earlier position on human thrival – one year later he was back with a new video series, pushing crypto – but he didn't, on balance, mind the fact that the whole world had suddenly heard of his father. When the TV channels came calling, that day and the next few, and then once or twice a year, Rohit answered.

What I don't know is whether Rohit ever watched the video. I'm going to bet no. But since I never have myself, I'm going to briefly hand over the narrative to someone who did. Lila knows I won't be reading what she has to say.

Tara asked me to describe the video. She admits it's a pretty redundant exercise – describing something the whole world has seen – but she says her story won't be complete without it.

The video begins with Tara's dad setting up the camera. When it's ready he steps back. And you can see the cubs in the background, three of them, maybe thirty feet behind him, at the edge of the water. And he starts talking.

'My name is Brahm Saxena. I am nobody. You might think, he's a human being, he's a man. I'm seventy-one years old. I used to be an accountant. All those things are true. But they don't matter. I am here today because, like you, I had forgotten what matters. I have spent my life forgetting, ignoring. Maybe wasted it.

But even if I wasted all this time. It is not too late to do what I must. For thirty-four years I delayed it, despite knowing.'

[The cubs, by the way, are half-asleep. They ignore him completely. They're also ridiculously cute. You can see why Americans like to keep them as pets, thinking they're just big cat-dogs.]

'I am not a man of power, or talent. But I have something to offer: this body. Behind me are three tiger cubs. Their mother is nearby. And so, thirty-four years late, but hopefully not too late, I am going to offer my body to them. You may say it is only a gesture. You may say, Who is he to make a gesture on behalf of our species. I am not doing it on your behalf. I am doing it only on

243

my own. No one has asked me to do this. But I know [and he looks behind him for the first time], I know that if you keep living the way you live – the way I have lived for seventy years – if you keep believing that humans are above all other life – I know what awaits you.

That is all. Now I will make my offering.'

[He doesn't say this at any point, but what the world media dubbed 'the Sister Network' – although no Sister has ever been proven to actually exist – anyway, they added a bunch of links below the video, trying to situate what he did in a broader context of atonement by humans as a species.]

He takes a knife out of his pocket. And he raises his shirt, and he slashes his left side in one quick cut. Not a deep cut, but one designed to maximise bleeding. We see enough of his side to know that there's not a gram of fat on him. He's all bone – if the tigers had their pick of which human was to be offered on behalf of our race, he would be some way down the list.

As he walks towards the cubs, the tigress appears. And snarls at him. And he reaches into his pocket again, and pops a pill. And he faces her, and namaskaars, and then he drops to the ground.

The video goes on. I know that the cubs start licking the blood. They do take a few bites. But the tigers leave him basically untouched. He's eaten later, by other creatures.

But the last thing I've seen is him falling. Beyond that – I haven't told Tara – beyond that even I can't go.

Janine was on a flight from Jabalpur to Delhi while my father was offering himself. But it was only when she landed in Hobart that she was met by TV cameras. She pleaded ignorance, and horror, and no one could ever prove she was lying.

My father had entered the park at noon, when it was closed to tourists. He had a special pass issued for zoological research. After dropping him off, the ranger drove to Jabalpur, from where she flew first to Mumbai, then to Sydney, before landing to a hero's reception in the Hazzard Islands, a Melanesian microstate that was at grave risk of becoming a Pacific Atlantis.

When Baba's will was read, it never occurred to Rohit that I might have written it. The will did not bring us close; such things are not in the power of legal documents. But still – not at once, but within months – Rohit found himself, for the first time in the annals of our family, at ease in my presence and with my existence. When he was blessed or cursed with a daughter, and I arrived bearing my weight in books, he was heard to say to the uncomprehending newborn: 'You're going to read ALL of these, so you can be as smart as Tara bua.'

My mother said nothing, but let me know that she knew.

In the first days after the offering, much of the debate, particularly in the Western press, concerned how to describe my father. He wasn't an 'eco-terrorist', clearly. 'Eco-warrior?' Not exactly. Suicide? That depended on what the pill he'd taken was. Some young conservationists complained that my father had chosen the wrong animal to feed himself to. Tigers, like pandas, carried the undue privilege of charisma. They already received too much funding, too much attention.

Postcolonial academics wrote essays opposing the Sister Network to 'global north' environmental movements. But my father appeared to be the only person known to possess a photo of Sister. When I went into his study, Bhagat Singh was still there on his desk, but Sister and her brother were gone. Journalists and governments were less interested in the movement's beliefs and activities than in the question of whether there really was a Sister. The movement must have a leader, but could it really be a girl in a yurt?

I never spoke to the press, but I did issue one written statement, which I sent to every journalist who got in touch.

I have seen it said, all over the world, that my father was crazy. Which is crazier – my father offering himself to the tigress and her cubs, or the fact that hundreds of millions of

245

Indians breathe the air that they do? What is your definition of crazy?

In Manda, an adivasi community that lived on the fringes of the reserve built a shrine to Baba. What he had done was beyond mere human comprehension. Whatever else he was, clearly he was holy. The state forest department, the park authorities, didn't linger on the matter of their rogue ranger. Thanks to my father, Manda vaulted straight to the top of the list of tiger reserves. From Seattle to Osaka, the tourists streamed in.

The dentists did not, however, yield to the temptation to upload their videos to YouTube – or sell them to Discovery – as the highest-quality footage of the tigress that had eaten Brahm Saxena. The silent old man whom they had ignored all morning had gone on to ruin the greatest moment of their lives. And, too often, that was what I saw, when I looked for my father, when I tried to place myself in the jeep and look into his eyes: I saw she-dentist, in the veranda, that afternoon, with a look that was trained at me but meant for him. I looked for my father, but found only everyone else.